MW01147920

The Curse on Long Autumn Valley

By

Andrew Craven

This is a work of fiction. All the characters and events portrayed in this book are either products of the author's imagination or are used fictitiously.

THE CURSE ON LONG AUTUMN VALLEY

Copyright © by Andrew Craven 2015

All rights reserved.

Cover art by Adam Burke

ISBN-13: 978-1517274221

Thanks to Carrie and our families for their support.

Special thanks to Barbara Morrison and Jenna Ritter for their help with the manuscript.

One

Yrion Blight stopped halfway between the woodpile and his family cemetery. His nose caught a sickly sweet scent, and he turned to see a low fog rising up from the dell to his right. It moved as if pushed by a wind he could not feel, crept into the cemetery and over the moss-covered gravestones of his grandfathers and great-grandfathers, five generations of Blights laid to rest. His father's was there too, the whitest of the stones, placed there only a month ago, just four mornings after Yrion's tenth birthday.

The fog reached the top of the hill and a riderless horse stepped out of the mist, silhouetted against the moon's white face. Steam rose from the beast, as if it had created the fog in its wake. It was the largest horse Yrion had ever seen, larger than any horse should ever be. The drifting fog enveloped its hindquarters. The horse seemed to be waiting.

For what? Yrion wondered.

Dread gripped him. He thought he could see its onyx eye staring him down.

Somehow he knew the answer. *A rider.*

The steed raised its front hoof and stamped it twice. Yrion could feel the thuds in his chest.

Not just any rider; it's waiting for me.

He didn't know how he knew it. He sensed it. He could feel it in his chest, as if the horse were speaking to his heart. He shivered, and his dread pushed that voice away.

As if in response, the beast bolted, galloping up the road that ran along the ridgeline. Its hooves rumbled like thunder as it disappeared into the maze of trees.

The fog followed it, slow and ominous; it frosted the moon's face, dampened the glow. Yrion shivered again. Frost gathered on the grass too. It felt cold enough to snow.

Yrion rushed to the woodpile, filled the crook of his elbow with a few logs, and hurried back into his family's cottage. He went straight to the fire, added two logs, and dropped the others in a messy pile next to the hearth. He sat cross-legged and blew upon the coals. Flames leapt up in seconds, and he held his hands to their warmth.

"Don't get comfortable," his big sister Laurel said from the kitchen table. "We're not through yet."

Laurel had been quizzing him all evening. Their family's auction was next week and it fell to Yrion, the only male left in the household, to do the bartering. Buckets, barrels, troughs, scythes, sickles, shovels, everything had to go. Laurel had calculated their asking prices and lowest acceptable offers. All Yrion had to do was memorize them.

"Asking price of the hame," Laurel said.

A dollar and a quarter? Yrion wondered. *Or two and a nickel?* His eyes tried to wander down to the slip of paper before him where all the figures were written down.

"No peeking," his sister added. "Use your brain."

He looked back at her. "Two and a nickel?"

"Two and a nickel is the *low*."

"Oh. Which one's a dollar and a quarter?"

His sister leaned back and growled at the ceiling. "A dollar twenty-five is the asking price of the sickle, the low for the scythe. We'll also take a dollar twenty-five for all five buckets. Thirty cents each."

Yrion didn't know how she kept it all straight. He knew he had to learn it but now all he could think about was that horse up on the road. It couldn't have been as big as it looked; it must have been a trick of the moonlight—for even the moon looked bigger on the horizon. And it wasn't waiting for him; it had stopped and stared for the same reason he had. Horses were curious like that.

"Yrion. *Yrion*," Laurel snapped.

Yrion looked back to his sister. She wasn't staring at the ceiling anymore; she was glaring at him. Her dark blue eyes could frost the blazing logs in the hearth.

"The asking price of the hame?" she asked.

"Oh. Two-sixty?"

"Two-*forty*. Mother, will you...what are we going to do with him?"

Lyra Blight sat in her rocker next to Yrion, a quilt draped over her legs, hemming her late husband's pants so they'd fit her son. Her close-set eyes peered down a high-bridged nose. At her temples, stripes of white streaked her dark red hair; they'd appeared in the past month, as if Corvus' death had caused her great stress. But that was the only change Yrion noticed. She was rocking peacefully now and humming a nameless tune.

"Perhaps take a break," she said, eyes on her needlework.

Laurel sighed and pushed herself back from the table. "I'm turning in," she said. She crossed the room, stopped behind the rocker, and leaned in to kiss her mother on the head.

Laurel's dark red hair matched their mother's—it was almost purple in certain lights. Otherwise, she took after their father: a thin, symmetrical face with high cheekbones, a nose that tapered to a delicate point, small ears that didn't jut out like Yrion's.

"Don't stay up too late," Laurel said to him. "Meeting tomorrow."

He turned back to the fire. "I remember."

Town meetings were another task he had to undertake in his father's stead. The thought of it dropped a weight into his belly. But when he pushed the thought away, the image of the black horse replaced it. He hugged his knees and rocked in place. So many things to worry about, so many things that frightened him. He didn't know how he would face them all.

"Mother," he said.

"Hmm?"

"Tell me again about the Nightsteed."

She resituated the pants on her lap.

"You're a little old for those stories, aren't you?" she asked.

Yrion slumped his shoulders. He was too old for a lot of things that still scared him. He picked a splinter off the hearth and flicked it into the fire.

"When boys and girls are lazy by day," his mother began, "their spirits become restless and wander by night. And if they aren't careful, they'll wander into the Hall of the Nightfather.

"Now, the Nightfather is the laziest that ever was. Grass grows too fast for him; seasons change too fast for him. And if vexed, he puts his curse on things, casts a darkness upon them to slow them down.

"One night, he heard a whinnying in the forest. He followed the cries to a clearing surrounded by a thick tangle of thorns, and there a monstrous horse—twenty hands at the withers—charged round and round, trapped on all sides by the thicket.

"'You see', the Nightfather said to the briars and brambles, 'your fast growing has gone and caused a ruckus.' He reached out and touched some of the thorns. They blackened and fell limp, and a small gap formed in the thicket.

"But then a very lazy idea came to him: 'If I had a horse to ride, I wouldn't have to walk.' So he climbed up a nearby tree, and when the horse charged through the gap in the briars the Nightfather hopped down upon its back.

"He soon regretted the idea. This horse wanted to run free, and it was the fastest and wildest that ever lived. Yelling 'whoa!' spurred it onward; pulling its mane spurred it onward. All the Nightfather could do was try to slow it with his curse. But the horse sensed that wicked touch, reared up and bucked him, but not before the curse turned its coat black as a moonless midnight.

"The curse preserved the beast, and it runs forever free. Some folk say they've seen it—the Nightsteed they call it—charging up and down Witching Hour Road."

"And what happened to the Nightfather?" Yrion whispered.

"Not far from where the Nightsteed dropped him, an old abandoned house sat wrapped and tangled in a hundred years of thicket. It was as good a place as any to call home, and the Nightfather decided then and there he was through with horses, through with just about everything. So he cursed the surrounding plants and crawling branches so that nothing could grow and disturb him, and he went inside.

"There he sits, waiting for Everdark, the far away time when all things—even the Nightfather—will find rest. And he does not like visitors coming and going. When restless spirits wander there, he uses his curse to imprison them in his Hall. If a boy wishes to avoid that fate, he best work hard by day to keep his spirit from wandering by night."

Yrion shivered and laid another log on the fire. He saw the others he'd dropped in the messy pile and began arranging them in a neat stack.

"Mother," he said, "I don't mean to be a lazy boy."

His mother kept rocking and knitting.

"Numbers just don't stick in my head the way they do for Laurel."

"Hush now. You'll find your place."

His place. If he didn't shape up, his place would be in the Hall of the Nightfather.

Yrion looked about him. An iron poker leaned against the hearth. Sprigs of sage and rosemary dried upon the mantle. A rug beater stood in the corner, his father's musket beneath it. Yrion knew nothing about working iron or growing herbs. Beating rugs made him sneeze and he was a bad shot—*Laurel* had the steady hands. She could do everything; Yrion couldn't do anything. And just when he'd gotten old enough to start learning, his father died.

Father died. It still didn't seem possible. Corvus had been such a presence, always on the move, getting things done, not a lazy bone in his body. All those years watching him hard at work…Yrion should have been paying better attention, not concerning himself with children's stories. He needed to put this Nightsteed nonsense out of his mind.

Maybe it was Banyon, he thought, *Uncle Cetus' draft horse*. That horse was always breaking loose. And it was big too. It must have been Banyon up on the road. Not the Nightsteed—there was no such thing.

Yrion was too old for those stories.

Two

Laurel dropped a few logs in the fireplace to rouse her brother from sleep. He lay curled up before the hearth as he had all night, their father's coat draped over him like a blanket. The air was cold, colder than any September morning Laurel could remember. She arranged the logs in a pile atop the ashy coals, a few of which still glowed orange. She blew a few times, and when they didn't ignite, she added two more logs.

"You're smothering it," he said.

"Then you do it."

He sat up. Laurel saw splinters tangled in the swirling cowlick on the back of his head. It looked like a bird's nest. He'd gotten the worst muddying of their parents' traits: his hair was a dirty brown mix of Mother's red and Father's black; he was soft and pear-shaped like their mother, with her big-bridged nose; he got his father's round ears, but larger; his hands were small and weak and clammy. The kid looked like he'd been pieced together in a hurry. He might grow out of it—if he decided to grow up at all.

"Have to let it breathe," he said. In seconds, the logs were crackling; at least he could light a fire.

Laurel moved out to the kitchen table, relit the oil lamp. The table was small and square, barely big enough for four place settings and a dish in the middle. She set out her quill, inkwell, blank sheets of paper, and her master copy of announcements. The announcements, drafted by the officials down in Brodhaven, needed to be duplicated and mailed to specified recipients. The recipients were too few to warrant the use of the town's only printing press, so the Brodhaven officials paid Laurel a dollar a week to transcribe them by hand.

She sighed and got to work. Her quill moved methodically, mechanically. It produced clean, consistent characters, evenly-spaced lines and paragraphs. She could write a letter, copy it, hold them stacked together in front of a light and the text would all but align, down to the letter. And she could do it without thinking about it, which was good because she would hate to have to focus on such an inane task, but bad because sometimes she focused too much on the inanity itself.

She was capable of so much more than this.

She understood all the laws drafted by the Brodhaven assembly. She had read more books before she was twelve than the local schoolmaster had in his life. She was the one who had calculated the prices for next week's auction. Yet the law forbade her from bartering. A woman couldn't auction property because a woman couldn't own property in Long Autumn Valley. Nor could she hold office, attend town meetings, or vote. A woman was permitted to copy letters, stitch clothing, cook meals—nothing that actually influenced the course of her life.

The law, instead, entailed it all on her kid brother who couldn't care less.

The little daydreamer can hardly lace his boots.

By the time the sun crested the hill out front of the cottage, Laurel had a neat stack of envelopes ready for delivery. Yrion sat by the fire, memorizing his auction bids. Their mother swept about the hearth, moving the broom around her son as if he were another piece of furniture. Laurel was standing at the wet-sink, scrubbing the ink from her fingers, when a knock came at the door.

"I'll get it," Yrion said, leaping up (the kid would do anything to get out of studying). But even their mother had stopped her sweeping and moved towards the door.

Laurel rolled her eyes and called, "Come in, Caelum."

The door opened before they reached it, and Yrion scowled at her.

Caelum Cronewetter stepped in. He wore a pale blue shirt that matched his eyes. His sleeves were rolled back revealing his skinny, dark-haired arms. His black hair swept to the left side as if he always kept his right cheek to the wind.

Yrion and Lyra greeted him eagerly, crowding so close he could barely enter far enough to close the door behind him. They always did this—fussing about him like house dogs, practically pawing at him—and it always embarrassed Laurel. But Caelum never minded.

"Morning, all," he said with a smile.

Laurel had to admit she was glad to see him too. She had so much going through her head, and he was the only person she could really talk to, the only person who understood her. He listened to her *modern* ideas about women in the Valley, even agreed with them. She couldn't talk to her mother about such things. And Yrion was, well, Yrion.

"Big meeting today, huh?" Caelum said to him.

Yrion looked at his feet. "I guess so."

"You'll do fine."

"Just follow Uncle Cetus' lead," Laurel said.

"I remember," Yrion said.

Laurel pointed to the letters on the table. "And take those with you."

"All right."

"And you need to mention the auction. Can't sell anything if no one shows up."

"All right, all right."

Their mother finally noticed the splinters in Yrion's hair and started preening him. "So," she said, "what are you two getting into today?"

Caelum, gentlemanly, held his hands together behind his back. "I thought I'd take Laurel on a picnic—with your permission, of course."

Her mother beamed. "Ooohh, how romantic."

"*Mother*," Laurel said. Her mother was shameless, always injecting *romance* into every interaction Laurel had with Caelum. Laurel didn't have time for romance. Silly notions like romance led to silly institutions like marriage. Laurel had more important things to do. Caelum and Laurel were just the best of friends, had been since their days at the schoolhouse.

She moved back to the kitchen, tore a loaf of crusty bread in half, and brought a piece with her. She told her mother she'd be back around noon then urged Caelum out the door ahead of her.

Yrion followed. "Did you bring Kernel?" he asked.

"Sure did," Caelum said.

Up on the road, a dainty roan stood roped to an ash tree. The sun's rays beamed between her doe-thin legs.

"Go get ready," Laurel said to her brother.

He scowled at her again and stayed by the door while she and Caelum walked up the steep hill. At the top, it leveled off where Witching Hour Road ran left to right along the ridge. Caelum unhitched Kernel's reins while Laurel slipped her bread into the canvas bag tied to the saddle's pommel. She felt a couple of apples or pears bulging at the bottom.

"You didn't have to bring anything," Caelum said.

"I can pitch in."

Caelum looked ready to say something else. Instead he stepped back and let Laurel mount Kernel first. Then he hopped up behind her, took the reins. With a flick of his wrist Kernel ambled up the road.

The Copperwood shaded them with a canopy of red and orange and gold. Long Autumn Valley got its name for its short springs and summers; the green drained from the trees in late July, but the changing leaves clung to the branches into mid-December. The Copperwood in late September embodied the real charm of the Valley. Eastward, to the right of Witching Hour Road, the forest rolled up and down over a series of interweaving hills and dells. The Blights—Yrion, technically—owned the first thirty acres. It was the only bit of their land that had any value.

A faint whiff of something bad turned Laurel's head to the left. There the hill continued to slope steeply down. After one hundred yards the trees ended and the land leveled off for a quarter mile stretch before rising up again at a tree-line at the far side. The swath between was the Blight's farmland where black blotches peppered a field of brown grasses and withered leaves. The blotches were pumpkins—and yams and squashes and parsnips and potatoes too. At least, they used to be.

Until the curse.

It had seeped in three months ago and taken only four days to turn the crops black—flesh, stem, seed, and all. It was as if every plant had been dipped in crude oil. Dark fumes rose from them and hung in a smoky haze over the fields. And they stank, a faint, sickly sweet odor, like rotting fruit soaked in animal blood.

But the curse hadn't just ruined her family's crops; it spoiled the land itself. Nothing would or could grow there anymore—except maybe more black, poisonous vegetables. It had ruined them, and there was nothing Laurel or anyone could do about it. And since it hadn't spread south to Uncle Cetus' farm or north to the Idlevice estate, it really did seem like a curse on her family, the first of several losses they'd faced this year.

"You're quiet today," Caelum said.

Laurel looked back to the road. "A lot on my mind."

"I brought you out here to take your mind off it."

Laurel didn't want her mind taken off it. She needed to figure all this out.

"Do you want to talk about it?" Caelum asked.

Laurel shifted in the saddle. "What's to talk about? We're broke. We'll burn through what the auction brings before spring. And I'm paid a pittance by people whose jobs I could do better myself."

"I know it," Caelum replied.

"And Mother's no help. She acts like nothing has happened, like Father is still alive and selling crops, shouldering our burdens."

"Grief's different for everyone, Laurel."

"And Yrion, I don't know what to do with him. If he'd focus one ounce of his attention on the auction bids instead of, of whatever it is he's doing—"

"And what about you?"

Laurel tried to wheel around in the saddle. "What *about* me?"

"With everything on your mind, have you had time to grieve?"

Laurel wasn't interested in grieving. Her father's death had been like a sudden blow to the head. She'd been dazed for a few days, numb and empty, but there was work to be done—the work helped focus her. As the days passed, she felt a little more focused, a little more normal, and whatever grief she was supposed to feel never came. She'd worked her way through it. Why hadn't everyone else?

"I've grieved enough," she said. "It's time to move on."

"Go easy on your brother."

"Someone's got to push him."

Kernel snorted and trotted a few steps. Caelum dropped the reins in Laurel's lap.

"You're upsetting her," he said.

Laurel had a *right* to be upset. Not that Kernel would know it. Laurel took the reins in her right hand and gently stroked the roan's neck with her left. Kernel eased back into a slow, lazy gait.

Before long, the road crossed into Idlevice lands. Off to the left, the Blight's fallow field opened wider, and the blackened specks of their cursed crops ended, giving way to dozens of little hills. Each hill was covered by a different crop—corn, wheat, barley, pumpkins—or a pasture dotted with sheep and horses, or pristinely manicured lawns of frosty blue grass. On the lawns, evergreens stood as tall emerald cones, planted to provide decoration here, shade there.

Witching Hour Road veered right and began to wind and climb a tall wooded hill. Laurel and Caelum had to dismount and lead Kernel on foot, back and forth, up and up. At the top, it turned right and began its long, serpentine run into the Uphills. Laurel and Caelum veered left onto a little trail and followed it a ways before tying Kernel to a silver maple. There they took their bag of food down a rocky footpath that led to a scenic outcropping and a grand view of Long Autumn Valley.

The sky rolled in broken sheets of puffy white clouds. Endless hills folded together all the way to the southwestern horizon. Barns and cottages dotted farm fields. Red- and orange-leafed trees divided the pastures. Far to the right, a long, steady line of a mountain range ran north to south, demarcating the western border of Long Autumn Valley. To the left, the Copperwood spread like a patchwork quilt over its own dominion of hills and dells.

Below the outcropping stood the Idlevice mansion, the grandest structure in the Valley: four stories, over seventy rooms.

Panes of glass formed two large windows in the center of the roof: one circle and one larger rectangle. Beneath the glass lay the main banquet hall where the Idlevices hosted their annual Ball of the Nightfather.

Laurel surveyed the mansion then let her eyes wander south. She could see in the distance how two hills pinched together where Idlevice land met her own; to her eyes, that little gap seemed shrouded in a patch of darkness.

"Do you think the Idlevices would buy our farm?" she asked.

Caelum looked at her. "So you've decided to sell?"

The way Laurel saw it, she didn't have much of a choice. "Our stretch of the Copperwood is still worth something. The curse hasn't crept up there, and there's no reason to believe it will. The Copperwood is strong."

Laurel could see what looked like reluctance or disapproval on Caelum's face, but he said nothing. He pulled the bread from the canvas bag, tore it in half, and passed her a piece. She wondered: was he keeping quiet because he didn't like the idea or because he didn't want to rile her up on what was supposed to be a peaceful picnic?

"You think it's a bad idea?" she asked.

"Not per se. The Idlevices have money."

"Then what is it?"

Caelum shrugged.

"Tell me already," Laurel said.

"It's Lady Idlevice."

Though women weren't permitted to conduct most forms of business in the Valley, Lord Percy Idlevice's health had declined these past few years and was now confined to a wheeled chair. He still managed to vote at the town meetings and sign the necessary contracts with local businessmen, but everyone knew his wife, Lady Vela Idlevice, coordinated it all, requiring only her husband's official seal to transact.

"What about her?" Laurel asked.

"Well. She didn't get where she is by…being nice."

"You're afraid she won't be nice to me?"

"Charitable, then."

Laurel didn't want her charity. This would be a business transaction. "I don't understand—"

"It's nothing. Forget I said anything."

Laurel wondered what he had against Lady Idlevice. *Being nice?* Lady Idlevice was a woman making her way in a man's Valley—and doing quite well. That no doubt required her to be things other than *nice* from time to time. Laurel could learn a lot from her, given the chance.

Caelum obviously didn't think so, but that was the end of it. Laurel picked at her bread. A breeze whistled out of the north, but the rocky hill behind shielded them from it. The Copperwood swayed and sounded like a faraway sea.

"What time is it?" she asked.

"You have somewhere to be?"

"No..."

Though now she did. She wanted to get off this rock, put her plan into action. She might be able to call on Lady Idlevice today, depending on how long this picnic went.

Caelum reached into the front of his brown wool vest and removed a silver pocket watch attached by a thin copper chain. Delicate engravings swirled across its front and back. He flicked it open. The engravings continued on the inside of its door, and a clean ivory face shone beneath a bubble of polished glass.

"Nine-fifty," he said. "They'll be ringing the bell in Brodhaven soon."

"Yrion had better be there."

"I'm sure he's fine."

"Or did he wander off? He'll do that, you know."

"Next month I'll be there and keep an eye on him."

Town meetings were reserved for the land- and business-owning men of Long Autumn Valley. In a few weeks, Caelum would become partner in Cronewetters' Clockworks , his family's business. The Cronewetters were craftsmen: metalworkers, potters, jewelers, engravers, copper-, silver-, and goldsmiths. Caelum's great-grandfather had made the watch Caelum carried, and Caelum had fashioned the new copper chain himself. They did fine work and had plenty of it, but theirs was a large family and the profits were spread thinly among them. Each Cronewetter had to earn his keep, and Laurel respected that. She wished the Blights had a family business.

"The boy needs a trade," she said. "Living in the woods with his mother and sister isn't teaching him anything."

"Why not have him come work with me?"

Laurel almost laughed. "Yrion? I think not. He's more daft than deft."

"Come now. Steady hands run in the family."

"If they do, they skipped over him."

"Give him a chance, Laurel. Everyone's gifted in some way."

Laurel shrugged. "If you say so. But let's not tell him till after the auction. I need to keep him focused."

Caelum nodded then reached into a hidden pocket on the inside of his vest and removed a small envelope. He opened its flap and offered its contents to Laurel. She looked inside and saw three thin wafers of dark chocolate. She inhaled their seductive scent and smiled. *Picnics aren't all bad,* she thought. When she reached for one, Caelum drew the envelope back.

"And what are *your* plans?" he asked. "After the farm sells?"

Laurel hadn't given that much thought.

Her father had wanted her married off by now—he even tried to arrange it several times. Most folk, *especially* her mother, thought Caelum would propose. If she had to marry someone, Laurel supposed she would prefer Caelum. But she *didn't* have to marry someone. Marriage was what women in the Valley did because the men wouldn't let them do anything else. Not Laurel. Laurel was going to do things differently; she was going to do more.

"Let's see what we get for it," she replied.

"Is there anything I can do?" Caelum asked.

"*You* could buy it."

Caelum looked out to the horizon. "All right."

Laurel looked at him. "I'm joking." She could see he wasn't.

"I have some money set aside," he said.

"A cursed farm is no good to you."

He thought about it for a little. "Maybe I could have it logged out."

Laurel nodded in consideration. It wasn't a bad idea. Only, neither of them knew much about logging or lumber costs. She would have to look into that.

She knew she was lucky to have someone like Caelum. He'd do anything for her. Probably the only reason he'd never proposed to her was because he knew she didn't want to marry. She found *that* romantic, in an ironic sort of way. And, if she understood him as well as she thought, he did too.

"Let's see what Lady Idlevice says first," she said. "I'd sooner be done with it."

"If that's how you want it."

Laurel snatched the envelope from him, took a piece of chocolate for herself. "That's how I want it."

Three

Yrion watched Kernel carry Laurel and Caelum up the road. Kernel looked much smaller than the horse he'd seen last night. Yrion's memory insisted the dark horse was half again as tall as Kernel, maybe more.

He went indoors. His mother stood in the kitchen, his father's slacks and vest draped over her forearm, her hemming complete. She had him try them on, and he found them itchy at the neck and collar. He had a lot of room to move, but the fabric didn't bend easily. Lyra knelt down and cuffed each pant leg twice.

"So they don't get muddy," she said. "You can unroll them when you get there."

Then she licked her hand and started smoothing out his hair.

"Mother," Yrion said, "do I have to do this?"

"Ten years old means you're officially old enough to vote, which is something every landowner should do—when time permits. And you have plenty of time on your hands these days."

"But…"

"Mind your Uncle Cetus."

Yrion squirmed away from her preening. "Yes'm."

He made it as far as the front door.

"Yrion," his mother said.

He turned and saw her holding out Laurel's stack of envelopes.

"Oh. Right," he said.

He stuffed them in his pocket and set off.

He went around the side of the cottage and passed between the woodpile and family cemetery. He could smell the curse wafting up from his fields—a sweet odor, like a rotting maple stump. It didn't bother Yrion as much as it did others, but he was sensitive to its presence; he could often smell it up over Witching Hour Road where Laurel and his mother couldn't. The smell today wasn't as heavy as it had been last night when the fog crept up to the road.

He followed the path that led down to the barn. A few chickens scratched aimlessly about, saw Yrion, and perked up. But they'd have to fend for themselves. Yrion used to feed all the animals—it was one of the few jobs he could actually do. But his father had sold off most of the livestock when the curse crept in; he couldn't grow the feed for them anymore.

The barn itself used to be a place of such bustle. Yrion missed the sound of his father sawing, hammering, shoveling, grunting. Now it was locked up, quiet. The rusted weathervane at the top of the cupola pointed due south, no matter which way the wind blew.

Past the barn, a little trail ran downhill through the Copperwood to where the fields began. Yrion turned left at the edge of the woods and followed the tree-line till he came to the end of his property. There, a long, raised mound stretched to the right along the southern border of his field. A muddy ditch ran along his side of the mound. Yrion's father and Uncle Cetus had dug this ditch and built this mound to keep the curse from spreading south to Uncle Cetus' land. The curse hadn't, though no one could say for certain that the ditch had anything to do with it. It was unpredictable like that; no one understood it.

Yrion scurried up the mound and walked along its crest. At the end, he hopped down and turned left along a wagon trail that ran between the Uncle Cetus' corn and pumpkin fields. Before long, a split rail fence began to follow the gentle bend of the trail. The fence was abnormally tall; a horse the size of Kernel could probably stoop and step through the lower gap. It enclosed a pasture, at the far corner of which stood a barn with dark wood siding, its doors flung wide.

Yrion scanned the pasture for Banyon, Uncle Cetus' giant shire, but didn't see him anywhere. That made him feel a little better: if Banyon had broken loose then it was very likely Banyon that he'd seen up on the road last night. But a neigh from the barn quashed that hope, and Banyon emerged and trotted over to the fence.

His coat was tan, his legs and mane black. He was massive, close to eight feet tall with his head up, and could hop right over a normal-sized fence. But even as he approached and poked his head over the middle rail to sniff at Yrion's clothes, Yrion thought the steed last night had been somehow bigger still.

"Best back away from him," a voice called from down the wagon trail.

Yrion took a step back and turned to see Cetus Boarsik lumbering up to meet him, a sledgehammer resting on his shoulder. Uncle Cetus' arms were bigger than Yrion's trunk, with black wiry hair that looked thick enough to break a pair of shears. The loose collar of his dirty shirt revealed a massive chest with the same thick hair which crept up his neck and got lost in his bushy black beard. A big man like Uncle Cetus needed a big horse and, when he stood next to Banyon, Banyon almost seemed normal-sized.

"That boy's got nothing for you," he said. When he reached out to pet the horse on the nose, Banyon moved his head away with a snort. Uncle Cetus snorted right back. "Don't fuss with me. I'm the one with the hammer."

"I think he likes me," Yrion said.

"Don't let him fool you. He'll bite your finger off and pretend he thought it was a carrot."

Yrion giggled.

"I'd sell him outright," Uncle Cetus said, "if anyone would buy him. But not many folk are big enough to show him who's in charge."

"How big is he?" Yrion asked.

"Biggest in the Valley, from what I hear. Eighteen hands at the withers."

Uncle Cetus hadn't mentioned it, but Yrion figured he'd ask: "Did he get out last night?"

"Banyon? Naw. When he gets out, he heads straight for the Nudniks' stable to strut around the mares. Not easy to drag him back home, but he's never hard to find."

"Oh," Yrion said. "Saw a horse up on the road last night. *Big* horse."

"Maybe you're seeing the Nightsteed." Uncle Cetus chuckled lightly but his deep voice made it sound like thunder. Banyon took a step back and snorted again.

Yrion stuffed his hands in his pockets.

Uncle Cetus took the sledgehammer in both his hands, dangled it behind his head, and began scratching his back with it. "You know, your Aunt Carina and I were talking. Why don't you and your family move down here with us? After you sell the farm, I mean. There's plenty of room."

Yrion didn't understand. He had a hard time memorizing the bids, but he was certain the farm was not on his sheet. "We're not auctioning the farm."

Uncle Cetus looked puzzled. "Well, even so, you have a place here with us."

Uncle Cetus wasn't really Yrion's uncle, nor was Aunt Carina Yrion's aunt. They were just kind and close neighbors who hadn't been able to make any children of their own. That made Yrion sad when he thought about it. He supposed everybody ended up cursed one way or another.

"Anyway," his uncle said, "I see Lyra's got you all dressed up for the meeting. You're going to have to go on ahead without me."

That weight dropped in Yrion's belly again. "You're not coming?" he whimpered.

"Naw. Piles to drive, then wood to split. Shelves to fix too. Carina's packing away yams, and I'll hear about it if the cellar isn't ready to receive them."

Yrion twisted in his boots and must have turned a little green because his uncle patted him on the shoulder and said, "I hate meetings too. For folk who'd rather steal from honest workers than work an honest day themselves. Now listen here: when Pavo Linenpest votes *yea*, you vote *nay*. And the other way around, too."

Yrion kicked at the dust.

"Chin up," his uncle said. "You're the head of the house now. Can't be scared of a meeting."

"Yes, sir."

Yrion continued down the trail, and Banyon followed beside him. Uncle Cetus watched them go, yelling, "Damn horse. I say that boy's got nothing for you!"

At the edge of the pasture, the trail branched off and Yrion turned and waved to Uncle Cetus. "Bye, Banyon."

Banyon stopped and watched him go.

Yrion's feet felt heavy, like he was walking through mud that got deeper and stickier with each step. He was alone, and not in a good way like when he wandered the Copperwood. He would have to stand among strangers and listen to them propose laws he probably wouldn't understand. Why couldn't Laurel go in his stead?—she actually *wanted* to. Yrion considered skipping the meeting entirely, but he knew Laurel would hound him with questions and he wasn't a very good liar.

He wished Father were here.

The wagon trail continued to bend back up the hill toward the Copperwood. The sun was just now cresting the treetops, but Yrion only briefly enjoyed its warmth before moving back under the shade of the trees. It really was cold for September; somewhere above the faint odor of the curse, he thought he could smell snow.

He followed the trail back into the woods, then onto Witching Hour Road south. The road wound lazily for three miles, then, in a final westward curve, it emptied onto a clearing at the

Copperwood's southern border. Puffy clouds drifted overhead, shading the landscape with dark patches that rolled over pastured hills all the way to the southern horizon. A flock of sheep grazed freely off to the right. The road rushed down a half-mile to Brodhaven. The town lay tucked between an interlocking series of hillocks. Slate-shingled rooftops jutted sharply from the dells.

A tinny bell echoed in the distance. Yrion had to hustle.

At the town's official limits, Witching Hour Road became a cobbled street and Brodhaven's main thoroughfare. Businesses crowded either side, leaning over the street, insisting folk could find their goods and services here. There were butchers, bakers, cobblers, coopers, farriers, lenders. Oldfather's Inn was off to the left; at four stories, it was the tallest building in Brodhaven. And to the right was Cronewetters' Clockworks, Yrion's favorite shop. If he'd had enough time, he'd have stopped and stared through its windows at all the wonders inside.

At the heart of Brodhaven, the thoroughfare widened into a broad circle ringed with peddlers' carts, and on the far side, the tinny bell outside town hall sounded for the last time. Yrion entered on the heels of the final arrivals. Two men closed the double doors behind him. The back quarter of the hall was shaded by a low ceiling. Some men were ascending a staircase that led to a balcony. Yrion found himself in a line, and it took him a few minutes to understand why; he was the last to sign his name in a big book: the attendance roster.

Yrion moved forward to just where the balcony overhang ended. Men crammed onto benches on either side of an aisle. The aisle stopped at a long, low table; clerks sat at it, sheets of parchment and broad, thin books before them. Behind them, an empty pulpit waited.

Men who couldn't fit onto the benches stood along the far walls where the light entered through tall windows crowned with semicircle panes. Yrion didn't know where to go and decided to stand behind the last row of benches on the right side. He peered around the shoulder of the man sitting on the end, scanning for familiar faces. He didn't see many.

At the front of the room, on the other side of the aisle, he saw the wheel of Percy Idlevice's chair. The old man's white hair was combed back over his liver-spotted scalp. A wool blanket lay across his lap and overhung the chair's wheels.

A few Whiteheads stood on the far side of the room, arms crossed, faces scruffy, brows furrowed. Yrion knew them by their long coats with the wolf's fur collars and by the way the other men gave them a bit of extra space. The Whiteheads were a big family who lived in the Uphills to the north. No one knew how big, but some folk said there were as many Whiteheads as there were *Blackheads*, the Whiteheads' word for anyone who lived south of the Uphills. There probably were a few actual Blackheads here mixed in with the Nudniks, Netherbrandts, Butterfields, Pennywills, Pettifogs, Cronewetters, Rotbottoms and a bunch of others Yrion didn't know.

Before long, Mayor Linenpest ascended to his place behind the pulpit. He wore a bright green shirt with gold buttons up the front. His hearty gut threatened to pop those buttons off but was held back by a thick, gold-buckled belt. He had a matching golden mustache that spread across his cheeks and flowed into his equally puffy sideburns which got lost up under his bushy, golden locks. But his chin was bare and red, and the skin of his throat bulged like a bullfrog's. A white mayoral sash hung from his left shoulder.

The mayor cleared his throat and spoke in a nasally voice: "Calling to order this, the seventeen hundred and thirty-seventh Brodhaven assembly, twenty-eighth September. Our doors have been shut; let no man open them until our business is through.

"We begin with announcements. Our next meeting, being the seventeen hundred and thirty-eighth, shall present my plans for the Witching Hour Railroad for public approval."

Some men grumbled at this, especially the Whiteheads.

"Naturally," the mayor said, "we encourage all Long Autumn Valley land- and business-owners to attend and voice their opinion. Notifications will be forwarded to those travelling abroad.

"Next, there are unconfirmed tidings of the curse west in the Valley, the uh"—and the mayor had to squint at his notes—"Tinpot family's farm. We have dispatched an official team to investigate. Charities will be established based upon their estimates."

Yrion remembered they had tried to set up a similar charity for his family, but his father would not allow it. Something about "not taking handouts" and "working for what they had" which Yrion didn't quite understand because Yrion had gotten everything he ever had from his mother and father and sister without having to work all that much.

"We'll now open the floor," the mayor continued, "to the general assembly for public announcements."

Hands shot up here and there. Some folk sidestepped courtesy and spoke their announcements aloud. The Whiteheads shouted outright, and Yrion couldn't tell if they were announcing something or just shouting for shouting's sake. He meekly raised his hand, guessing this was the proper time to mention the auction. Pavo Linenpest, meanwhile, had raised both his hands in an attempt to settle the assembly which seemed on the brink of all-out riot. Then, hands ineffective, the mayor produced a rusty cowbell from under the pulpit and began ringing it furiously till the crowd simmered and his voice could be heard.

"We have," he said, "a new addition to our good assembly." His eyes fell on Yrion, and he pointed the cowbell directly at him. "Young Master Blight, whose father has found rest—may his spirit never wander."

The whole room turned to look at Yrion. He was so nervous that he kept his eyes glued upon the mayor to avoid their stares. His mouth felt full of cotton.

"Welcome," the mayor said. "You have an announcement?"

Some sounds came out Yrion's mouth, but they weren't words.

"Out with it, boy!" one of the Whiteheads barked, and the riot began anew.

Mayor Linenpest banged his cowbell twice upon the pulpit, face flushed, and the commotion subsided. Then he said, "You may put your hand down, Master Blight."

Yrion hadn't realized he still had it up.

"What is your announcement?" the mayor asked.

The crowd turned to face Yrion again.

"Auction," Yrion replied. "Auction at our farm. Noon. Week from today." He didn't know what else he should say so finished with: "Tools." Then he dropped his eyes to his feet and stuffed his hands in his pockets. He noticed he hadn't unrolled his pants like his mother had told him to; somehow he'd managed to get mud on the cuffs.

"Splendid," Mayor Linenpest said, then re-announced so all could hear: "The Blight family will hold an auction at their farm, a week from today, October the fifth, at noon. *Tools*."

A few courteous seconds passed before the assembly devolved once more into a cycle of outbursts followed by cowbell followed by announcements. It went on for what seemed forever. When Yrion's feet and knees began to ache, he moved to a wooden post that supported the balcony overhead. He leaned against it and his thoughts soon drifted away from the bickering assembly...

The horse he'd seen *hadn't* been Banyon. Somehow he'd known that all along. But whose horse had it been then? There were no wild horses in Long Autumn Valley. He couldn't help but return to tales of the Nightsteed. Folk still claimed to see it charging up and down Witching Hour Road.

Yet, there had been that sense of impatience. The horse had stopped. It wanted a rider—it wanted *Yrion*. That wasn't part of any tale. The Nightsteed had bucked the Nightfather. Why would it want Yrion to ride it? It made so little sense, he considered the possibility that he hadn't seen a horse at all. Just fog and shadow and fear of the dark—that's what Laurel would say. That made the most sense, and he felt a little ashamed about getting so distracted by it all.

No Nightsteed, he assured himself, *no horse at all*.

The word *yea* brought him back.

He found himself sitting with his back to the post. He didn't remember sitting down, but his feet and legs didn't welcome him standing again. Another *yea* sounded and he moved back to his spot close to the aisle.

The mayor spoke a name Yrion didn't know.

"Nay," a voice said.

The mayor spoke another name.

"Yea," said another voice, followed by grumbling from the Whiteheads.

The vote! Yrion began to sweat. *What are they voting on?* Yeas and nays sprang up here and there like the call and response of birds and bullfrogs. The Whiteheads grumbled after every *yea*, but others expressed satisfaction with *hear, hear!* The opposite happened with the nays. After each, the panel of scribes sitting below the mayor's pulpit scratched an unbiased mark in their books. But none of it offered Yrion clues as to how he should vote. Uncle Cetus said to vote the opposite of Mayor Linenpest, but how had the mayor voted? *Had* he voted?

Yrion wanted to run, but he turned and saw the two men who had closed the doors were now standing guard at them. He considered hiding, but he'd signed the roster! *And* the mayor had already introduced him and would soon call his name. Could he simply *not* vote?

You should have been paying attention, Laurel would say.

"Yea," said a deep voice by the window.

"*Nay!*" shouted the Whitehead next to him.

"Nay!" concurred the next Whitehead, then "Nay! Nay! Nay!" said the next three.

For Yrion, that was as good a clue as he was going to get; the Whiteheads were rude and they scared him. So, when his name was called, he squeaked, "Yea."

It seemed to him that the Whiteheads grumbled particularly at his choice while Mayor Linenpest smiled and nodded to him. *What did that mean?* Yrion wondered. Did the mayor agree with his choice? Or was he just being courteous? Yrion lowered his eyes to the floor again. His feet were sweating so bad in his boots he felt as though he'd stepped in a puddle.

The votes continued a while longer, and at the last the mayor said: "And how do you vote, Lord Idlevice?"

Yrion craned his neck and listened.

"Yea?" the mayor asked.

Lord Idlevice didn't respond.

"Nay?" the mayor asked.

Lord Idlevice's decrepit right hand rose shakily from the armrest of his chair.

"Let the record show," the mayor said, "Lord Idlevice votes nay. And I cast my vote as *yea*."

Yrion felt like he was going to be sick. He'd voted wrong. For some reason, the Blights and Boarsiks and Idlevices sided with the Whiteheads despite the Whiteheads' rudeness.

The clerks, meanwhile, tallied up their counts while holding a hushed conversation, as if their calculations required no concentration. Laurel was like that—she'd do well as a scribe here, if they would give her a chance. Yrion had to focus just to write his name, and if he were thinking about the Nightsteed his name would end up looking like a horse.

When the scribes finished, they nodded in unison, and the centermost one scribbled something quickly on a scrap of paper and passed it to Mayor Linenpest. He read it and nodded.

"One hundred and forty-four yeas," he said. "Ninety-two nays. The yeas have it."

The Whiteheads let out a bitter cry and so did some others in the assembly. Feet began to shuffle overhead, and the Whiteheads came away from their spots at the windows. They moved like thugs through the crowd, and those who didn't step aside fast enough were shouldered out of the way. Yrion shrunk away to the support post.

"Henceforth," Mayor Linenpest continued over the ruckus, "only three-fifths of attendees need be present for votes to be held, rather than the previous four-fifths. Yeas still require three-fifths to pass. These new proportions will no doubt make this assembly more efficient. Again, we encourage all land- and business-owners to attend..."

Yrion didn't really follow what this new vote meant, but by then the Whiteheads had flung the doors open and were out in the street, probably shouldering women and children out of their way. The remaining assembly shook their heads and murmured and seemed glad that the troublemakers had departed. Yrion knew he was glad.

A cold draft continued to pull attendees from the room, and the meeting slowly dissolved without an official conclusion from the mayor. Lord Idlevice came rolling down the aisle, pushed by an olive-skinned man with slick dark hair. The lord was a large man with broad shoulders and large feet; Yrion would bet he was as tall as Uncle Cetus, if he could only stand. But Lord Idlevice wasn't even strong enough to hold his head up; it leaned heavily to one side on a limp stalk of a neck. His eyes rolled listlessly about in their sockets, and drool ran from the corner of his mouth down his sagging jowl. It didn't look to Yrion like the old man knew where he was. Even so, some of the men in the room bowed as Lord Idlevice rolled past.

Yrion stayed by the post and let the crowd inch its way out ahead of him. It took ten minutes for the surge to clear. A few handfuls of men stayed behind and held discussions in pairs or small groups. Mayor Linenpest was no longer behind his pulpit. Nothing left to do, Yrion took a step toward the door.

The mayor's voice stopped him: "Master Blight!"

Yrion turned and saw the mayor waddling down the aisle, an envelope in his hand. His belly stuck out so far he had to lean back to compensate, and when he got close it threatened to block his face from Yrion's view. He had to twist to the side to hand Yrion the envelope.

"Thank you for waiting," he said. "Give this to your good sister. Need copies right away."

Only then did Yrion remember that he had Laurel's letters in his jacket. He traded them with the mayor and said, "These need to be delivered." He stuffed the new one into his pocket.

"Of course," the mayor replied, then after a pause: "So will you be auctioning off your land as well?"

Yrion's brow crinkled. Twice now someone had mentioned this.

"Just tools," Yrion said.

"I see. Cursed land is a tough sell. Though, my plans for the Witching Hour Railroad detail landowner compensation—should the vote pass, of course." The mayor must have seen the confusion on Yrion's face. "We would buy your farm," he explained, a little louder and slower, "even if it is cursed, so you wouldn't have to walk away with nothing."

"That's good," Yrion said. *But who's walking away?*

"So you'll vote yea?" the mayor said with a smile. His mustache bent up in a big scoop on either side and made the smile look bigger than it was. Then he stuck out his hand.

Yrion didn't understand. "I thought the vote was next month."

The mayor chuckled. "It is, my good lad. Just getting a feel for how it will go."

Yrion shook the mayor's hand but didn't say anything. He remembered he was supposed to vote against Pavo Linenpest, and he didn't like all this talk about selling the farm. Yes, the fields were cursed, but the Copperwood was strong. And besides, Father was buried there, and all the Blights before him. They couldn't just walk away from that, could they?

Four

Laurel read the results of the vote in the letter Yrion had brought home. She couldn't believe it. For years Pavo Linenpest had wanted to run a railroad from south of Brodhaven all the way to the Uphills; now he was actually pushing for it to happen. The details were vague, but some aspects were a given: if the mayor's proposal passed, Brodhaven would claim eminent domain and force some landowners to sell their property; if the name 'Witching Hour Railroad' was any indication, the Blight farm lay directly in its path.

Laurel wanted to tear the letter in half, scribe work be damned. How was she going to find a private buyer now? Why would someone pay a fair price only to be forced to sell it to Linenpest for pennies on the dollar? Hadn't her family faced enough hardships this year, enough curses and bad luck?

She took a breath. Caelum's logging idea flitted about the periphery of her thoughts. There might be something there. She had to figure it out; she couldn't let their farm be swiped out from under them without fair compensation. Her mind began to churn.

Her brother stood across from her at the table, sullen and pantless, rocking from one foot to the other. Their mother sat next to him, blotting mud from the cuffs of his pants. He could have gone to the meeting in his underwear and still found a way to dirty those cuffs.

"Mayor Linenpest asked if we were selling the farm."

Laurel ignored him. A plan was forming in her mind—trying to, anyway.

"Are we?" Yrion asked.

"We have to," she said, watching the pieces swirl.

"But Father is buried here."

She tried to wave him away. "We need the money."

"What about the auction?"

Whatever plan was forming slipped away. She turned to her brother. "That'll make us thirty dollars at most—which you would know if you'd added it up."

He looked at the floor. "Uncle Cetus said we could stay with him."

Her mother gave her a quick, almost questioning glance.

"No," Laurel said. "They don't need us burdening them. And we don't need any charity."

Lyra went back to her blotting, and Laurel back to her letter. She still wanted to tear it to pieces.

"Can you believe this?" she asked. "Now they only need three-fifths present to vote."

"Mm-hmm," her mother replied.

"It's all part of Pavo Linenpest's plan."

"The mayor said it would make the assembly...better," Yrion said.

"Better for him. Instead of needing two hundred men present, he only needs one-fifty."

From the corner of her eye, she could see the blank stare on Yrion's face. He didn't understand the importance of what she was saying, of what Mayor Linenpest was up to.

"Townsfolk vote for townsfolk interests," she said, "and farmers vote for farmer interests. And since townsfolk live in spitting distance from town hall, they never miss a vote. Some farmers travel fifteen, twenty miles to attend; *they're* the ones who have trouble showing up."

Yrion's eyes brightened for an instant. "So this is a way to get farmers to show up!"

"No, Yrion. They *should* show up—they should be outraged by this—but that's not what the mayor's up to. He scheduled his railroad vote in the middle of the harvest, when farmers are too busy to attend. That used to mean no votes could be held—not enough men present. Now that's changed. Three-fifths of land- and business-owners are either townsfolk or close enough to vote like them; now they can start making decisions for the whole Valley. They'll be taking land from us before long, just you wait."

Yrion scratched his head. "The mayor said he'd buy the farm, not take it."

"Aye, buy it with taxes we paid him at a rate he can force us to accept. A real steal."

Yrion twisted the ball of his foot back and forth on the floor. At least he was *trying* to understand all this. "Why would townsfolk vote for a railroad?"

"Money," Laurel replied. "Plain and simple. The Uphills have lumber and minerals like iron, silver, and gold. Money will start rolling in by the train car right into Brodhaven. They'll get new streets, new buildings, new services. And I guarantee Pavo Linenpest will be skimming off the top."

"Oh," Yrion said. "Well, what about Caelum? Isn't—"

"*Yrion.*" Laurel was tired of explaining. Yes, Caelum was townsfolk. But the Cronewetters already got their silver and gold from Whiteheads, and they wouldn't damage that relationship by voting against them. And if more of the Whiteheads bother attending meetings, they might not be in this situation.

Laurel read over the list of addressees and found it longer than usual. The results of the vote needed to be copied and mailed to land- and business-owners abroad. Pavo Linenpest was reaching out to those who might help his cause, folk whose businesses might benefit from his railroad. The last name on the list caught her eye; it looked to be scribbled as an afterthought.

"Here you go, Mother," she said. "Jacob Le'fever still owns Rotbottom farm."

"You don't say," her mother replied.

"His address is outside the Valley, but he's getting notified about the vote. So he still has some ties to this place."

Thirteen years ago, Jacob Le'fever purchased Rotbottom farm, a cursed and abandoned plot of land that bordered the Idlevice estate to the northeast. No one understood why he'd made such a purchase; the land was useless. A few months later, he disappeared. Some said the Rotbottom curse took him too. More plausible (and insidious) rumors mentioned Vela Idlevice. In any case, Rotbottom farm remained abandoned to this day— who would want it? Now, maybe Pavo Linenpest did. Not even the curse could stop a train.

"I wonder if he'll return for the vote," Lyra said.

Laurel thought about it. "He might. Rotbottom farm touches Witching Hour Road. Jacob Le'fever might finally make his money back."

Those rumors about Vela Idlevice brought the lady to the forefront of Laurel's mind. Lady Idlevice, Pavo Linenpest, the railroad…it clicked. Laurel gathered up her writing supplies and the announcement. "I'll do these later," she said, then hurried off.

In her room, she stripped out of her dress—a tan thing woven from coarse fibers—and removed another from the cedar chest at the foot of her bed. Her mother had made it by hand, just for Laurel who took after her father and had grown too tall to inherit any of her mother's clothes. Her father had expected to see Laurel married in it.

How they used to fight about that. Her father pushed the issue as intently as any of his tasks on the farm, and Laurel, being Corvus' daughter, pushed back just as hard. And the dress her mother had made was the centerpiece of it all. 'If the dress is for my wedding day,' Laurel had said, 'then I'll never put it on.' And she hadn't. She locked it away in her cedar chest in some symbolic gesture of defiance.

Remembering those arguments still left a bitter taste in Laurel's mouth. That they wasted so much time fighting over such a thing. To marry or not to marry was her choice, simple as that; that anyone—even her own father— thought he could make it for her was seriously ridiculous, ridiculously serious. She felt her face warm, found her fists clenched, and pushed the memories away.

She slipped it on and did her best to observe herself in her handheld mirror. The dress's blue-grey color matched her eyes and complimented her crimson hair. It hugged her close beneath her bosom, flowed in pleats down to her ankles where it bunched in a hemmed, decorative frill. The fitted sleeves ended at her wrists with similar frills. Her mother had done well.

Atop her dresser, a matching blue-grey ribbon lay draped over a little wood figurine. Four inches tall, whittled from pine, the figurine resembled a girl in a dress that flowed outward to form a sturdy base for it to stand. Its arms curved upwards in front, as if it were carrying some invisible burden. Those arms were perfect for holding a pencil. Caelum had carved it for her when they attended the schoolhouse together, after seeing Laurel's fine penmanship.

She tied her hair up with the ribbon, took one last look in the mirror, and went out to the kitchen.

"Laurel," her mother said, shocked.

"Does it look all right? I only have these old boots."

Her mother looked her up and down. She looked ready to shed a tear.

"Beautiful," she said. "But where are you going?"

"I'm going to see Vela Idlevice. I want her to buy the farm."

"Vela Idle…dear, that dress is for special occasions."

"I want to make a good impression."

Her mother shifted in place from one foot to the other, like she and Yrion did when they were uncomfortable about something. "Should you be visiting so late in the day? It'll be dark soon."

Laurel walked to her and spread her arms. "Over two hours of daylight left."

Her mother seemed torn between objecting further and taking this opportunity to enjoy the dress on her daughter. She reached out and smoothed the creases on the sleeves with her fingers. Then she let out a sigh and nodded. Laurel leaned down and kissed her on the cheek.

"Work on those bids, Yrion," Laurel said.

He was sitting at the hearth again, stoking hot coals.

"All right," he said. "Take a shawl. I think it's going to snow."

"Not in September."

Laurel took a shawl anyway and found she needed it. The air was unseasonably cold and crisp. She hurried up the hill and turned north on the road. She moved quickly, as much to keep warm as to keep up with her heartbeat. She found she was nervous—a rare thing for her. Folk didn't often intimidate her because most folk were either men who thought they knew better than her because she was a woman or women who agreed with those men. But Vela Idlevice was different. She managed the estate for her frail husband; her annual ball was the event of the season, drawing guests from outside Long Autumn Valley. Laurel didn't want to just make a good impression in order to sell the farm; she wanted to impress the lady—because, maybe, the lady's admiration might validate, even bolster, Laurel's own ambitions.

Tributary paths branched left off Witching Hour Road and wound into the Idlevice's various fields. At the last, a wide carriageway curved gently left under a canopy of ancient willow trees. Stone pillars topped with copper finials guarded either side of the lane, signaling that this path led to the Idlevice mansion. Laurel took it. She'd never been down this road, never had any business here before.

After a half mile, the mansion came into view, and another quarter mile brought her to the main gates. The gates were forged of black iron bars, each bar topped with a spike, and they swung from two pillars that resembled those at the entrance of the carriageway. A twelve-foot high wall stretched to the left and right.

Laurel passed through, followed the carriageway another hundred yards, then weaved right around a circular fountain. A fat, urn-shaped spout stood in the center. On special occasions, perhaps, it would spit water, but it wasn't running now. The water lay cool and patient in the basin.

Then came the mansion itself. A turret rounded the southwest corner of the building. Tall, rectangular windows broke up its stony façade. Laurel scanned the windows for movement, some sign that someone had seen her arrive. Velvet drapes hid some rooms; sheer white curtains softened the shapes of furniture and plants in others. She brushed herself off one last time, tucked a stray hair behind her ear, and stepped up a four-stair, semicircular porch. The white doors were trimmed in gold-painted molding. The handles were gold too and curved like swans' necks.

Laurel knocked softly.

In seconds, the door opened and a gust of warmth rushed out. A servant stood there in a short black coat over a white shirt and straight black pants. His shoes shone like obsidian. His light brown face was cleanly shaven save for a thin line of a mustache. His dark eyes shone like his shoes, as did his hair which he parted on the side and combed to a small tail in the back. He ushered Laurel into the house with a sweep of his hand and closed the door behind her.

"Good evening," he said in an accent Laurel couldn't place.

Laurel cleared her throat. "Here to see Lady Idlevice."

"We weren't expecting visitors today."

"Oh. May I come back another time, when you expect me?"

"Your name?"

She told him, and he eyed her up and down, his gaze too sterile to be suspicious or judgmental. Then he hurried off with a stiff stride. Laurel glanced at herself in a mirror on the right-hand wall of the foyer. In such a setting, her fine dress didn't feel nearly fine enough.

After a minute, delicate footsteps drew near, and Vela Idlevice appeared at the end of the foyer.

The lady's raven hair was pulled back to a bouquet of thick, generous curls held in place by a sterling silver comb studded with violet jewels. Her violet gown pinched at her neck, hugged the contours of her thin body, then fell like drapes from her narrow hips. Her skin was milky white and her lips full. Her thin nose tapered to a delicate point. The only sign of age on the lady's face was the faintest hint of crow's feet at her eyes, but even they managed to enhance her beauty.

The lady looked Laurel up and down for the briefest of moments, her gaze more sterile than her servant's. The gown she wore when not expecting guests put Laurel's finest dress to shame—to such a degree that Laurel could no longer worry about it. Her plan was still a good one.

"Miss Blight?" she asked in a low, smoky voice.

"Lady Idlevice," Laurel replied.

"You're all shadow, girl. Come into the light and let me have a look at you."

Laurel moved out of the foyer and followed Vela to a spot where the sunlight could fall upon her. Now the lady was all shadow, a dark silhouette against the blinding sun. Laurel tried not to squint.

"My, you have grown," the lady said. "And grown fair. When was it I last saw you? In Brodhaven, walking along the storefronts with your father. I remember that hair—your mother's hair."

Laurel didn't know if she was blushing or if it was the sun warming her face. "Kind of you to notice," she replied.

"And how is your mother? I was very saddened to hear of your father's early rest."

"She is fine. Thank you."

"And are you fine?"

Laurel looked at the floor. "I am."

"So what brings you to my door?"

Laurel lifted her head. This was no time to be shy. This was a time for confidence.

"I'm sure you've heard of the Witching Hour Railroad," Laurel said.

"*Linenpest's* railroad," the lady replied. Venom all but dripped from her mouth. It was no secret in the Valley that Lady Idlevice despised the mayor—never invited him to her yearly ball. Laurel was counting on it.

"He's calling for a vote next month."

The lady's eyes narrowed. "How do you know this?"

"I'm one of the town scribes. I have to copy the announcement."

"I see. And is it ethical for a scribe to discuss the contents of these announcements?"

Laurel shrugged. "It's public knowledge already. Brodhaven would be more concerned that two women were discussing it than anything."

Vela's gaze held Laurel for the longest moment yet. Laurel could practically feel the lady sizing her up, deciding on whether or not this girl was worth her time. When the lady turned away, Laurel caught a glimpse of a smirk.

"Follow me, Miss Blight," Vela said.

She led Laurel to a room with the curved stairway with a white balustrade. Looking up, Laurel saw it wind round and round, up through all four stories. The ceiling above was a circular glass window which meant the stairs led to the Idlevice's famous ballroom. At the upper floors, the balustrade was wrapped with brown thorny vines and strands of cotton meant to look like spider webs.

Preparations for the ball, Laurel told herself.

They went left through a sitting room, then a study, another room with a large piano, and finally the room at the southwest corner of the mansion. Tall windows let the western light stream through sheer white curtains. Books lined low shelves on the south and west walls, but chairs surrounded a small tea table in the center of the room, making this room part study, part sitting room. Also at that table, Lord Percy Idlevice sat in his wheeled chair, his back to Vela's and Laurel's entrance.

"Percy, dear," the lady said, "this is Laurel Blight, Corvus Blight's daughter. You remember, our next-door neighbors? She's asked for advice concerning her farm."

Vela moved behind her husband's chair, took hold of its handles, and turned him toward Laurel. A wool blanket covered him shoulders to toes. His eyes were glassed over, and his head looked too heavy for his neck. But he managed to raise his right hand underneath the blanket.

"Forgive my husband's manners," the lady said. "His illness keeps him weak, but he insists on attending town meetings—his duty as lord. It'll take him a day or two to recover from it. You forget you're not a young man anymore, my lord."

Laurel nodded and smiled politely, and Vela wheeled him to the southwest corner where the windowed turret gave full vantage of his estate. Her servant, meanwhile, had reappeared in the doorway.

"I think some tea, Suhar," Vela said, and the man rushed off.

They sat at the table. Laurel kept her back straight, hands folded neatly on her lap.

"Now," Vela said, "let's talk about why you're really here."

Laurel could feel her face warming again. "I—that is, *my family*—need some advice. Mayor Linenpest wants our land for his railroad. I'm not certain we should sell to him."

"Oh? Why wouldn't you?"

"Because it's worth more than Linenpest will pay."

"Is it? To whom?"

Laurel dug her thumbnail into her palm. "Well…to you, perhaps."

"*To me?* Our estate spans three hundred acres. What good are a cursed farm and a few acres more?"

Laurel took a deep, quiet breath. "I don't want to sell to Linenpest," she said, "and I don't think you want me to either."

The servant, Suhar, returned with a silver dish bearing a matching teapot, cups and saucers. The conversation silenced while he poured the tea—which seemed an excruciatingly long process to Laurel. It gave her the unwanted time to second-guess herself. Maybe coming here wasn't such a good idea after all; it was so presumptuous. The lady was probably debating whether or not to ask her servant throw their guest out onto the carriageway and drink the tea himself.

Instead, when the tea was poured, Vela dismissed him and handed Laurel a cup and saucer herself. "How much land are you selling?"

"All of it," Laurel replied. "Eighty-three acres, thirty of them Copperwood."

"If the name *Witching Hour Railroad* is any indication," the lady continued, "Pavo Linenpest plans to follow the existing road—as far as he can, anyway."

Laurel nodded—she'd reached the same conclusion.

"And he'll use the lumber off the land to lay the rails," the lady added.

"But if someone else logged it out first…"

"They could make their profit and sell to Linenpest after. He needs the land either way."

Laurel found her validation. This *was* a moneymaking opportunity, and she didn't have to explain it or convince the lady of it. *It just might work! And* she'd get to spite Pavo Linenpest in the process.

"What about your brother," Vela asked, "the young inheritor?"

Laurel twitched at his mention. "Yrion is…young."

"Young enough to agree with any decision you make?"

"He'll put his signature where I tell him."

Lady Idlevice chuckled softly. "Only by unfortunate circumstance do you and I decide as men. For a time, anyway. And so long as the men are the ones to raise their hands or sign their names, no one seems to mind."

Laurel smiled again, politely, but earnestly too. She was glad to know she wasn't the only woman who felt this way. She sipped the tea—lavender, unsweetened, tasted like a meadow—while the lady considered her plan.

Finally, Vela took a sip of her own tea then set the cup and saucer on her lap. "I'm not going to buy your farm."

Just like that, Laurel felt deflated. All she could say was, "Oh."

"But you're right: I don't want Pavo Linenpest to get his hands on it just yet—and not simply because I despise the man. Lord Idlevice is already a landowner, and buying more doesn't buy him more votes."

Laurel hadn't considered that. Selling to her *or* Linenpest would mean they'd lose Yrion's vote at town meetings. The lady wanted to replace Yrion with someone with shared interests. But it also meant she believed they could actually win. Of that, Laurel wasn't so sure.

"What new landowner would want it?" Laurel asked.

"Well, Miss Blight, because we share a common interest, and because you've flattered me by asking my advice, I will help you find him. Lord Idlevice has many business associates."

Laurel stifled a stupid smile by drinking more tea.

"That would be wonderful," she said. "My lady."

They talked a while. About the Valley. About Pavo Linenpest's railroad. Laurel could never talk about this with her own mother—far too contentious. The only person with whom Laurel had truly discussed her modern ideas was Caelum. But Lady Idlevice, by virtue off her gender, shared not just Laurel's beliefs but her *perspective*. Laurel felt wholly at ease with her, as if they'd been schoolhouse friends too.

The sky greyed over just before sundown, and the servants began bringing in lamps, lighting the room so well it was as if the clouds hadn't come. But Laurel made certain to excuse herself before overstaying her welcome. Vela led Laurel back to the foyer, and Suhar opened the front door. A carriage was already waiting, and the lady insisted.

"Thank you," Laurel said. "For everything."

"Your visit was a splendid surprise, Miss Blight," the lady said. "I expect to see more of you."

Laurel nodded and left the house. It had grown cold outside, colder than Laurel expected. Light shone from the mansion windows onto two white mares standing before the carriage, their fine manes brushed as straight as a noblewoman's. A few white flakes drifted down from above.

Snow? Laurel marveled. *Yrion had guessed right.*

She climbed into the carriage, and Suhar closed the door behind her. The carriage moved forward without squeak or creak, and as it rolled around the fountain Laurel saw Lady Idlevice's silhouette looking out through the first window. The carriage quickly gathered speed, and by the time it passed through the gate, the mares were at full gallop. The light from the mansion faded, and a heavy blur of snowflakes rushed past.

Laurel's blood moved at the mares' pace. "That went well," she said aloud to no one, and in her mind she repeated: *That went well, that went well.* Her plan had proved to be a good one. With the lady's help, the farm would not only fetch a fair price but Yrion's vote would be replaced—a bonus she hadn't planned. Win or lose, things were looking good for her family.

Before long, the carriage halted and Suhar opened the door. Laurel stepped out onto Witching Hour Road, up the little trail from her cottage. Firelight fell in little orange squares through the front windows. The snow had picked up and was finding its way through the trees. She turned to thank Suhar, but he was already back at the reins, wheeling the carriage about. The mares thundered off, trailed by a cloud of dust and flurries.

Laurel found her mother rocking in front of the fire, needlework in her lap. Yrion lay curled up like a dog before the hearth, fast asleep under their father's coat. Laurel moved across the room and touched her mother on the shoulder.

"Did it go well?" Lyra whispered.

Laurel leaned over and kissed her on the head. "We're going to be all right."

Five

Yrion heard the thundering of hooves.

Stars streaked overhead.

Grass parted beneath him.

He came to a view of an open field.

I know this field, he thought.

Across a shallow dell, a tree-line began.

I know those trees.

A cottage nestled just inside their protection. A thin wisp of smoke swirled out its chimney.

I know that cottage.

The view lingered there, and a tightness began to build in Yrion's chest, like drawing breath after breath without exhaling. He wanted to move, knew he should, knew it was time, but the view was out of his control. The held-back breaths grew stale, chilled; he felt himself begin to shudder but couldn't exhale. The chimney wisp thinned, and when the breeze blew it vanished.

His limbs rattled.

His chest couldn't handle more breath.

He wanted to turn, to move one inch of his own accord. He wanted to exhale.

Then, a heavy thud sounded. It rippled across the dell, through the trees, and into the cottage, like a single heartbeat of the Valley itself.

Yrion sat up.

Air rushed out of him like a bellows. His father's coat lay jumbled in his lap. He shivered but was drenched with sweat. The last coals of the fire lay dying in a dim heap. The white light of the moon poured through the window.

He sat there panting. His heart raced. The images from the dream began to fade—smoke and forest and grass. But the feelings lingered, though he had trouble identifying them. Tension and intensity. Fear. An urge, a *need*. But a need for what?

Strange dream. Not much of a dream at all.

He shivered again and saw there was no kindling left for the fire, just a few splinters and chips of bark. He picked them up one at a time and flicked them onto the coals. They flared up like matches and quickly died. He put the coat on, hugged his legs tightly, and began to rock. He knew he should go to bed, climb under the heavy blankets and sleep like a bear in winter. But he was wide awake now.

He'd been trying to study his auction bids, but forcing numbers into memory made him sleepy. Really memorable things had a way of sticking on their own. Like the time Yrion rubbed his thumb along the freshly sharpened sickle; he still had a little scar from that. Or the time Father wore the hame and pretended he was an ox. That was easier to remember than 'a dollar twenty five for the sickle' and...*how much for the hame?*

Yrion didn't know how he would do it. The auction, selling the farm—everything was changing. And he was supposed to be changing too. As man of the house, he was supposed to have changed *already*. But he hadn't, and he didn't know how. He didn't know how he would *learn* how. Would he have to teach himself? He wouldn't be any good at that either.

He needed his father. For a month, a week. For a day. For one hour, even.

He felt tears welling up but he fought them back and decided he would get the fire going again. He tiptoed to the door, stuffed his feet into his boots, and slipped out into the night.

Snow was falling, just as he said it would. It lay in the thinnest sheet on the forest floor. It wouldn't amount to much; the ground was still too warm. Still, it surprised him—he'd gotten one thing right today.

Yrion rounded the south side of the cottage and stopped.

Looking through the trees and across his blackened farmland stirred something from memory. Slowly it came back to him. His strange dream. What had it been about? The field, the trees, the cottage. Tension. Fear—yes, that was a constant. The urge, the need.

A feeling of waiting.

Waiting, he thought. *Like that horse waiting for a rider.*

He wished he hadn't thought it. Especially not now, not here, right where he'd seen it just last night. And now he wished he hadn't come out here at all—he should have gone to bed. He turned and looked up to the road.

Nothing. No horse. No Nightsteed.

But that didn't comfort him much.

A breeze picked up and the leaves chattered overhead. He caught a strong whiff of the curse, sickly sweet, flowing up from the field. He hurried to the woodpile and loaded up his arms. He squeezed the logs tightly to his chest.

He turned back to the cottage and his arms went limp. The logs dropped on his feet but he hardly felt them. His breath caught in his throat, threatened to choke him. His chest grew tight again. The tension, the heart-racing intensity had returned. And he trembled.

There, only five steps away, stood the monstrous horse.

Its coat was long like a mane all over and was so dark Yrion struggled to truly see it. Steam rolled off its flank, and breath shot from its nostrils like a hot kettle, forming a low, creeping blanket of fog around its hoofs. It truly was the biggest horse Yrion had ever seen: if Banyon was eighteen hands at the withers, this horse was no less than twenty-one.

It lifted its lead hoof and dropped it with a thud that shook the ground.

Yrion felt the urgency, the impatience. He'd sensed it here last night, and he'd experienced it in his dream. What was more, he sensed the horse was feeling it too. He couldn't explain how he knew it. It was as if the horse were speaking to him—but not in words. Its heart spoke to his heart as if through black magic.

The Nightsteed.

What else could it be?

Ride, it told his heart. He didn't understand where. He didn't understand why. Only *ride*.

The Nightsteed stomped its hoof again. It had no time for questions. And neither did Yrion. He didn't just sense the impatience, he shared it. The Nightsteed's heart wasn't just speaking to his; his heart was speaking back.

Ride, it said. *Mount and ride.*

Yrion stepped closer and looked up. The Nightsteed's coat was thick and matted with dried clumps of mud and leaves and brambles. It smelled like the curse, the touch of the Nightfather. He reached out and tried running his fingers through the fur, but it was so tangled that they snagged. He gave the hair a tug, and the beast didn't seem to mind. Only when Yrion tarried did it wheel its massive head and snort. A glare from an unseen light source reflected madly in its glassy, onyx eye.

Yrion clutched a fistful of its hair. He lifted his boot high and took a few half-steps till it too snagged. He exhaled, and he climbed. The Nightsteed's coat was like a rope ladder, shifting precariously as he struggled upward. It took him five long steps to reach the top and swing his leg over. His little legs hardly straddled the horse's wide back, and it hurt his groin to try. Instead he knelt and let the insides of his feet grip as best they could.

The beast looked back at him with that glassy eye. Yrion understood that look too, comprehended what it said: he laced his fingers into its mane and squeezed tight with his feet.

The Nightsteed bolted.

Five effortless leaps and it reached the top of the hill. Another five and it was at full gallop. Yrion had never moved so fast in his life. The wind stung his eyes; tears streaked back across his temples. The beast's slaver slapped him in the face. Somehow, the Nightsteed continued to gather speed—*impossible* speed. Its long coat rippled like a banshee's shroud.

Yrion looked back and saw a trail of fog in their wake, as if the horse's hooves were setting the path afire. The Copperwood blew past on all sides. Witching Hour Road seemed to stretch on forever in a dark tunnel; yet, that too was impossible. At this speed they should have reached the steep, winding section that led into the Uphills. But the Nightsteed wasn't winding; it ran straight and so did the path.

Above, streaks of moonlight began to flash in rings around the dark tunnel; not a white moon, but orange, as if it weren't the moon at all but a dim sun. Yet, in those momentary flashes, the canopy itself remained black, as if the leaves themselves had blackened.

The flashes grew longer, stretched into visions like rooms connected by dark hallways. Visions of Laurel dancing with a man in black; the town hall packed full of wolves; a locomotive steaming across a frosty landscape; and his father.

His father looked tired; heavy bags hung beneath his eyes, as if he hadn't slept for weeks. And he looked dusty, like a figurine on a shelf too high to reach. He'd never seen his father in such a state. *Dusty?* Corvus Blight was always on the move. He didn't tire. What had happened to him? Where was he?

The scenes didn't pass by like stationary doorways. They flashed, and the flashes made Yrion's head swim worse than when he memorized auction bids. Yet they seemed so close, so real. They were just too brief. Yrion couldn't latch onto one, couldn't force it to stay put so that he might focus upon it. Maybe, if he timed it right, he could touch one. He would brush the dust from his father's shoulder, shake the weariness from him.

The flashing visions of Laurel and the train and the wolves gave way to constant flashes of his father. Without thinking, Yrion loosened his grip on the Nightsteed's mane. All he had to do was reach out. His father's image blinked as though Yrion were closing and opening his eyes at a deliberate rhythm to the Nightsteed's charge. If he could just *touch* the scene, it might steady, might come into focus.

He stretched.

His father looked so weary.

Stretched.

The scene was an inch from his fingertips.

Stretch. Stretch.

He clung to the Nightsteed's mane with his left hand, *stretched* with his right.

A sudden jolt occurred between his legs. The Nightsteed had looked back to see why its rider was tugging so. It caused only a slight change in the gallop's rhythm but the impossible speed compounded it.

And that was all it took.

Yrion's knees shifted off-center. He tried to reach back with his free hand to retake a hold, but it was too late. The momentum couldn't be stopped. The vision of his father was much further than an inch from his fingertips. And it was dimmer, transparent, vanishing.

"*Father!*" he squeaked.

He landed with a thud, and a blanket of fog rolled over him.

Six

"Yrion, dear. Yrion. Are you feeling all right?"

Yrion awoke to his mother's hand upon his forehead. Daylight shone in the hallway and bled into his windowless room. He was in his bed, covers up to his neck. Lyra moved her hand and placed her bare wrist upon his brow.

"Are you all right, dear?" she repeated.

Yrion blinked a few times. "I think so."

"You look like you had a rough night."

"What time is it?"

"You don't feel warm." His mother removed her wrist from his brow. "Midmorning. Time you were up. Laurel's already gone into town to deliver her letters. You don't want her to find you in bed when she gets back."

The thought of that helped Yrion throw back the covers and plop his feet on the floor.

"Oh, Yrion," his mother complained, "you've gone to bed *dirty*."

Yrion looked down and saw he was still wearing his father's coat. The coat was wrinkled and flecks of leaves clung to its fibers. He even had his boots on.

"I'm sorry, Mother. I woke up cold."

"Well," she said, "best get moving. You can help me wash your linens today."

His mother left the room.

Yrion tarried on the edge of the bed, looking down at his dirty clothes. He felt as though he hadn't slept a wink; in truth, he didn't remember going to bed at all. How had he gotten here? He remembered…he remembered…

His father. Dusty. Weary. Motionless. The thought brought Yrion to the brink of tears. What did it mean? What had he seen?

His mother's calls brought him to his feet. He stripped the linens from his bed and rolled them into a ball, took them out to the kitchen and dropped them onto a chair at the table.

"Yrion," she said, "I'd like you to—"

He pulled the front door closed behind him. He didn't have time for chores just yet.

The Nightsteed.

Had he dreamt it?

I put my boots on, he recounted. *I went outside.* He remembered stretching. He remembered falling. His knees ached. His ribs too. *It couldn't have been a dream.*

But what was the alternative? That a horse from folklore had shown up at his door? That he'd ridden it? That he'd seen his father dusty and tired?

He *must* have dreamt it.

Around the side of the house, a few logs lay scattered on the ground, right where he'd dropped them last night.

Didn't dream that.

But he saw no hoof prints. A horse as big as the Nightsteed would have left deep pits where it stepped. He dashed up the hill to Witching Hour Road, scanned about. He saw old wagon tracks and evidence of a much smaller horse—Kernel, probably. He saw old divots and loose stones. But no sign of the Nightsteed.

It must have been a dream, he told himself.

Yet that didn't feel true. Something had happened to Yrion. It was happening still. He sensed it, the way he sensed the Nightsteed's desire for a rider, the way he'd needed to ride. He felt it like he'd felt the oncoming snow.

He sniffed the air, smelled the rotting sweetness wafting up from his fields. He put his hands to his face and he could smell it on his palms, the smell of the Nightsteed's mane.

The distinct odor of the curse.

Seven

Jacob Le'fever felt the chug of the locomotive's engine pulse through the axles beneath him. He watched the frosty countryside stream past under the moonlight. It was colder here than he remembered. It had been thirteen years since he left Long Autumn Valley.

Thirteen years.

He'd received a letter from Brodhaven announcing a vote on the Witching Hour Railroad, and it presented him with a unique opportunity: he could finally unload Rotbottom farm at a profit. If the letter had come a week earlier—a *day*—he might have missed it, lost it in the shuffle of a thousand papers. He might have abandoned the farm for good, counted it as a loss. He didn't need the money, after all. He'd done well abroad, seen the world, made a fortune. He'd found what he was good at, and it had taken him far.

Business acumen, they called it. Buy, sell, trade; Jacob could do it all. Business had kept him away; now, it was drawing him back.

Thirteen years. Had it been long enough?

He leaned his head against the car's window, felt the cold against his brow. Mile after mile, the hills folded together all the way to the horizon, like icebergs under the moon. He'd seen real icebergs, seen spice roads wind over desert dunes, ancient ruins swallowed by jungle thickets, golden halls of foreign kings. But this countryside stirred something in him like no other. This place got into one's bones, and afterward he could call nowhere else home. Perhaps other lands invoked the same in other people. But Jacob, in so many ways, loved the Valley: the changing seasons, the views, the seamless mix of woods and farms, wilderness and agriculture. But it unearthed something else, too.

He wondered if he'd see her, wondered if he was ready to. He wondered if he cared either way.

Thirteen years, near enough to the day.

The memories rolled through Jacob's mind…

Night had settled into the Copperwood. They stood in a patch of holly and spicebush at the foot of a dead tree. The tree's leafless branches let the moonlight fall through.

Jacob held her hands close to his heart. "Vela, how long can this continue?"

Vela's dark eyes stared back, caught a glimmer of the moon. "As long as it can."

"But when will we be together?"

"We are together."

Jacob lowered their hands to their waists. "Not just here. Not just in secret."

Vela pulled her left hand away but Jacob held fast to her right.

"He doesn't love you," he said. "Not the way I do."

"That's why I'm here."

They were going in circles, and Jacob was unravelling inside. Vela had a way of answering his questions without giving him the answer he was seeking. It had a certain mystique, he supposed, but now was not the time for mystique. Now was the time for honesty. Perhaps she was incapable of honesty; Jacob's instincts said she was. But then she would do something—offer some small gesture of affection—to spark his passion, and he'd forget both instinct and reason, and he'd latch on to hope, to belief, the desire to believe.

"I bought that farm for you," he said. "To be near you."

"And we should live there, on cursed land?"

"I'll buy a horse then. We can ride out of the Valley together."

He saw a smile cross her face. "You're terrible with horses," she teased.

"I'll take you anywhere. If it's a fortune you need, I'll make one."

Vela squeezed his right hand. It sent a tingle up his arm.

"Is it time you need?" he asked.

"Not if time is hitched to a promise," she said. "I made that promise once already and you see how well I've kept it."

Jacob felt despair creeping in, fear of her rejecting him. Yet he needed her so, like a hunger.

"Vela, I can't...share you. Why would you ask that of me—of him, even?"

She yanked her hand away and it stung him, like pulling off a scab. "You didn't mind sharing me when this all started."

"But I wanted you so."

"And now you don't?"

"I want you more. I want more of you. I want all of you."

"And if you can't have all of me, you want none of me?"

They were drawing dangerously close to an ultimatum, one Jacob wasn't sure he was ready for. So many times and ways he had imagined demanding a decision from her. His passion imagined a romantic outcome. His reason insisted: whatever the outcome, it would be for the best; no more games. But fear held him back, fear of losing what little of her he had.

"I want—" he tried.

A thundering of hooves came out of the north chased by the howling of dogs. Torchlight appeared over the crest of the hill. Jacob's first instinct was to flee. He took hold of Vela's arm but found he could not move her.

The riders charged down the hill and wheeled clockwise around the thicket, encircling it. They all wore fine evening attire—black jackets and white shirts, roses upon their lapels. But their faces were hidden beneath pale masks in the Everdark tradition: weary, sad faces, the exaggerated semblances of tiredness. The riders had come from the Idlevices' Ball of the Nightfather.

The circle tightened which brought more light. The hounds snarled between the horses. The last rider to arrive urged his mount forward a step further than the rest and removed his mask. Jacob knew him; Vela knew him better.

"Who goes there?" Percy Idlevice demanded.

Neither Jacob nor Vela responded. One of Percy's servants or guests at the ball must have seen her sneak away, and it was plain that he had ridden out here to catch his wife in this very position. Nevertheless, Jacob watched as realization darkened Percy's face, a mixture of wrath and utter disbelief.

Everyone stayed where they were, caught in this breathless moment. Even the dogs had quit their baying. All were waiting for Percy Idlevice to make his move.

The lord drew a pistol from a saddle holster and pointed it at Jacob's chest. Jacob stared into the barrel. It was an old flintlock with a long curved handle, some Idlevice heirloom, made of equal parts wood and iron. Percy forced its hammer back with his thumb.

"Vela," he asked, voice quavering, "who is this man?"

Vela pushed Jacob aside.

"Percy," she said, "put the gun away."

Her voice was colder than Percy's stare and the iron barrel combined.

The gun twitched in Percy's hand as he struggled to keep it upright. When he didn't lower it, Vela approached his horse and mounted it with ease, sidesaddle behind him. She locked one arm around his trunk.

Watching her go to her husband sent a chill through Jacob; seeing her touch him made Jacob want to retch. He almost wished Percy would shoot him and be done with it. Vela took hold of the horse's reins in her hand and managed to turn it sideways while Percy kept his pistol aimed at Jacob's heart.

"Go," Vela said, as much to her husband as to Jacob.

Percy tarried long enough to say: "Begone, stranger."

Then he pointed his pistol skyward and discharged it, keeping his eyes—now wild with hate—on Jacob. He wheeled his horse the rest of the way about and galloped north. His posse was slow to follow, perhaps surprised that their master hadn't shot dead the man in the thicket.

When their torchlight disappeared over the hill, Jacob slumped to his knees.

Eight

Laurel stared in disbelief at the page. It was Thursday, and Mayor Linenpest's plans for the Witching Hour Railroad had been released to the public, printed by the local press on the front and back of a quality sheet of paper. That the mayor had gone through the trouble to use the press—had distributed the plans period—showed a great deal of presumptuousness on his part. He was confident he would win. That he had every reason to be made Laurel want to set the page on fire.

A simplified map of the Valley covered the first side. Brodhaven was located in the bottom left quadrant, identified by a picture of a bell. From there, a line representing Witching Hour Road curved gently into the upper right quadrant before arcing sharply to the left. The upper quadrants also contained a scattering of circumflexes to show the Uphills. Another line loosely paralleled the road and was crossed by a hyphen every half inch; this was the proposed path of the railroad.

The map wasn't detailed enough to show property lines, but Laurel had estimated correctly: the railroad would follow Witching Hour Road, shear off the Blight's stretch of the Copperwood, bend east past the Idlevice estate, then slice deep into the Uphills. A list of affected properties supplemented the map, printed across six columns in very small letters. Blight was on the list. Whitehead appeared over a dozen times.

Laurel turned the sheet over to read the details.

"Will we be seeing Caelum today?" her mother asked from her cutting board.

Laurel tried to keep reading. By 'we', her mother meant would *Laurel* be seeing Caelum today. Unlike Father, Mother didn't exactly pressure Laurel to wed, but it was obvious she wanted it, and she occasionally attempted (and failed at) her own subtler approaches.

"Such a nice young man," her mother said.

"Yes, very nice."

He was. And the sky was blue, and snow was cold, and the Valley was cursed. But what did that have to do with anything? Caelum hadn't asked Laurel to marry him, and she didn't want him to. They were old friends, best friends, and understood each other in a way that others couldn't. Onlookers only saw a boy and a girl, and to them boy plus girl equaled marriage.

Laurel blocked her mother out and kept reading, mouthing the words to herself. It didn't take long before she was reading aloud.

"Laurel, dear," her mother asked, "what's the matter?"

"...will enact, for administrative ease and considerations, the following mandates, should the Witching Hour Railroad vote pass. Private sale of properties with corners falling within the proposed pathway shall be restricted—all pending contracts shall be honored. A cooperative window will be provided for landowners of said properties, beginning today, October the third, and ending at sunset Friday, October the twenty-fourth. During this time, Brodhaven will offer eighteen dollars and fifty cents for every acre. After this window, and through construction, Brodhaven will reimburse displaced landowners at twelve dollars and fifty cents per acre."

Laurel slammed the page down on the table and crumpled it in her fist.

"Laurel..." her mother began.

"It's *thievery*! Eighteen-fifty an acre is dirt cheap as is—half what any acre is worth. No one will risk losing six more dollars an acre with the hopes of beating the vote. They'll take the eighteen fifty now, lose their voice at the meeting, and that's one less voice to oppose Linenpest's railroad."

Lyra set down her knife, moved behind Laurel, and put her hands on her daughter's shoulders.

"Eighteen-fifty isn't so bad," she said. "We can do a lot with that."

Laurel trembled. "Mother, our bit of the Copperwood is worth more than double that."

"We'll manage."

Laurel's feet began to tap, an effort to burn off the tension. "What would Father do?"

"He'd do what you're doing," her mother replied.

It all seemed so hopeless: the curse pushing on one side, this railroad pushing on the other. One way or another the Blights were getting squeezed off their land, but Linenpest was going to squeeze dozens of others off their land as well. If only a handful of them got the same idea that Laurel had, they might offer bigger plots of wooded acreage to profiteers. And there were only so many logging outfits in the Valley—only so many axes and hands to wield them. Why would they waste their time with a thirty acre stretch so close to Brodhaven when they might get a hundred acres in the Uphills further from the railroad's progress? Laurel's plans were falling apart before they had a chance to get started. If she didn't sell now, her family might end up with nothing. They might…

It took everything in Laurel's power to calm herself. This was exactly what Linenpest wanted: panicked sellers. She had to stay rational.

She skimmed over the list of affected landowners again and wondered. Whitehead was listed a dozen times. There were more Whiteheads than that—who knew how many? The Uphills spanned thousands of wild acres, and the railroad would only touch a fraction of that. To start anyway.

If all the Whitehead landowners attended the next town meeting, they might have a chance. The farmers too. Everyone outside Brodhaven had a stake in this. In a lot of ways, this vote trumped the harvest itself. Losing a day of work was better than losing land. Folk needed to realize this.

Laurel shrugged her mother's hands away. "I'm all right."

She spent the rest of the morning pacing about the house, jotting ideas down in the margins of the railroad plans. Suggestions. Arguments. Demands. At times like this, when she was composing not scribing, her penmanship was worse than Yrion's. She misspelled words. Drops of ink blotted the page. By the end, the rural railroad map had become a city of letters and crisscrossing phrases. But somewhere in the tangle were the right words.

After lunch, she was ready. She sat down, and the words flowed: constant, smooth, an act of cleansing. She wrote each line without rereading the one preceding it, transcribing from memory, and her strokes didn't stop till the letter was complete. It was short, but she knew every word was right. Her signature hadn't dried on the first copy before she began her second.

Before dinner, she had three stacks of letters written, and having spent years scribing, she knew a good many addresses by heart. She'd send them north, east, and west, to families sympathetic to her cause, families with some influence in their respective regions. She had to sell her farm either way, but if enough folk answered her letter's call, others might get to keep their land.

The letter read:

Landowners of Long Autumn Valley,

Wrapping a weasel in a sash makes him no less a weasel, and if we let him into the henhouse, we shouldn't wonder why we're short on hens. And when he offers to share eggs with us, it is neither gift nor compensation. The hens are our hens, their eggs our eggs, their houses our houses.

Land undefended is free for the taking. Silence is an invitation.

Declare your lands your own.

Vote against the Witching Hour Railroad.

Nine

Jacob sat up to what sounded like a pistol shot followed by a whistling ricochet. He turned. A blurry figure was standing next to his seat. Jacob put on his spectacles. It was only the car attendant.

"Brodhaven Station, sir," the attendant said.

Jacob looked through the car window to see they had arrived at his destination. The whistle must have been the locomotive's; the pistol shot must have been a dream.

Jacob thanked the attendant, buttoned his coat, and exited the car.

Yes, Jacob thought, *colder than I remembered.*

A dusting of snow had settled on the platform and beyond on tan grasses. Steam billowed from the locomotive's stack and gathered foggily on the platform. Jacob had to wipe the moisture from his spectacles. To the left, the line of trailing cars bent out of sight to the southwest; to the right, the tracks followed the same arc to the southeast.

Jacob was the only passenger getting off here. A young porter was pulling half the cargo out of the compartment beneath the car to find Jacob's luggage: a small black suitcase was all he'd brought, all he'd need. The porter found it, set it aside. Jacob picked up the suitcase, surprised the porter by slipping him a whole dollar, and let him finish restocking the compartment.

The platform hadn't been here thirteen years ago. It didn't look more than two seasons old. Opposite the train, a small, octagonal pavilion sheltered a few rows of empty benches. Beyond the platform, Witching Hour Road wound its way north over browning hillocks to the golden forests at the heart of the Valley. Carts pulled by horses and oxen were coming down the road. Some were filled with goods to be transported, some were empty and ready to receive. They spread out southeast and stopped at various cars behind Jacob's.

Jacob took a deep breath of the crisp air. It was a scent he couldn't describe but hadn't forgotten. Old. Ancient, even. Some of the first smells his nose had ever sniffed. Something in his blood, sent from mother to unborn child. It worried him. There was power in it. Dominion. As if the Valley were a set of jaws opened wide, and his nose smelled danger on its breath.

He had come for business not needing the money. Something was wrong with that. Rotbottom farm was single ear of corn compared to his harvest. Why then? Why had he come?

To prove that you could. To bury it.

Thirteen years had changed him, and it had changed this place. There was a platform beneath his feet. And soon, perhaps, a new railroad junction. He had moved on, no matter what the scents on the crisp air told him.

"Hello there," a voice came.

Jacob looked right and saw Pavo Linenpest ascending the platform stairs. The man—his waddle, his gut—was unmistakable. He was mayor now (so the letter from Brodhaven alluded). Somehow his stomach had grown larger than Jacob remembered. *See,* Jacob thought, *even Pavo has changed.* By the time Pavo reached the top of the steps he sounded ready to drop dead.

"Welcome," he huffed, "welcome. We don't get many travelers out this way. Not yet, anyway, but welcome. How was your journey? You know, I've ridden a few times, and I find it just splendid. The scenery, the rhythm—quite soothing, wouldn't you say?"

Jacob waited for him to come close, wondering if the mayor would recognize him in return. When he stopped a few feet short, Jacob knew he had.

"Why, Jacob Le'fever," Linenpest said. "Our letter must have reached you, yes? I hoped you would come. What do you think?"

The mayor gestured to the platform with a sweep of his hand.

"Very ambitious," Jacob replied.

"Took a bit of effort—and quite the personal investment on my part. But if you want the train to stop, you need a train station. Not many visitors, as I've said, but plenty of goods coming and going. Made my investment well worthwhile. And if the goods are flowing, travelers won't be far behind. And here you are."

"Here I am," Jacob replied.

"So glad you came. I thought you might. An opportunity for you, I think."

Pavo Linenpest came across as a fat fool, but the man was far from it. His candor put people at ease, made them trust him, but beneath it was a mind as shrewd as any, and every jolly gesture was carefully calculated. Jacob had done business with his kind before.

"Your letter encouraged me to return for the vote," Jacob said.

"Most certainly. I trust I can count on yours."

Jacob considered his response. He had the upper hand in the conversation, for Linenpest knew very little about him.

"I think not," he said.

"Oh? I wouldn't think Rotbottom farm was worth very much to you—unless it holds some *sentimental* value."

Jacob showed no reaction. "I don't like my things taken from me, even if they aren't worth very much."

And now the mayor had to consider his response. He was no doubt realizing his brand of charm was wasted on Jacob and that his plan to bring home votes from abroad might backfire.

"I see," the mayor said. "Will you be taking up residence again?"

"I haven't decided. Perhaps I'll spend my visit lobbying against your railroad."

Jacob was bluffing. He had no desire to involve himself in politics.

The mayor, trying to regain some ground, said, "With your reputation?"

Ah, Jacob thought, *so my flight from this place didn't go unnoticed.* He wasn't sure if that was good or bad or insignificant. Regardless, he countered: "As a successful business man with connections abroad? Certainly."

The mayor rubbed his chubby hands over his gut and weighed his options. "It falls to you, as a businessman, to decide what you value more: vote or profit."

Jacob wouldn't say which he valued more.

"Though," the mayor added, "if you've been travelling, you may not have received my proposed plans. They include a *fine* reimbursement incentive. I'll make sure a copy finds you."

Jacob nodded, satisfied. Whatever future dealings he had with Linenpest, the mayor now knew Jacob wasn't to be trifled with.

"May I give you a ride into town?" the mayor asked.

"I'll find my own way, thank you."

Jacob picked up his suitcase and moved past the mayor to the stairs. Before he reached solid ground, Linenpest called to him.

"Should I send the plans to Rotbottom farm," he asked, "or forward them on to Vela Idlevice?"

The comment disturbed the rhythm of Jacob's stride, slightly but perceptibly, a little more than he would have thought possible, far more than he wanted Pavo Linenpest to notice. Shame hadn't caused him to miss a step; no, it was the mention of her name. Melodious, even from the mouth of a pig. Jacob hadn't heard it spoken aloud in years, and it still moved him.

He kept walking but called to the mayor over his shoulder: "*Lady* Idlevice, to you."

Ten

Laurel peeled the yams and her mother chopped them. The yams came from Aunt Carina.

"I wish she wouldn't do this," Laurel said. "What is this, half their harvest?"

She gestured to the two overflowing buckets next to her feet. Aunt Carina had carried them here herself, and Uncle Cetus had carried the two other buckets on the far side of the table.

"It's just a bit of peeling," her mother said.

Laurel didn't mind the peeling. "Feels like pity."

"Laurel. Don't be an ingrate."

A knock came at the door around noon. Yrion was outside splitting wood (though Laurel hadn't heard the axe fall in a while). Laurel wiped her hands on the front of her apron and answered the door.

Vela Idlevice stood in the front yard. She wore a yellow dress that matched the sun. One hand held her skirt off the ground. A bundle of white cloth lay draped over her opposite forearm.

Laurel slipped off the yam-spattered apron, hung it on the hook, and pulled the door half-closed behind her.

"Lady Idlevice," Laurel said, "Can I help you?"

"I'm here to help you, Miss Blight," the lady said. "I have a prospective buyer I think you should meet."

"Today?"

"He's waiting in the southern study now."

Laurel looked up to the road and saw the lady's manservant wheeling their carriage about.

"Yes," Laurel said. "Yes, of course. I just need to wash up a little."

Vela let go of her skirt and opened the folds of white cloth to reveal a sky-blue gown trimmed with white and yellow fabric flowers that looked positively real. A pair of soft, matching slippers sat atop it.

"You can wear this," the lady said.

Laurel's eyes widened but she hesitated.

"When dealing with a man," the lady said, "look your very best. It's an advantageous distraction."

Laurel tarried a moment more. She didn't want to take it— this was far more charitable than a few buckets of yams. But she had asked for Lady Idlevice's help, and if this was the lady's way of helping, then it would be rude to refuse it. *Don't be an ingrate*, echoed in Laurel's ears. She closed the white folds and took the gown from Vela's forearm.

Laurel invited her in but hoped she would decline; the cottage was in no way presentable.

"Is your mother home?" the lady asked.

"She is."

"I'll say hello."

Laurel nodded and let Vela enter ahead of her.

"Lyra," Vela said, "wonderful to see you again."

"Vela," Lyra replied with a small nod. "Welcome."

Laurel saw something in that nod, a slight stiffness she had never seen before. Laurel hoped the lady didn't notice it as well.

Vela glanced about the cottage. "Apologies for dropping by unannounced."

Her mother offered tea and, thankfully, the lady declined.

"Mother," Laurel said while cleaning her hands in the wet sink, "Lady Idlevice has asked me to visit her for the afternoon. It's about the farm."

"Of course," her mother replied—and there was a coldness in her voice too.

"I'll hurry back." Laurel excused herself and rushed to her room.

She put the gown on. It squeezed her across the ribs and stomach, pinched her body into a thin hourglass. It pushed her breasts up high while the front dipped lower than anything she'd ever worn. The flowers bordering her bosom bloomed under the pressure. Below the cinch at her waist, the gown belled slightly outward; a thin wire frame stitched into the skirt enforced that shape. More flowers ringed the hem at the bottom.

Laurel did her best to observe herself in her handheld mirror. She felt ridiculous. It was a fine gown—very modern cuts and seams—but it revealed far too much. And it was so tight and delicate, she would have to sit very straight and very still and not breathe too deep else risk tearing it. She put her feet in the slippers and found them tightest of all; surely these were the wrong fit.

She supposed she should feel charmed, count herself lucky. How many girls in the Valley would kill to wear such a gown— and ride in Lady Idlevice's carriage? But if squeezing into a fine gown would sell the farm, Laurel would bear it. If she didn't, before winter ended she'd be starved enough to slough out of the dress with a shrug of her shoulders. Besides, when she set her discomforts aside, she thought she looked fine—looked the way one was *supposed* to look in such a dress. She tied her hair up with her blue ribbon and returned to her guest.

"Stop there," Vela said as Laurel stepped into the room.

Laurel obeyed, and the lady beheld her for a long moment, as did her mother. Laurel saw brightness in Vela's eyes, maybe a hint of pride, whereas her mother's stare clung to that iciness Laurel had noticed before.

"My girl," the lady said, "you look radiant."

Lyra went back to the yams without a word.

Laurel ignored her mother and approached. When she was within arm's reach, the lady reached up and undid the bow in her hair. Her red locks fell heavily upon her bare shoulders. With a sweep of her hand, the lady brushed some of them over the top of Laurel's head, forming an off-center part on the right side. Vela's own hair was pulled up tight, held in place with a jeweled ribbon. Laurel supposed her own ribbon was too plain.

"There," Vela said. "Radiant."

Laurel felt her face warm and looked briefly to the floor before turning to her mother.

"I won't be long," she said.

"Call your brother in, if you see him," Lyra replied.

"Thank you for sharing her, Lyra," the lady said.

"Mm-hmm. Good bye."

Laurel let Vela go out first. The lady took her skirt in her hand once more and moved up the hill with long, confident strides. Laurel caught Yrion watching from the corner of the cottage.

"Go help Mother," she said. Then she took her own skirt in her hand and followed the lady to the carriage.

Laurel sat in the backwards-facing bench, and Lady Vela sat opposite her. The carriage pulled away at a slow, dignified pace.

"Do I know this prospective buyer?" Laurel asked.

The lady gave her a thin smile. "I'm sure you've heard the name Pyxis Pettifog before."

Laurel had. The Pettifogs were shepherds and shearers, and their wealth nearly rivaled the Idlevices'. Their barn housed two dozen looms where the Pettifog mothers and daughters spun wool from the Pettifogs' enormous flocks which were rumored to exceed one thousand animals. Pyxis was the youngest son of this generation, and rather than tending sheep like his older brothers, he'd made a name for himself by designing many of the dresses locally in style.

Laurel looked down at her gown and then to Lady Idlevice's.

"You understand, now," the lady said, "why I insisted you wear it."

Laurel nodded. "But Pyxis Pettifog is quite wealthy. Why would he want our farm?"

"He stands to gain from it. That is the plan, is it not?"

"Well, yes. Only, I would think he'd prefer to see the land rather than me."

"In good time."

Laurel would never have considered Pyxis Pettifog as a prospective buyer. But this was, after all, why she sought Lady Idlevice's help. Besides, money was money and the Pettifogs had plenty of it.

When the carriage wheeled its way around the fountain outside the Idlevice mansion, Laurel saw another carriage parked in front of the door. It was black, trimmed in gold, and pulled by two black horses. Bright red curtains covered the windows, pinched in the centers like sideways bowties.

Lady Idlevice stepped out, led Laurel into the house and to the same study they'd sat in before.

When they entered the room, a man in his mid-twenties stood from one of the padded chairs around the tea table. His long, dark hair was pulled back and fastened in a tight tail by a silver ringlet. He was very tall and thin with a large Adam's apple. His face was just as thin, and his nose too, but he was handsome still. He beheld Laurel through large eyes that were only half-opened, as if he were scrutinizing her every detail. He wore a red velvet coat with stiffly padded shoulders, fastened off-center in the front by three gold buttons. His straight black pants tapered into a pair of high black boots. In a way, he resembled a soldier, only too delicate—a toy soldier, perhaps.

"Pyxis," the lady said, "this is Laurel Blight."

Mister Pettifog took Laurel's hand, bowed slightly, and brought her knuckles to his lips. He stared straight into her eyes all the while. Laurel found it an oddly formal greeting, but she reciprocated with a smile and slight curtsy.

"A pleasure to meet you," Pyxis said in a soft voice. He pronounced his words with a crisp deliberateness, like he could thread a needle with his tongue. He kept hold of Laurel's hand

and took a step back, eyeing her up and down. "The color suits her. Well done, Vela."

"Well done, Pyxis," Vela replied.

The lady sent her manservant off for tea, and the three of them sat down around the table. As Laurel took her seat, she noticed Lord Idlevice in his wheeled chair by the turret windows, in the same spot he'd been when Laurel last saw him. He gave no sign that he heard them, and the lady did not announce her return.

Mister Pettifog already had a drink in front of him, a clear, syrupy liquor in the bottom quarter of a bulbous glass. He crossed his right leg over his left and rested the glass atop his thigh. He gazed openly at Laurel, comfortable and confident, and took long sips of his drink.

"So, Pyxis," Vela said, "how is your family's business."

"So-so, he replied. "Revenues are high, but so are costs. The curse crept into one of Father's northern fields."

"I am sorry to hear that."

"My brothers didn't catch it right away, said it was a slow sort of transformation. Turned some weeds black but you could hardly notice. Unfortunately, the sheep won't avoid it—they're very *dumb* creatures. It turns their stomachs and they spit it up, but they go back for more."

"Them spitting up is costly?"

"No, but ingesting the weeds ruins the wool. Gives them coarse black spots, no good for spinning. And even the wool around the spots takes on that foul smell that won't wash out. All you can do is shear them, pen them up, and feed them a strict diet. Takes a month for the stink to go away. My brothers sold a few to the Whiteheads to avoid the hassle—at a loss, of course. *Dumb* creatures."

"The sheep?" the lady asked. "Or the Whiteheads?"

She and Pyxis chuckled, and Laurel hid her smile by taking a long sip from her teacup.

"Ah, well," Pyxis said. "What can you do?"

"Buy more land?" Laurel suggested.

Pyxis shrugged. "Always an option."

It sounded like an opportunity to Laurel.

"Pyxis," Lady Idlevice said, "why don't you show Miss Blight the shawl you brought. I'm dying to see it on her."

Mister Pettifog nodded with a smile. "As am I."

He reached into an accordion bag next to his chair and removed a lush bundle of fabric. He stretched it out in front of him. The shawl was crimson with a touch of purple, just like Laurel's hair, woven into a tapestry of blooming roses held together by a delicate netting of gold thread. Occasional drops of blue spritzed the rose petals and looked like morning dew.

They all stood, and Vela led Laurel to the inner corner of the room where an oval mirror rested in an angled stand. Laurel had never stood before a mirror so large—unless she counted the shop windows down in Brodhaven. The mirror was tilted in such a way that she was looking up at herself. (She wondered if this was how the wealthy thought everyone saw them).

Gently, Pyxis spread the shawl over Laurel's shoulders then lifted her hair out from beneath it. Her hair blended seamlessly into it, and the blue droplets matched her gown, as if the shawl were tailored for this very occasion. It felt softer than anything against her skin, so delicate that she wouldn't dare wear it anywhere but in an open room like this one for fear of snagging it on something.

Laurel was certain she'd never looked so pretty—not that prettiness mattered much. She saw it in an objective sort of way, recognizing the opportunity for vanity. For ladies surrounded by mirrors and adornments like this—and little else to occupy them—the opportunity must be great indeed. But, with that same objectivity, Laurel opted to appreciate her appearance for its usefulness: it was an 'advantageous distraction'.

"Silk," Pyxis said, placing his hands atop her shoulders. "Can you believe a worm could make something so beautiful? Makes me want to abandon wool altogether."

Laurel had read about silk but never thought she would wear it. "Will you go into the silkworm business, then?" she asked.

Pyxis shook his head. "I doubt I would fancy *wormherding* any more than shepherding. I'd rather import what I want and spare myself the disgust."

Laurel smiled politely in the mirror. When she tried to remove the shawl, Pyxis kept his hands on her shoulders.

"Keep it," he said. "You must be cold."

The fabric didn't exactly warm her, but…

Lady Idlevice ushered them back to their seats where her manservant had topped off the teacups and Pyxis' glass. Laurel thought things were going well but wondered how long these formalities would last before they discussed the farm. Perhaps, she considered, the lady was waiting for her to broach the subject. After all, Vela had arranged the meeting; wasn't that enough? So when a window of silence opened in the conversation, she tried to move things along:

"So, Mister Pettifog," she asked, "what are your thoughts on the railroad vote?"

"Well," he replied, "I don't yet attend the meetings, so it doesn't much concern me."

Vela wouldn't have considered him as a prospective buyer if he were a landowner—their cause needed more votes—but Laurel had to ask: "Are you not a business owner?"

"Not exactly. My older brothers bicker over their claim of land and sheep and wool. I don't have much of a voice in the matter. Honestly, I prefer it that way."

"But your dressmaking, your styles? I've seen them in Brodhaven windows."

"Oh, yes, that. I don't have a boutique of my own. Boutiques often front me the fabric and I sell what I stitch back to them. So I'm more of a hired hand, really. All profit, little investment."

"Quite the entrepreneur," Lady Idlevice said.

"Indeed," Laurel replied. "And is the entrepreneur interested in other endeavors?"

"Yes, Pyxis," the lady was quick to add, "would you be willing to make me a dress for the ball? I know it's short notice, but you can name your price."

That wasn't where Laurel was headed with her question. Twice now the conversation had gotten away from her.

"What about something like this?" Pyxis replied.

He reached once more into his accordion bag and produced a long black scarf that gave off a soft sheen in the light. He let them run their hands along it, and Laurel found it soft like velvet but thin like silk. Pyxis draped it over his arm and pulled it along, demonstrating how it clung to forms.

"This fabric will hug your figure like no other," he said.

"It's very fine," the lady replied. "But nothing *too* modern."

"Of course, of course. Tasteful. Elegant. Proper for our hostess."

Pyxis finished his glass of liquor then turned to Laurel.

"And what will you be wearing to the ball?" he asked.

It caught Laurel off guard. She hadn't been invited to the ball. Poor farm girls didn't belong at such things. It seemed Mister Pettifog had mistaken her for someone far above her standing—which meant Lady Idlevice hadn't told him who Laurel was or about the Blights' situation. Did the lady prefer it that way? It had to come out sometime if the farm was ever going to sell.

"You should wear what you're wearing now," Pyxis continued. "I'd be honored."

Laurel chose her words carefully. "It *is* the finest thing I've ever worn."

"Naturally."

More tea came and went for the women, and more liquor for Mister Pettifog. He pulled more fabrics from his bag and festooned Laurel, Lady Vela, and himself. But tea and liquor and fabrics didn't bring the conversation any closer to the purpose of Laurel's visit. If it went on for much longer, Pyxis might be too drunk to remember any of it.

Finally, she asked outright: "Mister Pettifog, when will you come visit our farm? It's for sale."

"Oh, Laurel, dear," Vela said with a chuckle, "let's not be presumptuous."

And though the lady smiled, Laurel caught glimpse of something in her stare, a tension in her lower eyelid that showed Laurel she was less amused than her laugh suggested.

Laurel felt her face flush. "Of course not."

Pyxis gave no sign that he noticed the tension. "Very soon, I hope," he said.

After that, Laurel let Lady Idlevice guided the conversation to topics she deemed proper, speaking only when spoken to, worried that her *presumptuousness* had angered Vela, or worse, had spoiled her chances of selling the farm to Mister Pettifog. They talked about Pavo Linenpest's railroad plans, the curse in other parts of the Valley, Vela's plans for the ball (very little of which she was willing to reveal). Not once did they discuss the Blights' farm, and at the end of it all Pyxis still didn't strike Laurel as someone who would be interested in the venture, profitable or no.

When the sun fell through the western windows, the lady excused her: "Miss Blight must be going. Her mother is expecting her."

"Of course," Pyxis said. He stood and kissed Laurel's hand again. "A pleasure meeting you."

"The pleasure was mine," Laurel replied.

"Percy," the lady called to her husband by the window, "Miss Blight is leaving."

Lord Idlevice did not stir.

"Good evening, my lord," Laurel said anyway.

Vela led her out of the study. Laurel couldn't help but think she'd done something wrong. When they reached the foyer, she turned to Vela, defeated.

"My lady," she said, "I hope I haven't embarrassed you."

The lady reached out and touched Laurel's shoulders. "My dear, you were positively charming, as I knew you would be."

"I don't understand. I—"

"We don't want to appear eager. Or worse, desperate."

"Oh," Laurel said. "No, that wouldn't do, would it."

"It would not. Let me handle the farm business."

Laurel sighed and nodded. It made perfect sense to her now. "Though, we don't have much time. The vote is in a few weeks."

"Brodhaven will honor all pending contracts—which includes logging rights. We have time."

Vela's driver opened the front door from the outside, letting the warm air rush out. Laurel pulled her shawl tighter around her shoulders only to realize it wasn't her shawl—or her gown or her slippers. She spread her arms to remove it but Vela stopped her.

"They're gifts," the lady said. "It would be rude to refuse them."

Laurel nodded. "Thank Mister Pettifog for me."

"I will. And I'll call on you soon."

Laurel reflected on the introduction during the carriage ride home. It hadn't gone anything like she had expected. It had been afternoon teatime at the Idlevices', a day most girls in Long Autumn Valley only dreamed of. Laurel had spent most of it trying to make it anything but that, and if not for Lady Idlevice's reassurances Laurel would have called it a failure. She supposed what really bothered her was leaving things in other people's hands. She understood the bargain she hoped to strike but not this layer of intrigue, of subtlety. She hadn't realized intrigue was needed—didn't the numbers speak for themselves?

Still, she trusted the lady. Vela had gotten this far for a reason.

Eleven

Yrion sat alone before the fire. He held his list of bid prices but tried not to look at them.

Hame equals two-forty, he told himself. *Two-o-five is the low. Two-forty, two-o-five the low.*

Sickle, one-twenty-five. Scythe, one-seventy-five.

Hame, two-o-five—no, two-forty.

He sighed and pushed his face hard into the paper. The auction was tomorrow. He wished it were over already; even more, he wished it would never come.

He hadn't been able to focus all week. He'd done his best to study during the days and help mother when he wasn't. He'd been keeping busy. He was so *tired*, and he looked it—even his mother said so. But still he couldn't sleep.

The Nightsteed.

He hadn't seen it since he'd ridden it, but he sensed it out in the forest, especially at night when the moon rose over Witching Hour Road. Every day before dusk he made sure to pile firewood up high by the hearth so he wouldn't have to go out in the dark. But the beast was still out there, charging through the Copperwood, waiting for a rider. Waiting for him.

But why?

More than anything, Yrion feared those visions of his father. They haunted his dreams. No matter how he exhausted himself in the day and studied into the night, he couldn't sleep a dreamless sleep, couldn't wake up any way but cold and trembling. Seeing Corvus so tired, so dusty, so *still*—that wasn't the Corvus Yrion remembered.

I'm trying, Father. I don't mean to be a lazy boy.

A log settled in the fire and startled him. It felt like it shook the floor. Sparks flew up the chimney, some ash puffed out of the hearth. Yrion turned his head away, saw the moon through the front window. The forest outside seemed to have stilled.

Yrion held his breath. The thumping of his heart swelled in volume. Thump. Thump.

Thud.

The floor shook again, though no logs had settled.

The pane fogged over, like someone had held a whistling kettle to it. Then a shadow passed over it and blocked out the moon.

Yrion gasped.

The Nightsteed.

He had to be dreaming. He'd fallen asleep and was dreaming. He looked back to the fire and, in a panic, stuck his hand close to the flames. He pulled it out immediately. It was hot, it was real.

The Nightsteed stamped its hoof again. The rosemary drying on the mantle fell to the floor.

Yrion squeezed his eyes shut.

"Go away!" he hissed. "Go away. I've got to study."

The Nightsteed neighed so loudly Yrion had to cover his ears. His mother and sister must have heard it. It sounded like a dragon in their front yard. Yet they didn't cry out or come rushing into the room.

The Nightsteed began stomping in a rhythm. Dust fell from the rafters. The furniture rattled on the floor. It would kick the cottage down before it was done.

Come out, its heart said to Yrion's. *Come out and ride.*

Those unspoken words tugged at Yrion—at his heart, at his spirit—and he felt compelled to go. To silence it, yes, but to sate something growing within himself as well. The Nightsteed's need for a rider awakened in him a need to ride, a need to break free. Like a spell, it seeped into him.

Stay, he told himself. *Stay and study.*

He rose from the floor, afraid, but more anxious than afraid. And more curious. Through the window, the Nightsteed saw him rise, and it stopped its tantrum. Yrion put on his jacket and boots without thinking and stepped outside.

The horse waited in the front yard. Yrion could smell it from where he stood, the sweet odor of the curse. Its accompanying fog covered the hillside; Yrion closed the door before it could creep inside.

The beast snorted, insisting Yrion climb up. But Yrion hesitated. *This isn't happening*, he tried to convince himself. *I need to get back in there. The auction is tomorrow and—*

The Nightsteed neighed. The sound cut through the forest with warning, so loud it moved the fog like a wind. Yrion cringed and covered his ears. The Nightsteed stomped its foot and nearly shook him to his knees. Quickly he stepped up and climbed its shaggy coat.

As soon as he threw his leg over its back, it bounded up the hill. Yrion dug his fingers in deep, squeezed his hands into fists. If it weren't for the tangles in the mane, he would have tumbled off.

When it reached Witching Hour Road, it charged full out, reaching its impossible speed. Again the road became a dark tunnel that stretched straight for longer than it should. The white moon turned orange and began flashing in passing rings.

Yrion would not look at those flashes, could not bear to see his father like that again. He would not have his dreams haunted for another week. Let the Nightsteed carry him where it would. If it needed a rider, if he needed to ride, he would ride. Let boy and beast tire one another out. But he kept his eyes straight ahead. The tunnel was like holding two mirrors up to one another, then stepping into that endless corridor which plunged toward a single pinpoint. And the Nightsteed charged down it—Yrion could sense the impatience between his knees—as if greater speed could get one to the end of something endless.

Then, as if in response to that thought, Yrion thought he *could* see an end to that tunnel. Perhaps it was trick of the mind or eye—this whole ride might be a trick—but it seemed that the dark pinpoint in the distance was growing. It was like the beam of a lighthouse pointed straight at them, only it was a beam of darkness—a *darkhouse*. The orange flashes became less frequent, and it gave the impression that the Nightsteed was slowing down.

Yrion's eyes tried to adjust. The darkness tugged upon them, as if trying to pull them from the sockets. It played tricks upon them, or his mind made up things that weren't really there: lines in the shadows, shapes in the shadows, shadows within the shadows.

At last, something materialized.

That steady black beacon, that darkhouse…it *was* a dark house.

A house tangled in a thick blanket of black vines, overhung by black willow limbs that drooped like ghostly shrouds. Heavy double doors, old and damp, spotted with black fungus. A house. Long and low like an oversized chicken coop. Yrion could smell the sweet stink of the curse, and knew what that house was, knew where the Nightsteed was taking him.

The Hall of the Nightfather.

The Nightsteed had come to take away the restless spirit of a lazy boy. Yrion must still be sleeping in front of the fire in his family's cottage. This dream had lured his spirit out of doors and put him on a wild horse to his doom. If he entered that hall, the Nightfather would curse him and he'd be imprisoned there till Everdark. His poor mother would find his cold body in front of a dead fire. The authorities down in Brodhaven would seize his land, and who knew what would happen to his family. All because Yrion was a lazy boy.

But I'm not, he insisted. *I've been working real hard.*

Yrion pulled on the Nightsteed's mane.

"No!" he shouted. "No!"

He used his right fist to pound on the beast's neck. But the Nightsteed charged on. It had found its rider and would not stop. Yrion could think of only one thing to do.

He released his grip on the mane and rolled sideways. He caught the glimmer of the steed's onyx eye looking back as he fell, but it could do nothing to stop him or its own momentum. Before he hit the earth, its impossible speed had carried it out of sight.

Crows cawed overhead.

Yrion didn't wake up in his bed, nor before the hearth. He was lying in the dirt on the side of Witching Hour Road. The faint remnants of a passing fog lingered with the scent of the curse. Soft, purple-grey light waxed through the dark treetops.

It was dawn.

He curled into a ball, fought back a sob. He was freezing. He was afraid. How had he gotten up here? Was his spirit wandering or was *he* wandering? If he had let the Nightsteed carry him to the Hall of the Nightfather, would he leave no body behind? Would he vanish from the earth?

Down the hill, the windows of his family's cottage were still black, but his sister and mother might be awake already. Yrion scampered down to the woodpile and loaded up an armful. He stepped through the front door just in time.

"Get this going," Laurel said from the hearth.

Yrion hurried over and placed his logs atop an already high stack. He'd hardly burned any last night. He hadn't been here. Laurel slid aside. The coals in the fire were dead cold, and she had too big a log sitting atop them. Yrion removed it, arranged some much smaller kindling, and had it relit in no time.

"You're up early," Laurel said.

He supposed it was a compliment, in a way; he was usually the lazy one, the last to rise.

"Couldn't sleep," he said. Then he ventured: "Did you hear anything last night?"

"Like what?"

Yrion didn't know how much he should admit, if anything. "A horse up on the road."

"You're always hearing things and smelling things."

He shrugged. "I guess I dreamt it."

But he knew he hadn't.

Twelve

Yrion was exhausted. His body ached. He'd found bruises on his elbows and knees. He felt as though he hadn't slept in days. The only thing keeping him awake was his nervousness about the auction.

The barn smelled of musty hay and wood dust, even with the doors open. Sparrows and doves nested in the rafters. An old owl perched high up on a truss, too proud to be chased away by the commotion below.

Bidders had come from all over the Valley: Nudniks from down below Brodhaven; some Netherbrandts and Pennywills out of the east; even a few Whiteheads came down from the Uphills. They arrived slowly after eleven-thirty, walked around the barn and examined the items for sale.

Uncle Cetus came with Aunt Carina—a woman as big as her husband and with hair just as thick and black on her arms. She could probably out-plow, out-bale, and out-dig most of the men here, the Whiteheads included. But when she laughed (which she did often) she showed how gentle she was. They stood by the entrance with Yrion, his mother and sister, and Caelum.

"I inquired down at Oldfather's Inn," Mother said to Aunt Carina. "An inn needs things laundered, and I can do that if nothing else. Wouldn't be much, but every little bit helps."

"Where will you go when you sell this place?" Uncle Cetus asked.

"Why not auction it off here and now?" Aunt Carina added.

"Oh, Laurel has some other plans in the works."

"Does she now? Good for you, girl," Aunt Carina said to Laurel.

"Whatever happens," Uncle Cetus said, "you'll all have a place in our house."

If they had to sell, Yrion would love to stay with the Boarsiks. And it seemed to him like a reasonable solution to their problem. No matter how much or little they got from the farm, they could combine it with the Boarsiks' then help out there.

"Thank you, Aunt Carina," Laurel said, "but we'll be fine, really."

As the seconds ticked away towards noon, Yrion began to fidget more and more. He felt hot in places he'd never felt hot before: his palms, the arches of his feet, the backs of his knees. He rolled the auction bids over and over in his mind. He'd brought his notes with him and kept them in his front pocket, just in case, but kept telling himself he wouldn't need them. Oh how he wished they would let Laurel do this. She would do it right; no one could swindle her.

He knew noon had come when Caelum nodded and slipped his watch back into his vest pocket. Yrion did his best to welcome everyone then moved to the left-hand wall. The bidders crowded in a semicircle around him, and Laurel, Caelum, and Mother looked over their shoulders. Mother smiled, maybe with pride. Laurel's gaze was as sharp and cold as ever.

The first item was a shovel. Its head came to a dull point, and a thin layer of rust tinted it brown. Years of use had smoothed its wooden handle, especially at the far end and close to the head, where Father's hands had held it most often.

"Shovel," Yrion said. "Starts at a dollar sixty."

Using fewer words made the talking easier, and when Laurel gave him a slight nod he knew he'd gotten the starting price right. But none of the bidders liked that price.

"One-fifty?" Yrion said.

One of the Nudniks said, "I'll give you one and a quarter."

Laurel shook her head slightly with a scowl, and Yrion said, "Won't take less than one-thirty."

Another Nudnik held up his finger, and the shovel sold for one-thirty. Yrion took the fellow's coins and dropped them in his pocket.

Most of the sales went that way, on the low side of what Laurel hoped to get. And with every piece that went, Yrion felt a faint pang of sadness. These were his father's tools, each a fond memory of him and a reminder that Corvus really was gone. His wooden mallet sold for sixty cents. But to Yrion, he was selling the memory of Corvus using the mallet to repair Yrion's rocking horse—Yrion had twice ridden the rails off that poor creature! Likewise, all five buckets sold to a Pennywill for a dollar twenty-five. Yrion watched the man carry away the time Laurel sassed Father and Father cooled her down by pouring a bucket of water over her head. Yrion hoped that, when it was over, he'd still have some memories left.

Calling up the highs and lows from memory took a lot of what Yrion could only call *strength*. He scrunched his face in thought so often it felt like it might stay that way—he'd have permanent wrinkles for sure. By the time he got to the hame he felt ready to faint.

"Hame," he said. "two-o-five." As expected, no one jumped on it, so he pressed on. "Won't go below one-forty."

Hands shot up.

"One-forty!" a Netherbrandt said.

"One-forty-five," countered a Whitehead.

"One-fifty," the Netherbrandt said.

Finally, some action, Yrion thought. But when he looked to Laurel, her eyes were wide and her lips pursed.

"One-sixty," a Pennywill said.

A Whitehead held up his finger. "One-sixty-five."

Why was she so angry? Yrion wondered. He dug into his memory and reviewed the figures he'd memorized. One-twenty-five for the sickle. Scythe, one-seventy-five. Everything seemed right. He wasn't supposed to, but he couldn't help but pull the square of paper from his pocket and look at his list of bids.

Hame, two-forty, it said.

A lump rose in his throat. He'd underbid himself by a whole dollar. He crumpled it in his fist and shoved his hands in his pockets. The coins danced a nervous jig in there, one he couldn't still.

"One-seventy," someone said.

A pause.

"One-seventy-five," said another.

A longer pause. The moment hovered there like a hornet ready to sting. Yrion couldn't bring himself to look back at his sister. The coins felt slippery in his sweaty fingers.

"Two-ten," a voice rang out.

Yrion looked up and saw Uncle Cetus lower his finger and cross his massive arms. The other bidders grumbled a bit, cheated out of their steal. Yrion stood there confused a few moments before saying:

"Sold. Two dollars and ten cents."

The auction finished out uneventfully, and bidders meandered away, the winners with their tools. Some offered condolences to Mother. "Good man, Corvus," they said. "He's resting well now."

When the last had gone, Yrion shuffled over to his family.

"You didn't need to do that," Laurel was saying to Uncle Cetus.

"What? Two-ten is a good price for a hame. Besides, I already bought Shamus"—Father's ox—"so I know the hame fits."

"Two-ten?" Caelum winked at Yrion. "Shows what I know. Would have guessed less."

Laurel glared at Caelum for an instant then turned to Yrion.

"Twenty-four dollars," she said, "and seventy cents."

She held out a little leather bag with both hands. Yrion couldn't have kept track of the total if he'd wanted to. He fished all the coins from his pockets and dropped them into the bag, glad to be rid of them.

Caelum whistled. "That's a big haul. What do you think? Want to be an auctioneer one day?"

Yrion blushed a little. "Nooo."

"Well," he said, "what do you think about coming to work for me?"

"Need you to start pitching in," Laurel added.

Yrion was even more dumbstruck by that than by Uncle Cetus' overbid on the hame.

"Really?" he asked. "Do you mean it?"

"Come down tomorrow," Caelum said. "I'll show you around."

Yrion's hands found their way into his pockets again. "Do you think I can? Do the work, I mean."

"Why not? You did all this." Caelum swept his hand across the emptied barn.

"Now, you mind Caelum," Laurel said. "Don't touch anything without his say so."

"Laurel," Caelum said. "He'll be fine."

Yrion couldn't believe it. Cronewetters' Clockworks was his favorite shop in Brodhaven. And Caelum was so nice. He wondered what he'd be doing there. He'd sweep the floors just to be around all the fine trinkets. And now he'd have money to contribute, like Laurel—like the man of the house should.

He wasn't a lazy boy. He wouldn't end up in the Hall of the Nightfather.

Thirteen

Laurel walked Caelum up the front path to the ash tree where Kernel was hitched. Afternoon was slipping toward evening on what had turned out to be a fair-weather day for the auction. Uncle Cetus and Aunt Carina had gone home, Uncle Cetus with the hame up over his ox-like shoulders. Caelum was the last to go.

"That was the least amount of money we could have made," Laurel said. Everything had sold, but at a bargain to the bidders. They knew how desperate cursed landowners were. Laurel supposed she expected it, but that didn't make it sting any less.

"But you have to admit," Caelum said, "Yrion did great."

"I don't know—"

"Come on, he made one mistake. Which is how many less than you expected?"

Laurel had to admit she was proud of her brother—though definitely more *relieved* than proud. This had been tough for him, but *he could do it*. Now that the auction was over and he had a job, she wouldn't have to ride him so much anymore; that would be Caelum's duty for a while. She'd be free to focus on the farm's sale.

"So tell me about your visit with Lady Idlevice," he said.

Laurel took Kernel's reins while Caelum unhitched her. "Visits, you mean."

"More than one? So she's really going to buy your farm?"

"No, but she's offered to help me find a buyer. Met one interested party already."

"Really?" Caelum waited for more.

Laurel felt strange saying it. "Pyxis Pettifog."

She could see Caelum thought it strange too.

"Really?" he said again.

"I didn't get it at first either. But he has money to invest. Why not make some more?"

Caelum paused. "I guess so. I mean, it makes sense."

Laurel could read discomfort on his face—the same hesitation she'd seen on their picnic when she mentioned selling to the Idlevices. She could see he was trying to compose himself, to cover it up.

"Is there something I should know about him?" she asked.

Caelum shook his head. "No. I mean, what's to know?"

"You tell me."

He bandied a little: "He's a socialite. Has a reputation for extravagance, a taste for strong drink." Then he looked away from her. "And women."

Laurel grinned wickedly. "Oh, I see."

"But none of that really matters. He's just a buyer."

"You're jealous."

Caelum's brow furrowed. "Should I be?"

"*Should I be?*" Laurel mocked.

Caelum waved her away. "Just be careful."

"Careful to what? Not bore myself to death sipping tea?"

He put his boot in Kernel's stirrup and threw his leg up over the saddle. "Obviously, you have a handle on it."

Laurel grinned at him again. "I do."

"Tell Yrion eight o'clock tomorrow," he said.

"Eight o'clock."

Kernel trotted away. Laurel watched them for a while wondering what Caelum was so worried about. Between his apprehension and her mother's tight-lipped coldness about Lady Idlevice, one might think they *wanted* to take Linenpest's eighteen-fifty an acre. Laurel wouldn't; she'd get every cent this land was worth.

She returned to the barn. The north and south doors were still tied open. She passed through, and her eyes wandered over its emptiness. All it housed now were birds and mice. And memories. She remembered the time she and little Yrion were sitting in the buckets, pretending they were barrels going over a waterfall. Yrion (of course) tipped his over, right onto his fingers. He howled at that and Father forbade them from playing the bucket-barrel game again. Father put his hand on Laurel's shoulder then and said to her, "You have to watch out for him, you hear?"

I have been, she thought. *I will.*

She pushed the memories away. No sense dwelling on the past; she had to move on—they all did. She looked up and wondered if a buyer would knock the barn down for the slate on its roof and its ancient beams. After all, without farmland, what good was a barn? Or a cottage for that matter? Should *she* try to squeeze some money out of them before the place sold?

She unhooked the rope loops on the southern doors and walked backwards, pulling them closed. She hefted up a long plank that was standing against the wall and dropped it into the doors' lock slots.

When she turned she was startled to find someone standing in the northern doorway. The silhouette of a man: tall, wide stance, wide shoulders, arms crossed. He wore a heavy coat that hung down to his knees. Its fur collar was so high it looked like a headboard—a reliable sign the man was a Whitehead or Whitehead cousin.

"Auction's over," she said. "Nothing left to sell."

"What about the farm?" he said with a heavy Uphills accent. 'Farm' came out in two syllables like 'fah-arm'. His interest startled Laurel more than his sudden appearance. She put her shoulders back—*don't appear desperate*—and approached him slowly.

"Been in my family for six generations," she said. "But we might consider selling."

"The lady said you were more than considering."

The lady?

"I'm sorry, sir, I didn't catch your name."

With the southern doors closed the man's face was shadow. Laurel moved into the doorway next to him, and when he turned she recognized him.

"Willem Whitehead," he said.

The Whiteheads' bloodline intermingled with others all through the Uphills and farther north, but there remained a core family who oversaw them all, a pseudo-nobility headed by Wilfred Whitehead, which made his eldest son, Willem, a sort of prince. Willem had long, wavy blonde hair and matching stubble on his cheeks and chin. His massive arms threatened to tear through the sleeves of his coat. He looked like some medieval seafaring raider who had just stepped off his longboat.

Laurel extended her hand. "Laurel Blight. Pleased to meet you."

Willem didn't reply, nor did he take her hand. His pale eyes scanned her up and down, but she couldn't read his intentions at all.

"You mentioned the lady," she said. "Do you mean Lady Idlevice?"

He nodded. "Said you didn't want that Blackhead Linenpest to get his hands on it."

To Whiteheads, anyone south of the Uphills was a Blackhead, but Laurel didn't take offense. What bothered her was, considering Willem's princely status, why he would want to buy the farm. Yes, it was a moneymaking opportunity, but the Whiteheads had thousands of wooded acres and logged them already. Why move operations south—and for a mere thirty acres? Perhaps Mister Whitehead was surveying it for one of his distant, unimportant cousins.

"And she sent you down here to have a look around, I take?" Laurel asked.

Willem nodded, grimly.

"Well," she said as she pulled the left hand door closed, "as you can see the farmland is no good. But the Copperwood is strong. Our share stretches up over the road and then some."

She moved around him to the right-hand door. He kept his feet planted and swiveled at the waist to keep his eyes on her.

"Let me lock up," she said, "and I'll show you the property's corners."

"I've seen enough," Willem said.

For a moment, Laurel considered that maybe she'd failed to be tactful, that Willem had seen through to her desperation. She quickly discounted the notion. He had shown up alone and gotten right down to business. *None of that good impressions fuss.*

She pulled the right door closed and let it bump into Willem's left arm.

"You want in or out?" she asked.

Willem's mouth twisted in the thinnest of smiles, and he stepped back from the doorway. Laurel laid a thin plank across the outside of the doors and turned to him.

"If you've seen enough," she said, "best be on your way. There are other interested parties—aside from Mayor Linenpest."

Willem's smile grew a little wider. "When you see me again, I'll make my offer."

With that he departed, strode down to the tree-line then turned north along the edge of their cursed farmland. Laurel watched him go. A very strange exchange, she thought. Why would he make an offer without seeing the whole property? Or had he already explored it uninvited? In any case, an offer was good—she hadn't gotten that far with Pyxis Pettifog after a whole afternoon of chitchatting.

When Willem was out of sight, she went to the cottage and found her mother standing outside the door. Lyra's arms were crossed, and Laurel thought she saw her foot tapping.

"What was that all about?" Lyra asked.

"*That* was Willem Whitehead."

"I know who it was. What did he want?"

Laurel opened the front door. "Guess he's going to make us an offer. Where's Yrion?"

"Off somewhere. What kind of offer?"

They went in and stood on either side of the kitchen table while Laurel recounted her encounter. Lyra listened quietly, and Laurel saw that coldness return to her mother's manner. By the time she'd finished, her mother would barely look at her. Laurel thought, maybe, her mother didn't want to sell; maybe Lyra had a sentimental attachment to the place, like Yrion did. Now that offers were coming in, maybe reality was finally setting in.

"We have to sell," Laurel said. "There's just no other way."

Her mother shook her head. "It's not that."

"Then what?"

Still her mother held back, started rocking from one foot to the other like Yrion did when he was antsy or nervous or in trouble.

"If you're not going to tell me," Laurel said, "can you, I don't know, hide what's bothering you a little better? We're never going to get anything done otherwise."

"It's not—" her mother began, but even then she struggled with the words. "It's not Lady Idlevice's place to be doing what she's doing."

Laurel gave her a puzzled look. "I asked her for help."

"Help selling the farm."

"Isn't that what she's doing?"

Her mother looked at the ceiling.

"Didn't I just say Willem Whitehead is going to make an offer?" Laurel asked.

"Aye, and Pyxis Pettifog is interested too."

Laurel paused. "The lady thinks so."

Her mother finally looked at her. "In our muddy little farm?"

"The Copperwood is strong. It's—" Laurel was almost stuttering.

Her mother stood there, patiently, while Laurel flipped back over the memories: Pyxis' gown and shawl; making a good impression; Willem Whitehead's blatant stares. The pieces fell into a queer place. Her mind picked them up, shook them about, and reexamined them. They fell back into that place. An idea had been introduced, and now she couldn't view it any other way.

Her words came out flat, as if this epiphanic conclusion had knocked her over the head. "She's marrying me off."

Lyra went about filling the kettle for tea. Laurel couldn't believe it. How had she not *seen* it before? Her thoughts churned; her mind felt like mush. She was as slow as Yrion sometimes. What was plain: she had to put a stop to it. Lady Idlevice's introductions came at a price Laurel would not pay, one she hadn't fathomed someone would ask. But now the question was: would the lady still be willing to help her? Really, *could* she help her? Was Laurel's profitable plan profitable enough on its own?

The water boiled, and Lyra poured it into two cups. They took their tea to the chairs by the hearth. Laurel didn't know what to say. She thought the topic of marriage had died with her father. Yet here it remained, as if his ghost were finding ways to bring it up again, to haunt her in this very particular way. How long would she have to argue this point? For the first time she felt *wearied* by it.

Her mother must have seen the weariness. "We can take the mayor's offer," she said.

"No."

"The Boarsiks can give us a place to stay—"

"No." Laurel would not rely on someone else's charity to get them out of this.

Her mother sipped her tea and let Laurel stew—like her father. Laurel knew she was as stubborn as he had been, and awareness of that stubbornness didn't lessen it. She would figure this out yet. She had to. With Father gone, she had to put things in order—*patriarchies* be damned.

"How did you do it?" Laurel asked. "Marry Father, I mean."

Her mother slowly nodded. "Well, we spoke the words—"

"No, I mean, how did you *arrange* it."

"Oh." Her mother thought about it a moment. "Suitors didn't line up for me the way they've started for you. Handsome men marry pretty women, and rich men marry pretty women. The rest of us sort of…pair off."

"So Father pointed at you and that was that?"

"No, dear. I pointed at him."

Laurel shook her head and chuckled, a little embarrassed by her mother's forthrightness. "All right. But why *him*?"

Lyra thought a little longer on that. "He was a quiet man, your father. Always something on his mind. And he couldn't sit in a room for long. People thought him strange, but I saw something there. A man itching to do something gets something done. If I couldn't marry a rich man or a handsome man, I at least could marry a busy one. That's all I needed, really."

To Laurel's surprise, for all her mother's clumsy attempts at subtlety and fawning over romance (when it came to Caelum), she'd married for the most practical of reasons. And Laurel had to admit: she admired it! Her mother had chosen as well as she could. Maybe Corvus wanted Laurel married not because of some deep-seated support of patriarchies but because he wanted his daughter to be practical like her mother. He'd never put it that way; Laurel wondered if she would have felt different about the subject if he had.

"And what did Father need?" Laurel asked.

Lyra looked into the cold, blackened hearth. Ash sat in a little pile of grey and white.

"Your father needed to work," she said. "And when the curse took his land, I think it took a piece of him with it—like taking a wheel out of one of the Cronewetters' clocks. He didn't know how to stop the bob from swinging. It just…tore the rest of him up."

Fourteen

Yrion opened the door of Cronewetters' Clockworks. It swung against a course of four brass bells that played a mysterious chord, one he associated with wonderment. Behind the glass display cases, a few Cronewetters—a grandfather, an uncle, a cousin—worked at personalized stations. They had giant magnifying glasses strapped to their heads and didn't look up when the bells chimed.

The shop ticked to a chaotic rhythm like the buzzing of a mechanical beehive. Clocks hung from hooks in the ceiling; they sat atop tables; they stood on the floors, some taller than Uncle Cetus, with polished brass tubes staggered down their chambers, golden pendulums swinging away. There were pocket watches, too, atop cloth-covered shelves inside glass display cases. Some sat open like clams revealing ivory faces. Some had no faces at all, just a clear lens that magnified the little gears and springs inside. The watches' hands were as intricate as any grandfather clock, only shrunken down; the second hands looked as thin as spider strands.

Though called a 'Clockworks', the Cronewetters made more than clocks here. They made rings of silver and gold, set with diamonds and emeralds and sapphires; bracelets and tiaras, necklaces and pendants; silverware sets polished to a mirrored sheen; oil lamps with etched-glass doors; candelabras in the likenesses of men, a candle for each hand and one atop the head; mugs and steins engraved with mottos and sigils.

Yrion's favorites were the pewter statuettes: knights with lowered lances riding atop charging destriers; warriors with swords pointed skyward; wizards with arms spread, little jewels affixed atop their staffs; a wide-winged phoenix rising from a mountain of flames.

Yrion could hardly contain his excitement over getting to work with such things—or at least near them, to see how they were made. It would be like living in a daydream. And if he set enough money aside, maybe he could buy a little statuette for himself.

When the clocks struck eight, the place erupted in rings and dings and chimes, and Caelum appeared in the doorway at the back of the room. He saw Yrion by the statuettes and approached.

"Which one do you like?" he asked.

Yrion liked them all, really, but was looking at one in particular: a little castle atop a mountain, a giant serpent coiled about its towers. He pointed to it.

"Why that one?" Caelum asked.

Yrion wasn't sure why he liked any of them. It wasn't the dark grey metal they were made of—which wasn't nearly as pretty as gold or copper. He guessed it was the figures and places themselves. Yrion wanted to know the wizard, to fight alongside the warrior, to see a snake wrapped around a mountain—though a snake that big could swallow the Idlevice mansion in one gulp. He supposed, maybe, he didn't wish to *be* there so long as such places were real *somewhere*.

"I wish I could go there," he said.

Caelum smiled. "I saw a blacksnake climbing a stump of a tree that had been struck by lightning. The stump was kind of jagged, so it gave me the idea."

"You *made* this?"

"Sure did. These are training, part of my apprenticeship. When I've perfected them, I'll move on to clocks and watches."

Yrion kept his wide eyes on the castle. "Why would you want to do watches?"

Caelum chuckled. "Well, I want to get better. It's much harder to make a watch than a figurine. You've got to be very precise or it won't keep time. And the higher the skill, the higher the price tag."

Yrion hadn't thought of that. "You think I could make watches one day?"

"Maybe. Do you want to make watches one day?"

Yrion shrugged. He could probably think up dozens of ideas for statuettes—he'd seen lots of stumps in the Copperwood. But watches seemed less exciting.

Caelum led him into the workshop through the door at the back of the showroom. More Cronewetters sat tightly packed at workbenches, some of them boys younger than Yrion. They looked up only long enough to see who entered, then returned to their tinkering.

The workshop held all the same treasures as the showroom but in varying degrees of completion. Grandfather clocks stood doorless and faceless, their gears exposed and half-assembled. Rings and pendants lay in unpolished piles atop chest-high tables. Figurines stood as featureless blobs, waiting to be defined by Caelum or another apprentice.

The place glowed a rich, flaming yellow from the many lamps, and the air was thick with the smell of their burning oil. Windows on the right hand wall provided a little light but (because they faced an alley) not nearly enough. Candles provided a little more, and wax sat in hardened, wickless pools on the tabletops. The ceiling was black from smoke.

Caelum explained that this was where most of the work was done, that many generations of Cronewetters had worked here. They stopped at an L-shaped desk tucked into a corner. It was covered with all the same materials as the other desks but also a plump pincushion spiked with dozens of tiny needles.

Yrion pointed to the cushion. "You sew here, too?"

Caelum picked it up. It was orange and resembled a pumpkin. "Not too much," Caelum said, "but here's a good test."

He selected a tiny needle not much thicker than a hair and held it out to Yrion. Yrion had to shift his viewpoint till the light caught it just to see it. He took it, though he could barely feel it between his fleshy fingers. Then Caelum reached out and plucked a hair from Yrion's head; Yrion squeaked.

"Sorry," Caelum said with a smile. "Put your arms out."

Yrion did so.

"Now," Caelum said, "thread the needle."

Yrion looked to the little wisps in his fingertips. He had to bring them halfway to his nose just to see them. They danced wiggly dances, and he realized how unsteady his hands must be all the time. He propped his elbows up on his belly to steady himself, but the hair and needle still danced. He made a few unsuccessful stabs, held his breath, failed at a few more.

"When my grandfather made me do this," Caelum said, "he said a boy who could thread this needle with a hair on the first pass had the hands of a watchmaker."

Yrion looked at Caelum. "How many did it take you?"

Caelum smiled again. "More than one."

Yrion smiled then too, but when he looked back to his fingertips, he had trouble refocusing on the hair and needle. One was missing.

"I dropped the hair," he said. "No, I dropped the needle."

Caelum laughed and patted him on the head. "There's a hundred needles on this floor. Keep your boots on."

Yrion dropped the hair. Maybe he'd never be good enough to make watches.

"How long does it take to make a statuette?" he asked

"Depends," Caelum said, "on the intricacy and the size. Mountains are easy because real mountains are rough and random. Soft curves like a wizard's cloak are tough to keep smooth. Tight corners get pretty tricky. I can do a castle in a couple days. Others take weeks—like my latest one."

Caelum brought a three-wicked candle from another table and set it next to a statuette in the middle of his workspace. The statuette struck Yrion with an undeniable likeness that stood his hair on end. Caelum had made a horse that could be only one horse.

It stood about ten inches high, locked in a frozen charge, its front legs pulled close to its body, its hind legs half-hidden in a cloud, its mane blowing in a still wind. It looked real enough to charge off the table. Its eyes gleamed wildly in the candlelight, and slaver trailed from the corners of its open mouth. A little boy hugged its neck, his body up off the mount, his pajamas whipping as fiercely as the horse's mane.

"*The Nightsteed,*" Yrion whispered.

Caelum slid the candle closer. "I've been working on this for over a month."

Caelum ran his finger down the horse's mane but stopped before reaching the clinging boy's outstretched body. For a moment, even his steady hand seemed to tremble.

"When I carve the mold too shallow," he said, "the boy is too fragile. Too deep and he slows the whole thing down. This one I'm not sure about; it's fragile, but—what do you think?"

The steed's hair wasn't long enough, and if someone really tried hugging the Nightsteed's neck his face and shoulder would be battered blue. But the size of the horse compared to the boy, the way it emerged from the pursuing fog, even the boy himself just barely holding on, they were exactly right.

Yrion was entranced, eerily connected to the statuette. For, of all the ones he'd seen, this *was* real somewhere, just up the hill from Brodhaven. His voice came out thin and wispy: "Have you ever seen it?"

The boys at the other tables giggled, and Yrion backed away a step. He didn't know they were listening.

"No," Caelum said. "But I imagine this is what it looks like."

"So real," Yrion whispered to himself.

The four bells rang out in the showroom.

"Customer," Caelum said. "I'll be back."

Caelum hurried off. Yrion clambered up onto his work stool. He stared at Caelum's Nightsteed, watched the candlelight gleam off the metal and cast shadows into the folds of its ears, the cups of its hooves. He swiveled the statuette by its base. The details astounded him with their lifelikeness; Caelum had somehow captured the very experience of Yrion's rides. The way the steed's slaver whipped back. The look that bordered on madness in its eyes.

Yrion stroked the horse on the nose, found it cold to the touch.

He almost thought the beast would turn its head away.

He caressed its short mane.

If he worked hard, maybe someday he could make one with a shaggier coat.

His finger trailed up over the boy's back.

He'd make the boy look like himself.

Click.

The pewter boy snapped free and dropped on the tabletop with a clink.

To Yrion, it sounded like a bell had dropped from a steeple.

He nearly cried out: *I broke it!*

The little pewter boy lay armless, belly up, now lifeless and fake. The Nightsteed looked wrong too, just another figurine. Caelum's month of hard work snapped off by a fat, clumsy finger.

Yrion came off the stool and started to shift back and forth from one foot to the other, panic-stricken. What would he tell him? What *could* he tell him? Caelum had invited him into his shop, offered him a job, and already Yrion had broken something.

He could hear Laurel's words: *Don't touch anything without his say so.*

What would she say when she heard about this?

That got him moving. He rushed back through the workshop, past the preoccupied Cronewetters, and out through the showroom. Caelum was with a customer, and Yrion heard him pardon himself: "Yrion?"

Yrion couldn't look at him. He let the four brass doorbells answer.

Fifteen

Jacob stood outside Cronewetters' Clockworks. The shop's title was written upon its bay window in gold letters applied directly to the glass. Inside on the sill, their watches and clocks sat on display, better than ever, a mixture of modern styles and the quaint charm of Long Autumn Valley.

Plenty of other businesses displayed this blend of trends, a mix of old and new. Like Jacob, in a way: a mix of nostalgia and thrill. The town had doubled in size in thirteen years, and if this vote went the mayor's way, things would grow even faster. Plenty of business opportunities. Jacob would have done well here, could have been a part of this boom. With his experience and capital, he could do well here still.

But his good sense advised him against it. He'd already done well, and stood to do far better back east. The wisest thing to do would be to sell the farm and leave this place behind for good.

Jacob had been meaning to do that for three days now, but Pavo Linenpest had been avoiding him. Twice Jacob had sought an audience with the mayor to settle the sale of Rotbottom farm, and twice the mayor's clerks told him Linenpest had been 'called away'. Jacob knew better. Linenpest was stalling—and not for any bargaining advantage. There *was* no bargain; the terms of sale had already been laid out by Brodhaven's railroad leaflet. The mayor was simply inconveniencing him, a little victory after Jacob's curtness on the railway platform.

In the meantime, Jacob had been staying at a local inn, taking in the town. He needed to visit Rotbottom farm, *his* farm—a good businessman wouldn't sell it without one final assessment. He'd hoped to rent a horse to spare himself the long walk but hadn't found one to his liking. He wasn't a good rider or fond of horses; they were such unpredictable creatures.

Yet, he wondered if it were really the lack of a horse that kept him from the farm. It was a place of vivid memory and concentrated feeling, and the road to it passed through the Copperwood where memory and feeling were stronger still. From the Cronewetters' doorstep, he could see the canopy of that forest in the distance, golden orange like clouds on an evening horizon. Could he walk through that place?

Just then, a boy burst out of Cronewetters' and forced Jacob to take a step back. Jacob's heel collided with something solid, and he nearly fell over backwards. He spun about quickly—as much to regain his balance as to find what he'd crashed into, expecting he would see a wheelbarrow or a peddler's cart.

It was an old man in a wheeled chair.

The chair was finely crafted and quite modern—Jacob had only seen this model in cities on the eastern coast. The old man had a wool blanket wrapped about him like a cerement. An olive-skinned foreigner was pushing him along, and he glared at Jacob.

"Goodness," Jacob said—to the old man, to the foreigner, back to the old man, "excuse me."

The foreigner allowed himself to give Jacob a slight, condescending nod, but by then Jacob had lost interest in him. Jacob was transfixed on the old man; he recognized him—though nearly every part of Jacob insisted he was mistaken, insisted what he thought he saw was not possible. The old man's face was thirteen-years-etched upon Jacob's mind, unforgettable, unmistakable, no matter how strange the circumstances that wheeled it before him. But thirteen years had aged Percy Idlevice like thirty-nine, withered the lord to a husk of his former self. His once-dark hair had fallen from his pate and what was left clung to the sides like a faded crown. His beard had paled and thinned as well, exposing blotchy jowls.

Jacob had always hated the man. He knew jealousy fueled it, but it was hatred nonetheless. Lord Idlevice's wealth had paid for something Jacob wanted long before Jacob had wealth of his own. Lord Idlevice's power—his *pistol*—had driven Jacob from Long Autumn Valley, in fear and in shame. And of all the ways Jacob had dreamt of the lord's demise—usually by some fantasy-vengeance on Jacob's part—he had never once imagined what lay wrapped in the wheeled chair. To his surprise, he now pitied the man, something he would never have thought possible. Thirteen years had changed Brodhaven, changed Percy Idlevice; Jacob had to let himself change too.

"Lord Idlevice," he said and bowed. "Excuse me."

Percy didn't look at Jacob; his eyes wandered across the sky, but Jacob doubted they were seeing the sky either. The lord was all but gone, his heart ticking long after the brain had stopped thinking. Still, waveringly, laboriously, the old man's right hand lifted off the armrest in a vapid salutation.

Jacob nodded again, stepped aside, and let the two pass. A few doors down, they stopped at a carriage parked in the street. White, trimmed with gold, hitched to two white mares—Jacob hadn't noticed it before. Its appearance tickled something on the periphery of his thoughts. What was it? He'd seen carriages before, even finer ones, but carriages had never interested him. Why this one? Why now?

Instinctually—or through some preternatural sense—Jacob swiveled to the door of Cronewetters' Clockworks and entered. The bell above the door rang an enchanted chord, while Jacob looked right, back the way Lord Idlevice had come, then left to where the carriage awaited. He stooped a little, peered between two tall clocks that stood inside tubular bell jars, each like a crystal pillar. There he waited, eyes fixed upon the carriage. The clocks' glass refracted the light and distorted his vision so that only a thin strip of window remained in focus.

His heart jittered. He had to press his palms to the sides of his jacket to dab up their sweat. Time seemed to stretch, as if the ticks and tocks were compounding: if one clock's tick marked the passing of one second, two score clocks made it feel like two score seconds.

She came out through the shop where the carriage was parked.

Jacob watched her blurry form as if through tears. The beat of his heart drowned out the clocks. He didn't know if he was breathing, didn't know if he needed breath anymore.

The Valley had changed. Brodhaven had changed. Pavo had gotten fatter, Percy older. His own reflection in the glass showed grey in his short-cropped beard and more at his temples. Wrinkles creased the corners of his dark brown eyes beneath the wire frames of his spectacles.

Lady Vela Idlevice hadn't aged a day.

She wore an indigo gown that hugged her every perfect curve. Her dark hair absorbed the dress's color and appeared indigo too. Her lips alone were painted a deep red that Jacob could see nearly a block away.

She crossed the sidewalk like a shadow. She lifted one leg in but stopped. Time might have stopped too. She turned her head, slowly, as if her own preternatural sense had connected with his. But Jacob could not meet that gaze—whether she could see him or not. He cringed backward and thumped into a display case behind him. Atop it stood a circular rack, each concentric tier a little smaller than the one below it; the tiers held little pewter figurines. They all shook from the jolt Jacob had given them. One spun on its base—to, fro, side to side—then toppled. Jacob stuck his hand out just in time and it landed in the palm of his hand.

Jacob let his heartbeat settle and his breath return. His palm felt hot and wet enough to steam.

She hadn't seen him; she hadn't sensed him.

Coincidence, he told himself. *People's heads turn.*

Jacob felt as though he'd dodged a pistol shot. He had come close, close to—

"May I help you?" the young clerk said from across the room.

Jacob looked at the figurine in his palm. It was the likeness of a bearded king upon a throne.

"No," he said. "Just looking."

Sixteen

Laurel knocked on the Idlevice's front door. She was wearing the blue dress her mother made—comfortable, appropriate for a farm girl, nothing to impress anybody. She had come to put a stop to the lady's matchmaking. However, she'd walked the whole way here and had yet to figure out how not to come across as an ingrate. This might be the last time she and Lady Vela interacted. She might have to go about selling her farm alone and in a whole other way.

So be it. What alternative did she have? Marry some rich stranger? That might have worked for Lady Idlevice, but it wouldn't for Laurel. There was nothing ungrateful about that. Still, she caught herself shifting from one foot to the other and stopped it before the door opened.

Suhar, the manservant, welcomed her in and led her out of the foyer and down the right-hand hall. They had to stop and step aside while two servants lugged a heavy wooden table past. Two other servants holding tall stacks of table cloths followed in their wake. Preparations for the upcoming ball, Laurel guessed.

They continued on and came to a glass-enclosed tea room. Lady Idlevice sat at a wrought iron table, an open bottle of wine in front of her.

"Laurel," she said, "how wonderful of you to come."

"My lady," Laurel replied with half a curtsey.

"Please, sit. Help me finish this wine."

Her manservant produced a fresh glass in an instant and filled the bottom inch. Laurel sat and sipped it. It was heavy and rich and made her nose twitch. She set the glass on the table with no intention of touching it again.

"No?" Vela chuckled.

"An acquired taste," Laurel said.

"Most things are. So what brings you here?"

Laurel ran her finger along her chair's armrest, still unsure how to begin.

"Willem Whitehead visited me," she said.

Vela raised her eyebrows.

"And I realized something," Laurel said. She paused, mustering confidence. The lady waited patiently. "They're suitors. Your prospective buyers, they're suitors."

The lady took a long sip of wine. "He's rich, isn't he? Charming too, in a rugged way—an *acquired* taste."

Laurel hadn't noticed Willem's charm. Charm was irrelevant.

"And there aren't many loggers out there," Vela continued. "Linenpest has his, promised them contracts already. The Whiteheads might be the only other option."

Laurel didn't see why it would make that much of a difference. Hers was still a profitable plan—*wasn't it?*

"I suppose you intend to marry the Cronewetter boy," the lady said.

Laurel shifted in her seat. How did Lady Idlevice know about Caelum? "He's a friend."

"Come now. Young men don't go riding with young women to be friends."

"He's an *old* friend."

"Well, maybe *he* will buy your farm."

"Oh. No. Though, he offered in a way." She said it almost dreamily, then snapped out of it: "He doesn't have that kind of money."

Vela chuckled. "Even *old* friends don't offer to buy farms with money they don't have."

Laurel's brow furrowed. She hadn't come to talk about this. What she and Caelum had was difficult to explain. She wouldn't call it love, really. Not that she didn't love him. Only, the word love, with all its romantic and marital connotations, didn't accurately describe it. Love, to her, seemed more like a fantasy, like something her kid brother would daydream about. And the only thing worse than thinking one *had* to marry was convincing oneself she really wanted to for love's sake.

"Well," the lady asked, "do you want to sell your farm or don't you?"

This Laurel could answer. "Yes. I just don't want to marry. Anyone. Ever."

The lady's eyebrows rose. "Ever?"

Whatever plans she'd had for Laurel, Laurel had probably just put a torch to them. But the lady didn't look upset; if anything, she looked astonished, almost as if she liked the idea. Nervous, Laurel took another unpleasant sip of her wine.

"I thought I'd have my work cut out for me," the lady said, and when Laurel didn't respond she added, "If I'm to help you, I need to understand you."

Laurel wasn't sure how much she should say. Most of what the lady had accomplished she owed to her marriage to Lord Idlevice. Laurel wouldn't get much help if she started condemning the lady's life choices simply because they differed from her own viewpoints.

"I think," Laurel started, "that is, I *worry*, that folk want me to marry because they don't believe I can do much else. They believe it about a lot of other women too, maybe *all* women. That belief is keeping me from what I want to do, from what I'm good at—or would be, given the chance."

The lady exhaled long. "My," she said, "you are modern."

Laurel looked at her lap.

The lady poured the rest of the bottle into her glass, letting the last drops drip, drip, drip. Then she took the glass in her hand

and eased way back in her chair. "Say you sell, make every penny you're due. How long will the money last?"

Laurel didn't answer because she didn't know. She could stretch the money a long way, but it would eventually run out. Her dollar a week from scribing wouldn't be enough.

"Will your brother pick up the slack?" the lady asked.

Not likely, Laurel told herself. She didn't yet know his wage at the Cronewetters, but it wouldn't be much. She truly didn't know how they would manage. She'd always just imagined they *would*; they would find a way—*she* would find a way. That was why she was here, wasn't it?

"Women's opportunities," the lady said, "are—*limited*. Marriage is our best chance at improving our situation. Or securing it. Protest it if you like, but it's the harder path, the *martyr's* path. Is that your intent? To be a martyr?"

Laurel swallowed. She wanted to change the Valley, but she had no delusions about her importance in it. It wasn't about martyrdom. She was *capable*, all women were, and their womanhood shouldn't preclude them from opportunity. That was simple logic, not righteousness.

"If not," the lady continued, "you might consider marriage for its benefits."

This all sounded eerily familiar to what Laurel's mother had told her just the day before. Lyra had married Corvus because he could provide. Vela had done the same—but as a much prettier woman, she'd managed to marry wealthy. Laurel admired this rational approach; *that much* she could identify with. If she would have accepted one of her father's arrangements, her husband could be providing for her family already.

Still, something about it didn't sit right with her. Though fully rational and pragmatic, something Laurel strove to be, she felt a warning within her. The thought of needing a provider went against one of her core beliefs. Or maybe that was just her father's inherited stubbornness talking. If there was nothing pragmatic about a belief, shouldn't she squelch it?

"Of course," Vela said, "there's still hope the vote won't go Linenpest's way. You know, I read a letter recently." She rose from her chair and moved to a little table by the doorway with a good many letters and papers atop it. She took one from the top and passed it to Laurel. "One about weasels and henhouses."

Laurel froze, letter in-hand. She hadn't mailed one to Lady Idlevice.

"Daring words," the lady said.

Laurel opened it. Sure enough, they were Laurel's words in Laurel's script. She couldn't believe it. She'd composed those letters in a fit, and it had proved a cathartic exercise. But no sooner had she mailed them than she'd forgotten about them.

"How did you come by it?" Laurel asked.

"Oh, it's making its way around certain circles. Someone suspected I had written it. Not I, I said. I'd have compared Pavo Linenpest to a pig, not a weasel."

Making its way around certain circles? Without the envelope, Laurel couldn't discern who the original recipient was.

"Did you write it?" the lady asked.

Laurel looked at the lady then back to the letter. She wasn't particularly worried about the wrong folk seeing it; no one could prove she wrote it. Besides, its authorship wasn't important. She pretended to read it again, admitting nothing.

"Do you think this will change anything?" she asked.

"It might. It's travelled far already."

Laurel thought about it and decided she wouldn't gamble anything on the hopes the vote would fail. The numbers favored Linenpest; he knew it, everyone knew it. Laurel's letter might rally a minority, but it would remain a minority. She needed to sell the farm, to stick to her plan—whatever that was now.

A rumble of thunder snored in the distance. Laurel looked out through the glass walls of the tea room to see a patch of dark clouds gathering to the southeast.

She stood. "Storm coming."

"I'll have my carriage take you," the lady replied.

"No, no. I need to walk off the wine."

Vela smiled. "I should have to walk to Brodhaven and back."

Laurel thanked her for her hospitality and turned to leave.

"Laurel," the lady said before Laurel made it out of the room. Laurel turned back. "I'll stop sending you suitors."

"Thank you, my lady."

Seventeen

Yrion ran out of Cronewetters' Clockworks and didn't stop till he reached the Copperwood. There, he veered east off Witching Hour Road and plunged into the forest. Exhausted, knees wobbly, he ricocheted from one trunk to the next, stumbling like a wounded criminal fleeing a murderous mob. Tears blinded him and made his course all the wilder.

Caelum had worked so hard on that figurine. How could Yrion ever look at him again? Why had he thought he could ever work there? Yrion ruined everything he touched. He couldn't remember bids, couldn't pay attention at meetings—couldn't do *anything* right. Worst of all, he couldn't provide for his family, couldn't be the man of the house. What would Laurel say when she found out?

Maybe nothing. She'd known I couldn't do it all along.

Deeper and deeper into the forest he went. If he'd ever gone this far east, he couldn't remember it, and through his blinding tears the Copperwood here seemed wholly foreign, wholly hidden from the world. That was for the better. He wanted to get away, to go even deeper if possible, to be wholly hidden himself.

He came to a gully, let himself half-stumble, half-slide down its steep embankment. Its base was mushy with water that had worked its way to the lowest point. He followed it, not knowing which way it was taking him. His boots squished and flung specks of mud onto his jacket and pants. He caught a faint whiff of sickly sweetness, the smell of the curse that had drifted off some faraway field—maybe his own—and become trapped down here with the muck. This was where he belonged, down with the muck, down where nincompoops like him didn't look so bad, where his faults could blend with the faults of the land.

Soon he found a crack on the right, a jagged ravine cut into the hillside, barely wide enough for his shoulders to fit through. Water trickled out its base and fed the muck in the gully. Yrion stepped up to it. With the sky all grey, and the Copperwood's thick canopy, and the thinness of the crack, hardly any light shone in. He could see the roots of trees sticking from its steep walls, stretching for the water. Such an unwelcoming place. No one would find him here. Hidden, wholly hidden.

He crouched beneath a low-hanging root and slipped in.

The surrounding walls dripped with moisture. Boulders broke through the surface in places, their faces slippery with red moss. Yrion moved over and under roots slick with black slime. The crack turned right and its opening disappeared behind him. It was like a dark fold in the earth, filled with sweet stink and cold sweat. He couldn't hear the trees swaying overhead, only his mucky footfalls and the faint flow of moving water.

Then, as unexpectedly as the crack had appeared, it opened again, and a wide basin stretched before him. Embankments rose on either side in two gentle humps like burial mounds. The humps met in the tight curve of an oval one hundred yards away. Atop them, a single row of evergreen trees rose up to compete with the Copperwood canopy. Their trunks leaned heavily inward, and their drooping boughs almost met in the middle. Here, what light managed to filter through had a cold, dark green hue Yrion had never known in this forest.

As a centerpiece, a single birch tree towered in the middle of the basin. Its white bark flaked in dry sheets. Its base was a braid of three roots that grew together into a single trunk. High above the overhanging evergreen boughs, the birch spread its branches like celebrating hands tossing fistfuls of gold.

Yrion had never seen a birch so tall. He moved towards it, lured by its strangeness. The basin was flat and level, and across the span lay the thinnest sheet of cold, clear water. It barely covered a layer of smooth stones so level they appeared intentionally groomed. Yrion walked atop them, and with the water so shallow, it seemed as though he were walking atop that too.

Close to the tree, he saw its exposed roots and supposed this basin was once filled with much more soil that had long since been washed away. He wondered where so much water would have come from. Even now he couldn't determine the source of what remained. It was as if the water were bleeding from the tree itself.

One root curved in such a way that made a little seat for Yrion. Here he began to relax a bit, though he could not say where *here* was. Somewhere below Rotbottom farm. How had he never come across this place before?

What was certain: he was hidden, wholly hidden. With mounds and evergreens as walls, and the thin crack, dank and unwelcoming, at the far end. No one would find him here; no one could find this place at all, unless they stumbled down the same wild course Yrion had taken.

Overhead, the sky had darkened as if a summer storm were coming. Or perhaps it was the overhanging evergreens casting their shadows. Yrion wished it were summer so that he might stay here longer. Tonight this pool might freeze over. And at some point, he'd have to go home.

He began to weep again.

He'd let everyone down. When he wasn't being a lazy daydreamer, he was breaking things. What would his father have said?

He wouldn't have said anything. He would have kept right on working.

Mother and Laurel, they needed Corvus, not his foolish son. His foolish son needed him too, maybe more so.

What would Yrion do? What *could* he do? He didn't know how to *do anything*. But the Valley kept right on changing, with him or without him. Death, this damned curse, the Witching Hour Railroad. Even here, in this strange cubby of the Copperwood, he couldn't hide from it, couldn't get far enough away.

Thud.

The sound cut Yrion's weeping short.

Thud.

Eerie and familiar. On the other side of the tree. Ripples hurried across the pool's surface.

Yrion sprang from his seat and turned.

The Nightsteed stepped from behind the birch tree, appearing like a ghost in broad daylight. But even in broad daylight, the beast was all shadow. A thick fog gathered over the water behind it, and Yrion smelled the curse stronger than ever. The trees overhead swayed—the sky *had* darkened with storm clouds—but down in the basin the air was still.

Yrion backed away a few steps. The Nightsteed looked down at him and dropped its front hoof like a sledgehammer. Yrion knew what it wanted, knew better than to question it, knew better than to resist. And in that strange way that accompanied the beast's presence, he had no intention of resisting; he wanted it too. The beast's heart spoke to Yrion's, and Yrion's spoke back; they spoke in unison.

Ride.

Yrion wanted away from this place, away from Long Autumn Valley, and the Nightsteed wanted it too. Perhaps, like him, it felt trapped in the Copperwood and had been running to and fro, seeking a way out. Perhaps it needed a rider to guide it. None of that was in the tales, but it didn't matter. Only one thing mattered.

Ride.

Yrion clambered up the shaggy coat. The Nightsteed neighed. With mounds and trees all around, this place was like the clearing in the story of the Nightfather, fencing them in. But no fence or foliage could pen this horse. It charged and passed through mound and tree like they were apparitions. Nothing in this world could stand in their way.

They returned to the dark tunnel, passed under the black-leafed canopy and through the flashing scenes. Yrion had no interest in them. He kept his eyes on the endless road, that corridor between two mirrors, focused on the single pinpoint of utter darkness ahead. It pulled his thoughts to it, like a needle pulling black thread. It sucked at his very heartbeats, capturing their pulse and funneling them towards it. Slowly, fed by thought and thump, the pinpoint grew. The flashing scenes with their fruitless temptations sputtered out, and the darkhouse appeared in the distance.

The Hall of the Nightfather.

Seeing it sent a chill through Yrion. The black vines curling about its roof seemed to reach out to him. The sweet stink of the curse grew stronger—he could almost taste it. He clung to the Nightsteed's mane, afraid to go on, but more afraid to face what lay behind. This was his path now. *Ride. Ride.*

The house rushed at him, but the Nightsteed did not slow. How would it stop? Would the hall's double doors magically open? What would be inside? Yrion squinted, braced for impact.

But no impact came.

In a darkly blinding instance, Yrion found himself standing before the house. He hadn't dismounted; he hadn't been thrown. The Nightsteed had simply vanished. Not so much as an echo of its hooves remained. It had abandoned him, and it had taken with it that shared urge to ride, leaving a stillness in the air, a stagnation that trapped the smell of the curse—or perhaps it was the curse that did the trapping. Nothing moved, nothing sounded—save Yrion. His own racing heartbeat was a comparable racket.

He stood upon a stone porch. It was coated in a thick layer of dust and old dirt. Black leaves had gathered into piles at the base of the house's walls. Black vines slept atop the roof, black limbs hung like men at the gallows. A sooty circular window punctuated the house's shallow gable. The stink of the curse permeated it all.

Yrion stepped up to the double doors. Their wood was cracked and splintered and grey save for the black speckles of fungus. The planks had shrunk and warped and no longer formed a tight seal. Rusty hinges and brittle studs barely kept them standing. It was dark inside, like his locked up barn back home; he wondered if it was just as empty. No candlelight or lamplight shone through the crack under the door.

He didn't know what awaited him, but he'd come this far. If this was truly the Hall of the Nightfather, Yrion would be imprisoned here till Everdark with all the other lazy children's restless spirits. He'd tried his best not to be a lazy boy, but his best hadn't been enough. In any case, he was a clumsy boy. A nincompoop. He couldn't provide for his mother and sister. They were better off without him. One less mouth to feed.

But perhaps something else lay beyond it. The tales hadn't gotten all of it right about the Nightsteed. At the very least, he'd finally get some answers.

He raised his fist to knock.

Something disturbed the silence before his knuckles could touch wood. It came like a gust of wind that he couldn't feel. It had the ominous power of a storm, rising up from some depth where sound itself went to die.

A voice.

Yrion whirled. The fog had closed in like a wall of clouds. A few strides away, a rocky shoreline touched the black waters of a bog or a moat. The fog hung over them so thickly he couldn't tell how far the waters stretched, but they were as motionless as the vines and trees, as smooth as the surface of that faraway basin he'd just fled.

The voice came from that mist, swirled about him like a swarm of bats.

"*Yrion,*" it said.

His heart pounded at a Nightsteed rhythm.

His own name, spoken in a voice he hadn't heard in months, a voice he could never forget.

"Father?" he whispered.

Yrion's voice carried far less power—was but a mouse's squeak.

He strained his eyes, thinking Corvus might appear in a rowboat to ferry Yrion away from this dark place. Or come walking atop the water and carry Yrion away in his arms. But he saw only fog and black water.

"*Yrion,*" his father's voice repeated, not above a whisper, but one that cut the fog like a blade.

"Father!" Yrion shouted. He stepped closer to the water, cupped his hands to his face. "Corvus Blight!"

The fog swallowed his words.

"*Yrion.*"

Yrion stepped blindly forward, and his ankle rolled. He fell to his knees, then to his hands, splashed into icy water. It felt like needles and knives against his skin. He winced and sucked in breath with a squeak.

When he looked again he saw blood staining the water in little wisps that swam into the spaces between the river stones. He could *see* stones, *see* his hands; the light had returned. And sound too: wind through the trees, leaves rolling through the forest. He lifted his head and found himself in the basin again, on his hands and knees, soaking in the pool. Ripples radiated from him. He pulled his hands from the water to inspect his palms and found two round patches of bare red skin that stung worse in the open air.

He felt ready to weep again, but not from his wounds. They were tears of half-joy, half-fear.

Father.

Corvus had called to him, called him back from the door of the Nightfather. But where was he? Here in this basin? Somewhere in the Copperwood? In his grave in the Blight family cemetery? *Yrion*, his voice had said, but there were so many things hidden in that voice, in that single word. Warning, longing, but contentedness too, maybe even a hint of pride. But how could one feel all those things at once? And what did they mean together? What did any of this craziness mean?

Thunder pealed overhead, and rain began to fall, starting as a few heavy drops that spattered the pool's surface with little dimples. He could hear the shower drawing closer, a calamity of wind and rain, the Copperwood thrashing. The flaky white bark of the birch tree began to fall like snow. He would be drenched in seconds.

He stood, knowing better than to hide under a tree during a storm.

But before he took his first step, he saw something sticking out from the sole of his boot. A jagged bit of blackness. He lifted his foot and plucked it off: a single maple leaf, black-veined, black-stemmed, black-bladed. Black as if dipped in Laurel's inkwell. Black that couldn't be wiped away. Black brought back from the Nightfather's doorstep.

"Father," he said and slipped the leaf into his pocket.

Eighteen

Laurel set the package and the letter down on the table. The letter was scribe work from Brodhaven, which she received almost daily. But she'd never received a package before. It came wrapped in brown paper, cross-tied with twine, shaped like a book but half the size in every dimension. It had 'Laurel Blight' written across the top in a fair, feminine but unfamiliar script.

She cut the twine below the knot and pulled the paper away. It was a small wooden jewelry box, delicately thin and sanded to a glassy finish. The beveled edges of its lid had a shallow rope-like pattern carved into it. The rich orange stain had soaked into the grooves and accentuated the pattern.

Laurel lifted the lid to reveal a padded velvet interior. A silver pen rested in the center—one of the recently invented reservoir pens she had heard about but never seen. Its nib looked as sharp as any knife, its barrel plump like a wasp queen. Laurel tested its weight and balance. It felt strange in her hand compared to her feather quills, strange but comfortable.

The box's lid had a small envelope pressed into its velvet recess.

Her mother approached and Laurel passed her the pen.

"From Caelum?" Lyra asked.

Laurel had thought the same at first, but this wasn't his handwriting. Inside the envelope she found a note. It read:

Laurel,

Do the things you're good at.

Vela

A thoughtful gift, a luxury Laurel would never have bought for herself. But why had it been given? If anything, Laurel ought to buy Lady Idlevice a gift—a token of appreciation for her help. Laurel didn't consider it charity: she didn't *need* such a pen for her scribe work; she might not even use it if it couldn't outperform her feather quills. So what then? Simple kindness?

Also inside the envelope, Laurel found a card of an aged, earthy color, like a papyrus scroll but stiffer. She had to read its print twice, and it confused her more than the pen. The words made her sweat, made her fingers tingle. She put the card face down in the box.

"What is it?" her mother asked.

"It's an invitation," she said, "to the Ball of the Nightfather."

Her mother passed the pen back without a word.

Laurel was too stunned to think. "Why would she invite me?"

Her mother gave her a brief, expectant glance.

The Idlevices' ball was the most important social event of the year; nearly everyone with money would attend: old money, new money; lords, ladies; socialites, suitors. Vela had stopped sending the suitors Laurel's way; now, she was bringing Laurel to the suitors—and to every other prospective buyer the Valley had to offer. If Laurel didn't want suitors, fine; here was buffet from which she could choose according to her own standards and priorities. Here was a chance to have it her way.

Do the things you're good at.

"It's a very nice pen," her mother said.

"Should I accept?" Laurel asked.

"Or you can come with Yrion and me to the Boarsiks' dance."

Which meant her mother didn't want anything to do with this ball business, so Laurel eased away from it: "If he's well enough to go."

Yrion had caught a chill after Monday's storm, came home sopping wet and hadn't been out of bed for three days now. He'd made it one day at the clockworks before something got him out of it. Hadn't made a dollar. It was as if he did these things on purpose to get out of work. Though, he did look rough—was sweating through the sheets every night.

In any case, Laurel was going to have to work this out on her own. Her timeline was shrinking fast—just over two weeks to get something binding from a buyer. She was starting to feel the pressure every other landowner in the railroad's path was feeling: throw away the vote and get the eighteen-fifty an acre now, or else risk six dollars an acre on the unlikely chance the railroad would be voted down. Most folk weren't as stubborn as her; no doubt some had already sold to Linenpest. Laurel was trying to do something different.

Now she asked herself: *why?*

She wanted to get an honest price for the farm. She wanted to provide for her family. She wanted to win the vote. She wanted to change Long Autumn Valley's patriarchal ways. She wanted to live a different life than that of the typical Long Autumn Woman. But if she tried to have it all, she might end up with nothing.

Do the things you're good at.

So what *was* she good at? Scribe work—that's what the pen was for. But was she going to be a scribing spinster her whole life? If she followed that path, she'd be forced to sell this fancy pen to put food on the table. And writing letters wasn't going to get her farm sold.

Do the things you're good at.

Laurel was good at lots of things. She had a sharp mind. Lady Idlevice liked her plan (though she'd envisioned an alternate version of it). And Laurel had lots of options. So what was important to her? Principles or practicality?

She went in circles about it for the next two hours then decided some scribe work would help clear her head. She laid her writing supplies out on the table—her new pen included—and opened the letter from Brodhaven. It read:

Ms. Blight,

Your services as scribe are no longer needed. Thank you for your years of diligence.

Sincerely,

Pavo Linenpest

Laurel had to read that *three* times. Then she simply stared at it—stared *through* it. She felt like she was going to be sick. It couldn't be, it couldn't be. Not now.

No longer needed? That didn't make any sense. She was the best they had. Her diligence kept their scribe costs down. She was never late, never made a mistake. And there would be a lot of announcements after the railroad vote passed...

Her own words came roaring back to her: *Vote against the Witching Hour Railroad.*

Her letter. The one making its way around certain circles. That had to be it. There was no other explanation. But she hadn't signed it—how could they have known she wrote it?

Maybe it's your perfect handwriting.

She'd copied hundreds of letters for Brodhaven. Her penmanship was the unspoken voice of the town's official business. To the reader, her damned letter probably *looked* like official business.

"Laurel, dear," her mother said from her rocker, "are you all right?"

Laurel was trembling and hadn't realized it. "Fine," she lied.

She'd put her family in serious trouble. With her brother sick and her mother's occasional odd job, they didn't have a single steady stream of income. How could she have been so reckless? How could she tell her mother?

"Have you heard back from Oldfather's Inn?" she asked.

"Nothing yet," Lyra replied.

Laurel *wouldn't* tell her. She'd find another way. She had to.

Caelum stopped by later that afternoon, unexpected but timely. When Laurel saw him tying Kernel off to the ash tree, she went up to the road to meet him.

"Surprised to see you here," she said, trying to be cheery.

"Came to check up on Yrion."

When she drew close, she found she couldn't look directly at him, and he knew something was wrong.

"Laurel, what's the matter?" he asked.

She was almost too embarrassed to speak. "My, uh, services are no longer needed."

Caelum's brow wrinkled, and a lump rose in Laurel's throat. She choked it down. "I lost my job today."

Caelum brought her in close, hugged her. "What happened?"

"I wrote a letter," she said—and, hearing it aloud, she couldn't believe how stupid she had been: "A political one. Told folk to vote against the railroad. Likened the mayor to a weasel."

Caelum winced. "I'm so sorry."

"So stupid," she said, and no matter how she tried she couldn't fight back the tears. She couldn't, apparently, do anything right. And she couldn't see through the tangle of troubles, didn't know which thread to start with. She backed out of Caelum's embrace. "Vela Idlevice invited me to the ball."

Caelum paused, tasting the idea. "That's exciting."

Laurel could tell he was pretending. He knew she didn't like dances and fancy dresses. "Is it?"

Caelum shrugged. "Might be a sight to see."

"You don't want me to go."

"I didn't say that."

Laurel looked away. Absently, she started scraping at the road with the toe of her boot.

"What?" Caelum asked.

Laurel exhaled. "The lady is trying to set me up with someone."

Caelum stiffened.

"Apparently," she explained, "the only way someone will buy this place is if they can have me along with it. I'm sort of a buyer's dowry."

After a few moments, he relaxed a little and let out a nervous chuckle. "Well, that's how she got where she is."

Laurel jammed her hands in her pockets, kept kicking at the dust. She looked at him, but again found she couldn't for long.

"Laurel," he said, "you're not actually *considering* this."

Laurel supposed she was—if only in a theoretical way. She knew it sounded bad. But it *was* what her father wanted. When he was alive, she could be as stubborn and righteous as she wanted. She didn't have that luxury anymore.

"I have to take care of my family," she said.

Caelum stared at her hard—she could almost feel his eyes pressing with determination. "*I'll* take care of them."

"I don't want *you* to take care of them. *I* need to take care of them."

"And this is how you're going to do it? By marrying some rich fool—like *Pyxis Pettifog*?"

Laurel crossed her arms. It did sound bad when he said it that way. But it was her choice, one of the few she had. She had to keep her options open, didn't she?

"The Laurel I know wouldn't even consider this," Caelum said.

Laurel could almost see the arguments swarming like hornets about Caelum's head. "She might."

"The Laurel who hates dances suddenly wants to dance? The Laurel who wants to make her own way in the world suddenly wants to be another man's property?—and not just another man, but the kind of man who would view her as property as...as proven by such a *ridiculous* arrangement!"

Laurel didn't need this now, not from him.

"She might," she said again, this time with a clenched jaw.

"The Laurel I know—"

"Maybe the only Laurel you know is the one you're in love with."

Her words knocked him back a step. He'd never told her he was in love with her. But everyone knew it—even Lady Idlevice. Even Laurel. She'd known it her whole life. But loving her didn't give him the right to tell her who she was; nothing did. "Maybe you don't know the real me at all. Maybe you resent my choice because it doesn't end with you."

Caelum's face had gone pale, and the stiffness in his posture slackened.

"You're right," he said. "It's your choice. I won't try to make it for you. Or take it from you."

He turned, unhitched Kernel from the tree.

"What am I supposed to do?" Laurel shouted. "Marry *you*?"

"I never asked you to marry me."

"If I'm going to marry someone to take care of me, shouldn't I pick the best candidate?"

"I never asked you to marry me," he said again, low, as if mumbling in his sleep.

He led Kernel away, though it looked like Kernel was leading him. His strides were short, his knees weak. He didn't look back.

Laurel watched him go. Why had she said those hurtful things? He was only looking out for her.

She didn't like this any more than he did—couldn't he see that? But Pavo Linenpest wasn't leaving her many alternatives. Neither was the curse. Neither had her father. She was running out of time and options, and she didn't need him or her mother or anyone trying to close doors she needed left open. Not for love, not for some misconstrued interpretation of who they thought she was or what she was capable of. If they wouldn't support her decisions, they needed to stay out of her way.

She stormed back to the cottage, gathered up her writing supplies, and tossed them into the fire. Everything but Lady Idlevice's pen.

Nineteen

Yrion had many dreams, dreams of his father.

In some, Yrion wandered the Copperwood, trying to call his father's name, but had no voice. He screamed and screamed but his father's name would not sound. He could say Copperwood and hello and help, but he couldn't say Father or Corvus or even Blight.

In others, he found more black leaves in the Copperwood and believed that his father was buried beneath them—that Corvus Blight wasn't dead, not truly, merely covered by layers and layers of fallen leaves. Yrion dug everywhere, and this time calling his father's name didn't matter because Corvus couldn't hear through the leaves anyway.

In still others, Yrion didn't have to search at all. Corvus was there, out in the field, working, as Yrion always remembered him. Once in a while, he'd stop and wipe the sweat from his brow, turn and see Yrion watching, and beckon to his son to join him. Yrion wanted to, but something always got in the way: he had to put his toys away first; he had to go tell Mother first; he had to go to the barn and find a shovel first; all of which dragged endlessly on so that he never made it down to the field.

In the hazy windows of consciousness between dreams, he remembered his father's voice. Sometimes, he heard it so clearly he would sit up and look about the room, trying to catch a glimpse of Corvus in the doorway, Corvus at the foot of the bed. His eyes found nothing. Yet, Yrion sensed his father's presence, the way he could sense the coming snow. It lingered like a scentless scent, and it made him miss his father more than ever.

Yrion didn't realize he was awake, staring at the ceiling, until he heard his mother's voice.

"Well, good morning," she said from the doorway. "Or afternoon, I should say."

Yrion knuckled the sleep from his eyes. His body felt very stiff.

"What day is it?" he asked.

"It's Sunday, nearly midday."

"*Sunday*?" He'd been in bed nearly a whole week!

Lyra moved next to the bed and put her wrist to his forehead.

"Sunday," she said, "and the fever has finally broken."

Yrion knew he'd gone through a few days and nights but not so many. He felt oily all over, and on his hands he still caught the faint scent of the Nightsteed's mane, the stink of the curse. The cuts on his palms had scabbed over.

"Do you feel good enough to get up?" his mother asked.

"Maybe for a little."

"Just long enough to change out the bedclothes. You've been sweating and stinking the whole house up."

"I'm sorry, Mother."

Lyra cupped his cheek and smiled.

"Go check on the fire," she said. "We haven't had a nice one going since you lay down."

Yrion almost rose but tarried a moment.

"Mother," he asked, "do you ever think about Father?"

"Every day."

"Do you miss him?"

"Mm-hmm."

"Me too."

Yrion didn't know how to ask what he wanted to ask. It sounded mad.

"Do you ever *feel* him?" he asked. "Like he's still here?"

Lyra sat on the edge of the bed.

"Your father isn't a restless spirit," she said.

"But how do you *know*?"

Her tone sharpened a bit: "Do you think your father was lazy?"

Yrion wanted to talk about the Nightsteed, the Hall of the Nightfather, all the strange things he'd seen. But how could he? Who would believe such a things if they hadn't seen them for themselves? Yrion had seen them—and heard them and smelled them—but even he had trouble believing them.

"That day," his mother said, "I woke up and found your father still in bed. That never happened before, not once. He'd get up hours before dawn, practically in the middle of the night. He had that much he wanted to do." Her eyes wandered to an empty corner of the room. "When I saw him lying there, his back to me, I knew he was finally resting."

Yrion wiped the tears from his cheeks. His mother shed none. She and Laurel were strong like that. And Father was too. Yrion wondered how he'd ended up so soft, so lost.

"And do you?" his mother asked. "Feel his presence?"

Yrion had. At the doorstep of the Nightfather. In his fevered dreams. But he had to be strong. He had to figure things out on his own. That's what men did. They didn't ride the Nightsteed; the Nightsteed was just a children's story. They didn't visit the Hall of the Nightfather; that was where children went. And when men died, they didn't hang around and whisper their son's names; they found rest.

"I just miss him," he replied—which was at least half the truth.

Twenty

Jacob walked up Witching Hour Road. He hadn't found a horse to his liking and decided not to wait any longer. He had business this way; Rotbottom farm was this way. It was Monday, and though the mayor had yet to make himself available to Jacob, Jacob had negotiated a settlement with other Brodhaven officials. Money would exchange hands later this week. In the meantime, he would pay one last visit to the farm, have a look around.

The warning in the back of his mind told him to turn back.

But what was this warning? Certainly not his business sense, those rational thoughts that had made him his fortune. No, they would demand he visit the farm, perform a visual inspection, and be certain he would get every cent it was worth. Besides, he was a grown man, perfectly capable of managing his own affairs, of walking the streets and roads of this valley or any other.

He came to the edge of the Copperwood. In his travels, few places matched this place's beauty. Unlike the bourgeoning town of Brodhaven, the forest hadn't changed in thirteen years. The sky was overcast, but even so the rich canopy of leaves colored the light in hues of saffron and apricot. The air here hugged him close and exuded a distinct scent, something sweet but old and mysterious.

He entered the forest and it immediately swaddled him in nostalgia. Every stride carried him further into the past. The branches above him swayed in celebration, praised his return and beckoned him onward. Before long, his years of travel became like a dream, and this nostalgia he felt was the present, true world.

He followed the road mindless of his movement, progressing as if upon the rails Pavo Linenpest planned to lay here, rolling onward till he came to the bend in the road. Right, to the northeast, lay Rotbottom farm. But on his left, a lane passed between two stone pillars. It led to the Idlevice estate.

There he stopped.

The warning in his mind pleaded that he follow the road. It would lead him to profit, to success, safe and sure. Between the pillars, lay ruin, an impossible dream.

But something new competed with this notion, something he had carried with him the world over, something that had been sleeping a troubled sleep for thirteen years and had awakened between two bell jar clocks in the Cronewetters' shop.

She hadn't changed.

The image of her stepping into her carriage, turning her head, it was all he saw when he closed his eyes at night, when he opened his eyes in the grey light of dawn, like some vestigial memory from infancy, vivid but without context, a hot flash from a fevered dream. Her movements were ethereal, spectral, inexplicably fluid, transcending sight, more like the interplay of scent and memory.

What good were surety, safety, and success compared to that? Jacob hadn't come up this road—hadn't returned to Long Autumn Valley—for business. Business had been but a pretext. *She* was the reason he'd come, the reason he'd amassed his fortune to begin with. His business sense owed its very existence to her. He had labored, he had suffered. Why then should he not dream? Where would the world be without dreamers?

He ought to turn left here, plunge down that lane and arrive triumphant at her front door. Percy Idlevice was no longer a threat—the man's heirloom flintlock pistol was no doubt hanging on a wall where it belonged. The man could literally no longer stand in Jacob's way. And Vela was there, lonely, in need of someone to care for her, to carry her away from such loneliness.

But what if she wasn't?

Jacob reeled from that thought and followed the road to the right. More thoughts chased him, driving him onward like coyotes nipping at his heels, lashing him like whips punishing him for such reckless hopes:

What if she'd forgotten him?

What if she abandoned him?—she'd done it before.

What if she was happy?

Maybe some dreamers shouldn't dream; maybe some dreams shouldn't be dreamt.

Jacob moved almost at a trot. The road continued to bend but before it began its zigzag path up a rocky hill a lane broke off to the right and loosely followed the hill's base. A mile later, the trees ended in a clear-cut line and a wide, bare expanse of land opened up. Brown, lumpy hillsides crowded together, looking like a bad harvest of potatoes piled into an oxcart. The hills were spotted with tight clumps of dead grass; every tenth clump, a few blades of black grass sprouted like rogue hairs. Otherwise, no vegetation grew.

This was Rotbottom farm, a one hundred and ten acre bald spot shaved into the Copperwood, every inch of it cursed, as if in punishment for ravaging a sacred place. At its far borders, the trees resumed unsullied. Perhaps they were the only thing keeping that black plague at bay. That anyone would buy such a miserable plot—were they, in turn, to be cursed as well?

No, Jacob decided. No, he knew nothing about that. Good things had happened to him in this ugly place, and bad things had happened under the beauty of the Copperwood. The curse was something separate altogether, something no one could predict. Some wedding days are sunny, some stormy, and neither one foreshadowed a thing about the marriage.

In any case, the place wouldn't be Jacob's much longer. Soon the Witching Hour Railroad would come chugging right through here, then weave its way north to the Uphills.

Jacob walked on. The clumps of brown and black grass threatened to turn his ankles at every step. The dry stuff crackled beneath his boots. He crossed over the domelike hills, up and down, in as straight a line as he could manage.

The Rotbottom farmhouse stood in the center of the property. Moss clung to the mortar and brownstone walls. Paint flaked off the posts and frames to reveal deeply cracked, dull grey wood. Wrens flew in and out of the eaves. The roof sagged in a deep bow, and bare wood shone through in patches where shingles had fallen free. Shattered pieces of slate lay scattered about the front yard. Most of the windows had been broken.

Next to the house, an old gnarled tree stood in the yard. Its grey, leafless branches contorted in spirals as if it had died a painful death. Lumpy knots covered it like warts. A murder of crows argued in its limbs. They flew off when Jacob approached.

He stepped onto the porch. The boards groaned beneath his boots, and broken glass crunched. He removed a tarnished key from his pocket and jiggled it into the lock. The house had settled so much that he had to put his shoulder to the door to open it; it rubbed a semicircle across the floor as he pushed it inward.

Everything was as he'd left it: a great stone hearth spanned half of the right-hand wall where ancient ashes waited to be swept up; a few mismatched utensils lay in a tin tray atop a wobbly table; a chair, half pushed-in, waited next to it, draped in a canopy of cobwebs. Just as he'd left it.

Time hadn't changed this place. Nor the Copperwood. It was as if these places from memory had all been sleeping, waiting for his return. And the things that hadn't slept had since moved into positions that only benefited him: Brodhaven's offer to buy the farm; Percy Idlevice's failing health; Jacob's growing fortune.

But what about her? She hadn't aged a day. Could she be waiting for him too?—sleeping, waiting to be awakened? If not, he would leave this place and never return; half of him was demanding that already. But if she *were* waiting, if what they once had could start again…

Twenty-One

Yrion examined himself in his sister's mirror. He wore a tattered pair of pants which his mother had snipped short; frayed threads fell like overgrown hairs over his old, holey boots. He wore one of his old white shirts; its wrists were frayed like the pants and had been intentionally stained with mud and tea. Atop it, he wore his old coat. He'd outgrown it, but it showed all the proper signs of wear for the occasion.

He held his mask up to his face, and a pale, weary face stared back. Long crow's feet webbed outward from the corners of the eyeholes; puffy bags sagged beneath them; the eyebrows were raised in the center, making the face look very tired. His mother had made it from wheat paste and tobacco leaves, and she'd done a fine job; it really looked like the face of a restless spirit loitering in the Hall of the Nightfather.

The Everdark festival marked the harvest and the end of a long year's work. The best harvest foods were served—like pumpkin and sweet potato pie—and it gave everyone a reason to dance. At the end came the Dousing of the Lights—*Everdark*—to signal the end of the party, the end of the season. It was the one holiday the hardworking folk of Long Autumn Valley celebrated.

Yrion didn't need a festival immersing him in such fantasies. He'd been living them. The Nightsteed, the Nightfather's hall—he was convinced they had contributed to his illness. While bedridden, Yrion hadn't once heard the Nightsteed's thundering hooves. And though he'd had countless vivid dreams about his father, he came out of them rested. But now that his body was strong again, his mind seemed to have weakened. In the mirror, he was already looking unrested again, even without his Everdark mask, and he felt that way too.

Besides, this year's festivities wouldn't be the same. It was the first year without Father, and *no one* danced like Corvus

Blight. He took dancing as seriously as any other task. By the end of the night, he would be the only person on the floor.

"Yrion," his mother called from the kitchen, "the day's getting on."

Yrion came out of his room with his mask on and spread his arms.

"*Perfect*," his mother said, "don't you think, Laurel?"

Laurel glanced at him from her seat at the table.

"He looks the part," she said and went back to her task.

She had her own mask cut to pieces, reduced to something that only covered her eyes and the bridge of her nose. She was adhering bits of cardinal and blue jay feathers to the strap.

"Such a shame," Mother said.

"It's a masquerade, Mother," Laurel said. "I'll make a new one next year."

"What if you get invited to the ball next year?" Yrion asked.

"Then I'll already have my mask."

Their mother sighed and told Yrion to come along.

Yrion's shoulders slouched. "Aren't we going to watch the carriages?"

"I told your Aunt Carina we'd be down after lunch," Mother said, "and already dinner's sneaking up."

"Sorry, kid," Laurel added—but she didn't sound it. "Have to get moving myself."

The Blights had their own little Everdark tradition: being the Idlevices' neighbors and living so close to Witching Hour Road, they would watch the decorated carriages roll past on their way to the Ball of the Nightfather. But this year Laurel was actually going to the fancy ball; she'd get to see them close up and talk to the lords and ladies that rode in them. Yrion would not only miss the carriages, he wouldn't have anyone close to his age to tag along with at the Boarsik's.

"Is Caelum going to the ball?" he asked.

"It's invitation only," Laurel said.

"Oh. Was he invited?"

"No."

"Oh. Do you think he'll come to the Boarsik's?"

"Yrion, I don't know what his plans are."

Yrion wasn't sure if that was good or bad. He'd spent a week in bed after the day he'd run out of Cronewetters' Clockworks, and all this week regaining his strength. Soon he would have to return to the clockworks and apologize to Caelum for breaking the statuette—he owed him that much. The thought of that confrontation put a knot in his stomach. Yrion wouldn't blame Caelum if Caelum fired him on the spot.

"I expect you'll be home late?" Mother said to Laurel.

"Don't wait up," Laurel replied.

Lyra handed Yrion two baskets and picked up two of her own before sidestepping out the front door. Her baskets overflowed with strips of musty old cloth, dried gourds, and wreaths of grey twigs spotted with orange and red berries. They would use these to decorate the Boarsiks' barn. Yrion's baskets were heavy with turnips. Laurel said they didn't have turnips to spare, but Mother refused to show up empty-handed.

They followed the same path Yrion had weeks back: south along the edge of the Copperwood, right at the big dirt mound, then left down Uncle Cetus' wagon trail. From here they could see the barn, its doors shut, and Banyon trotting about his pen.

"Look at him go, Ma," Yrion said.

"He's a wild one, isn't he?"

"A little bit. But I like him. And he makes Uncle Cetus so cross—on purpose, like."

Mother chuckled. "Oh, I've heard."

When they drew close, the horse spotted them and trotted over to greet them.

"Hey, Banyon," Yrion said.

Banyon, like a proper gentleman, escorted them along the fence line. At the end of the fence, they turned right to the far side of the barn where the doors were flung wide. Aunt Carina was sweeping dust out in great brown gusts.

"Haloo," she called.

When they stepped up, she leaned the broom against Yrion's chest and took his baskets.

"What do we have in these?" she said. She lifted them close to her face, testing their weight. "Turnips?" She gave Mother an admonishing look.

"Leftovers," Mother assured her. "We'll work them into something or other."

"Aye, no worries there."

Yrion started sweeping now that he was holding the broom. Inside the barn, Uncle Cetus was disassembling the animals' individual pens which were held together with black iron pins and hinges. Their massive corner posts—nine feet tall and a foot wide on all sides—stood in square holes in the barn's floor. Uncle Cetus handled them as easily as Yrion handled the broom.

"Where are the other animals?" Yrion asked.

Uncle Cetus hefted a post up on his shoulder. "I set them loose in the south field. Banyon ain't one for sharing."

Yrion moved the broom aimlessly about.

Overhead, gourds already hung on varying lengths of twine from the rafters. A fist-sized hole had been punched into each. Before nightfall, candles would be placed in them and they'd light up the barn. Mother's wreaths would hang from the posts, and her strips of cloth would loop and droop as streamers between the rafters. And Aunt Carina would have a great many other decorations to add. Even now, she and Mother were discussing it, amongst other things.

"In our day, remember," Yrion heard Carina saying, "it was a *true* celebration of the season's end."

"I remember," his mother agreed.

"Pushing work aside for celebration's sake—especially *this* celebration—seems a bit backwards, doesn't it."

"Aye, but who are we to question the likes of Pavo Linenpest?"

The Everdark festival hadn't always fallen on the third Saturday of October. It used to happen when all the crops were harvested which, year to year, farm to farm, happened anywhere from mid-October to early December. For simplicity's sake, officials down in Brodhaven voted to fix the day of celebration when the weather wasn't so bitter cold and the harvests weren't all packed away for winter.

Aunt Carina led Lyra out of the barn to discuss the outer decorations. When they were out of sight, Uncle Cetus stretched his back with a sigh.

"Take a breather," he said to Yrion and sat down atop his stack of posts.

Yrion slowed his sweeping to a lazier pace. "Banyon will be all right out there?"

"Oh, he'll be fussing all night, wanting a roof over his head, but he'll be fine. I'll throw a blanket over him if he'll let me."

"He followed me down the fence line again."

"Looking for handouts again."

Yrion kept his broom moving. Uncle Cetus tried to scratch a spot on his back that his arms were too muscular to reach. He stood and put his shoulder blade to one of the posts left standing and rubbed it up and down like a bear against a tree.

"Have you given any thought to what I said?" Uncle Cetus asked. "About bringing your family down here to stay, I mean."

Yrion hadn't, really, though it sounded nice. "Naw. Don't want to be a burden."

"Now listen here: your father helped me raise this barn and put up that fence and a whole lot else. Weren't no generations of Boarsiks on this plot before your Aunt Carina and I settled. He was a good man. Or maybe he was just glad to have something to do. But glad is glad and good is good, and I'll take either where I find them. So no more of this burden business."

Yrion looked at his feet. "Yes, sir."

"Besides. You ain't staying on for free."

"No, sir."

"Plenty of work needs done."

"Yes, sir. Only, Laurel's got her own plans."

Uncle Cetus scratched at his beard. "Well, I would say, since you're the man of the house, it's your decision to make. But I don't make half the decisions around here neither."

Yrion shrugged. He had too many other things on his mind.

"Anyway," Uncle Cetus said. "Guess you're not going to the fancy ball either, huh?"

"It's invitation only," Yrion replied.

"Just doesn't seem right, does it? We can be fancy too."

Uncle Cetus stood up, held out his arms, and began waltzing about with an imaginary partner.

Yrion giggled, overturned his broom, held it at arm's length, and bowed to it.

"You see?" Uncle Cetus laughed. "Fancy as can be."

"*Cetus!*" a voice bellowed.

Uncle Cetus stopped in his tracks, and they both turned and saw the women had returned. Aunt Carina had her massive arms crossed and her foot tapped away.

"The party doesn't start till sundown," she said.

Yrion was a little frightened, but Uncle Cetus laughed: "Just practicing, dear."

"And you need it, but first things first."

"Yrion," Lyra said, "when the sweeping's done, you can hang the streamers."

"Yes, Mother," Yrion said.

The women left again, this time going down to the house. Yrion righted his broom and resumed sweeping.

"You heard them," Uncle Cetus said, as much to himself as to Yrion, "back to work. But before you do the streamers, we'll try to get the blanket on Banyon."

Twenty-Two

Laurel looked herself over one last time in the mirror. She wore the sky-blue gown Pyxis Pettifog had given her. She ran her hands down her ribs and over the hourglass cinch the gown forced at her waist. She'd done her hair up in a heavy bun and secured it with a yellow ribbon that matched the silk flowers trimming her bosom. She teased the baby strands at her hairline as best she could; when she held her mask up to her face, its feathers concealed most of them.

She wore her heavy brown boots but held the slippers in her hand. If she tried to walk to the estate in them, they'd be ruined before she reached the Idlevice's carriageway. Besides, the things were so tight, she didn't want to wear them longer than she had to.

She sighed and set the mirror face down on her dresser. Next to it, her invitation was propped against Caelum's wooden figurine. She hadn't heard from him since they'd argued about the ball. They'd never fought before, not like this. And she'd never been hurtful to him, never been cruel. She didn't want to take back all she had said, but part of her wished she could take back how she had said it.

Yet part of her was still angry about it. Caelum was judging her, condemning her decisions. He insinuated she wasn't in her right mind, that she was being irrational, when she was being anything but. He sounded like every other man in Long Autumn Valley, telling women what they're feeling and how they should be thinking. Who was he to tell her whom to marry and why?

And who said she'd actually have to marry anyone? Maybe all Laurel needed was the power of suggestion, the feigned possibility of marriage. A coquettish performance tonight—a few innuendos to a few rich men—might attract a buyer. *Do the things you're good at.* Well, she could play the damsel in distress, a girl in need of saving.

She pushed thoughts of Caelum away; she'd been thinking them long enough. If she sold to Linenpest now, she'd get scat; if she sold to him after Friday, she'd get half scat. Brodhaven would honor pending contracts, which left her a very small window.

She snatched her invitation off the dresser and hurried out of the house.

Witching Hour Road was at its busiest. Carriage after carriage clattered past on their way to the Ball of the Nightfather. Each was decorated in the Everdark tradition. Some were covered with musty, moth-eaten cloths and sheets. Others had brown and grey vines and brambles woven about them and looked as though they'd emerged from some deep, dead thicket. Some carriages were custom-made just for this occasion, constructed of old barn wood; they looked like wheeled shanties rolling past. White cloth streamers trailed behind them like defeated banners. Even the drivers were dressed the part, all wearing fancy coats and slacks that had been purposefully tattered, and they covered their faces with weary masks of the restless souls imprisoned in the Hall of the Nightfather.

But that was the extent to which the wealthy participated in the tradition. Inside those ramshackle carriages driven by dusty servants, noblemen and noblewomen were wearing their most extravagant clothing, procured and tailored for this very occasion. Just like Laurel.

She kept to the left side of the road, held her gown up in one hand and her invitation, slippers, and mask in the other. When she passed through the stone pillars at the end of the Idlevices' lane, she stepped behind an old maple and changed into her slippers. She left the boots there and walked the rest of the way to the mansion. By the time she passed through the gate, her feet hurt and the toe of her left slipper already had a fray in it. At this rate, the delicate things wouldn't survive the walk back to her boots.

The fountain spat water in a geyser shaped like a trumpet's bell. Carriages were jammed horse-to-cart all the way around it, unwilling to unload their passengers anywhere except directly in front of the mansion. Laurel moved past them, and didn't have to wait long for a gap in the procession. Suhar was accepting invitations at the door, and when she stepped up he smiled and gave her a slight bow.

Laurel passed him her invitation and he added it to the stack in his hand.

"Welcome, Miss Blight," he said. Then he tapped his eyebrow twice with his finger to remind Laurel to don her mask. She did so, and he gestured for her to enter.

She walked through the foyer and into the great room with the spiral staircase. The doorways to the left and right which led to the tower room study and the tea room (respectively) were blocked off with folding panels—black frames with white cloth pulled taut between. Stringed music floated down the atrium ahead, along with laughter and chatter which lured the new arrivals onward and upward.

Laurel began the long, counterclockwise ascent up the stairs. The servants had finished decorating the marble balustrade with dried vines and shredded strands of cotton. It looked like some massive colony of spiders nested in a great, smoky, upward swirl. Dark blue sky shone through the circular skylight as the sun began its rest in the west.

At the top of the stairs, a wide upper landing stretched to the left with a full view of the atrium on one side and a series of tall windows and glass-paned doors on the other. The doors opened onto a balcony which provided guests a view of the fountain and carriageway below and a grand overlook of the southern landscape, rivaled only by Caelum and Laurel's picnic spot. To the immediate right, a wide doorway was clogged with guests waiting to make their entrance into the legendary ballroom. They advanced one couple at a time, each giving the previous couple ample space to dissolve graciously into the revelry.

Laurel waited alone, glad this was a masquerade. Never had she felt so out of place, so vulnerable, and never had she needed such feelings less than tonight. Her fine gown didn't look nearly as fine as others she saw: gold-threaded dresses with skirts so large their wearers looked like bells; bodices with jewels stitched right into them; fold after fold of silk frills billowing from sleeve and neckline. Laurel's homemade tobacco leaf mask certainly couldn't compete. The men's were made of leather, of animal fur, of carven wood, even of steel, fancy things trimmed with chains and metal studs and spikes. The women's were even more extravagant: silk padding of every color, or pale carven ivory, all trimmed with exotic bird feathers and so many jewels that some looked like crowns across their faces. Some had long, beaky noses; others had domelike foreheads spiked with little horns. But men and women alike had eyeholes and eyebrows slanted downwards to portray the oh-so-tired faces of the spirits awaiting Everdark in the Hall of the Nightfather.

Laurel's entrance was fast and she moved immediately to the left side of the room to gather her wits. The room was laid out like a long hall without any windows along the walls. Tapered redwood columns ran single file down each side of the room and supported the twenty-foot ceilings. Between them lay the hardwood dance floor, and above it a skylight that matched the hall in length. The last remnants of daylight fell through it, yet already the room beamed with candlelight from chandeliers supported by long iron arms on each column. The far end of the room had a raised sort of stage and ended in a set of closed double doors. Next to the stage, violin and cello players sat in a semicircle, providing the hall a subtle, melodious backdrop.

Tables lined the walls and some spaces between the columns, topped with a lavish spread of foods: honey glazed goose stuffed with carrot mash; roasted duck with cranberry dressing; lamb skewers dipped in apricot jam; smoked pork rubbed with rosemary; charred beef crusted in coffee; fried river trout; apples and pears in a cinnamon stew.

Servants rushed in and out of doors on the right hand side of the ballroom. They moved amongst the guests carrying silver platters topped with crystal glasses filled with sparkling wines or steins of beer or whole silver tea sets. They offered strong coffee in tiny cups with handles so small one could only pinch them with the thumb and forefinger. They presented little plates with more food samples: clams and crawfish and seared pheasant strips and dumplings.

And the guests—so many guests. Perpetual lines stood at the food tables. Those satisfied with the pickings brought by the servants gathered in tight clusters beneath the skylight and were surrounded by a slow, counterclockwise current of walkers.

Laurel snatched a flute of white wine from a tray and moved against a pillar. She watched the current of guests flow past and wondered if she'd made a mistake coming here. She didn't know how to begin this task she'd undertaken. With all the masks, she couldn't identify a single person, and, mask or no mask, she would probably know less than one in thirty. Every so often, the eyes of a gentleman would linger on her as he passed, and she would feel a brief moment of conflict: disapproval of his shamelessness mixed with a nervous uncertainty of how she should react yet encouragement that this mad plan of hers could actually work. More often than she could consciously help—more often than was wise—she found herself sipping from her little flute. It was empty within minutes, and a servant appeared within seconds to carry the glass away. She would not have another.

A hand touched her elbow and Laurel was relieved. Lady Idlevice had slid in next to her and was watching the crowd too.

"My lady," Laurel said.

Vela wore a form-fitting gown, black as night, cut straight across her chest to reveal her bare shoulders and a massive ruby over her heart. She wore elbow-length gloves to match, and simple silver bangles on her wrists. The gown was trimmed with raven feathers, as was her black velvet mask which had a long black nose like a raven's beak. Silver strands were woven into her sable hair which was secured at the top of her head with a silver comb set with three rubies of its own. The gown, Laurel presumed, was the one Pyxis Pettifog promised to make for her— simple but avant garde. Lady Idlevice wore it well, outshining her guests with a perfect balance of taste and sophistication.

"Here," the lady said and pressed something into Laurel's hand.

It was an ivory mask that shamed Laurel's homemade one. Its cream color complemented Laurel's complexion. Thin ripples of crimson worked their way across it in rivulets, like dye dropped in a glass of water. It was cut like her own mask, meant to cover only the upper part of her face, but at its temples red and orange maple leaves overlapped and spread back the bands that secured it to the head. The leaves would blend seamlessly into her hair; she would look like a woodland nymph, if a weary one.

Laurel pulled off her own mask, passed it to Lady Idlevice, and donned the new one. It attached with a single button in the back from which dangled a copper-threaded ribbon. It fit comfortably across her cheekbones, as if custom made for her. Vela gave her a quick glance and smiled.

"Perfect," the lady said.

Laurel reached for her old mask but saw it was not in Vela's hand.

There it was, on the floor behind the lady's foot. Before Laurel could bend down for it, the train of a passing woman's long gown swept it into a cluster of shuffling feet where a heavy black boot crushed it. It split into three different pieces which were kicked in three different directions. Laurel could only shrug it off; she had a better mask now.

"I'm glad you chose to come," Vela said.

"Thank you for the invitation. And the pen."

"I hope you'll put them to good use."

Laurel wasn't so sure about the pen; she was no longer a scribe. "So what now?"

The lady didn't seem to be listening, but said, "Let them come to you."

"I don't know that they will."

"They will. Which reminds me: Willem Whitehead accepted my invitation."

Laurel tensed involuntarily at his mention. "Does that surprise you?"

"I invite the Whiteheads every year—their family is older than the Idlevices. But they've never accepted. Seems you made quite an impression on Willem."

"I appreciate the warning."

"Give him a chance, Laurel. He might surprise you."

Laurel looked out across the room and went about pushing her reservations aside. If this was the game she had to play, she would play it and play her very best. And who knew? Maybe she would enjoy herself while she was at it.

"I suppose one dance won't hurt," she said.

She looked back to the lady but found the lady wasn't there. She scanned about, saw Vela in another conversation two pillars away. Laurel was on her own. But she was ready.

"Good evening, Miss Blight," a voice said.

Laurel turned and saw a man standing before her. He wore a trim red velvet coat with three large gold buttons running off-center up the left breast. His pants matched the jacket, his black boots matched his black hair. As a courtesy, he peeled back his ebony mask—a thin, effeminate thing similar to Laurel's.

Laurel curtseyed. "Good evening to you, Mister Pettifog."

Twenty-Three

Jacob moved in the shadows of the carriages jammed along the Idlevices' lane. Lanterns lined the carriageway, and light poured from the front windows, but the lawn was dark, dark enough with all the commotion for him to move unnoticed. As the line of carriages began to bend towards the fountain, he diverted right onto the grass. He walked briskly, but not fast enough to draw attention; he'd purposefully arrived at this, the most hectic time for the doormen.

A black shadow cut a definitive line off the corner of the house; whereas the front windows blazed with light, the windows on the eastern side were dark, as if all their radiant potential had been diverted to the south side, the only façade the guests would see.

He crossed into the darkness and slowed his pace, let his eyes adjust. Then he swung wide around the glass tearoom. Behind the tearoom stretched a wide stone patio surrounded by a knee-high rock wall. Jacob kept off those stones till he reached the back corner of the house. There he approached a windowed door. The room beyond was as dark as the lawn.

Jacob had been here before. Thirteen years ago. They'd used this very door to sneak away from the party. He raised his hand to the knob. Would it turn? Would she still leave it unlocked? Much had changed; some rare, wonderful things had not.

It will turn, he told himself. It will turn. She hadn't changed. She'd left this door unlocked for thirteen years, waiting for him to walk back through it. She was up there now, waiting for him still.

His laid his fingers upon it, gently—seductively—let them slide over its cold metal. He inhaled. Squeezed. Rotated. The knob turned, smooth and sure, and the door swung open, soft and quiet as a cloth curtain in a breeze.

Validation. Thirteen years to this very night. The same setting, the same stakes. Thirteen years had punished him.

Thirteen years had tested him. Now, thirteen years offered him a second chance. Now, thirteen years favored him.

He moved through the house like a cat. Every step, every turn, every nuanced detail remained preserved in his memory. He didn't know the whole house, but he could have walked this particular route with his eyes closed. Up and over and around. He ducked from servants here, waited for them to pass there. It was as if he were reliving that night thirteen years back but in reverse. He half-expected to bump into his younger self.

A long, labyrinthine path led him to the fourth floor where he emerged from a door that opened onto the balcony. There, costumed guests sipped from crystal glasses and observed the glowing fountain and carriageway below. The last hint of dusk had vanished in the west, and the crowd was near its peak. Jacob pulled the door closed behind him and set out among them as if he belonged here.

Jacob's own costume was so inelegant as to be nondescript—save by one word: black. Black boots, black slacks; black shirt, black cummerbund, black jacket; black gloves to cover his hands, a black cowl to cover his head. Even his mask was black—eye holes with a weary slant, brow with a weary furrow—and dulled by a matte finish. Even his brown eyes would look dark, surrounded by so much black. Black to hide his identity.

He could see her again—*must* see her again. He could watch her tirelessly work the room. He could dance with her again—*would* dance with her again. But he could not risk—could not bear—being rejected by her again. This night would be the test. When he saw her—when he *touched* her, he would know, know whether to reveal himself to her or to leave the Valley, alone and forever.

Jacob went in from the balcony, moved with the surge of couples headed for the ballroom. Rather than wait for one of their grand, timed entrances, he slipped in inconspicuously, made his way to the nearest pillar, and scanned the crowd.

Plump ladies in gold dresses. Powdered-jowl ladies in blue. Ladies with curls piled atop their heads like beehives. Ladies with masks so bejeweled they looked as though they'd fallen face-first into a ringmaker's junk drawer. Jacob dismissed them one by one like paging through a book in search of that single, brilliant, truth-speaking passage.

Then he saw her, dark among the dancers, sultry as a sentient vapor. Jacob cringed behind the pillar, slunk around its other side and peeked out for a better view. The ruby at her chest shone like a blood-dipped sunset. Her face was covered by a black mask with a bird-beaked nose. But Jacob knew her—unmistakably so. He would know her in the dark: by her scent, by the sound of her footfalls, by the touch of her hand.

Would she know him in the same way? The thought startled him, excited him. If she did, that would be proof beyond doubt, absolute validation of his hopes, of dreams he'd dreamt but half-feared to dream.

He watched the crowd part ranks for her then draw close—but not *too* close, out of respect and awe and worship. That Jacob had once been closer still left him breathless.

He could wait there all night, watching her, but he had come for more.

He had come back for it all.

Twenty-Four

Laurel let Pyxis Pettifog lead her onto the dance floor. A waltz had started and other couples were already joining in. Laurel and Pyxis squared off, waited for the proper beat, and began. Laurel had learned these formal dances from her mother when she was a little girl, before she was old enough to realize she wanted nothing to do with them. They came in handy now, though she was just barely keeping up with the steps.

Pyxis, on the other hand, moved with absolute grace, his chin up, his spine straight—as if he had been taught to dance before he learned to walk. Other dancers gave him a wide berth as he twirled Laurel through the crowd, and the bystanders watched him as he passed by—especially the younger, presumably available ladies. Pyxis was, after all, very handsome. And rich. And eligible. And his dressmaking made him a bit of a local celebrity. Laurel wondered if the onlookers could see through her own clumsy steps to the poor farm girl beneath.

"It's nice to see a familiar face," she said.

"It's nice to see you in that dress again," Pyxis replied.

Laurel smelled strong drink on his breath and realized, despite his graceful movements, Pyxis Pettifog was a little drunk.

"It's the finest thing I own," she said—remembering she had said something similar before.

"It would be, wouldn't it?"

Laurel chose to take that as pride in his workmanship rather than condescension. All the same, she said: "Aside from our bit of the Copperwood, of course."

"Of course. Have you had any luck convincing someone else of that?"

Laurel chose her words carefully (to not appear desperate). "There are a few interested parties."

Pyxis winked at her. "I know of one."

Laurel had to remind herself to expect innuendos like this. Every time she talked about her farm, her hand in marriage would be the subtext. Such a silly game. She would rather speak plainly about such things. But this was why she had come; this was how she would sell the farm.

"You know, Miss Blight," Pyxis said, "I read a letter recently."

Laurel's jaw clenched. "Let me guess: one about weasels and henhouses."

"That's the one. I heard you wrote it."

That damned letter. But it didn't matter now if she admitted it; she'd already lost the job.

"So bold," Pyxis said. "And ironic."

"Oh? Ironic how?"

"That it's female."

Laurel couldn't keep her eyes from narrowing.

He said, "What I mean is, women can't own land—or sell it or vote or any of that. So it's ironic that a woman is writing about the subject."

"Well, someone needs to."

"Do you think it will sway the vote?"

"Everyone seems to be talking about it, so that's something."

Pyxis shrugged. "None of my business anyway."

"But Mister Pettifog," Laurel said, "your family owns land. And a lot of it."

"True. But families like mine and the Idlevices are insulated, in a way."

"Land is land, isn't it? What Pavo Linenpest is proposing sets a dangerous precedent for us all."

"Technically, perhaps. But Linenpest would never try to appropriate our lands. He wants the Valley to grow—to put it on the map, as they say—and knows he can't do that on his own. We Pettifogs aren't just wealthy. We bring wealth to the Valley—we *attract* it. Half the dresses here are my design—even Missus Linenpest wears them.

"And the Idlevices, well, they have a fame all their own. Even if they don't get along with the mayor, he wouldn't touch their lands. You've seen how his railroad bends around their estate."

Laurel didn't like the smug way Pyxis said it, but she knew it was true. Linenpest's railroad cut across poor lands, many of them belonging to Whitehead cousins and second cousins. But not even rich Whiteheads were spared, for they kept their wealth to themselves in the Uphills and wanted nothing to do with putting Long Autumn Valley on some *Blackhead* map. If Laurel was to have any hope for the mayor's railroad to be struck down, she needed people of influence to oppose it.

"Perhaps, Mister Pettifog," she said, "you'd be willing to help a poor farm girl?"

Pyxis smiled. "What did you have in mind?"

"Well, you're an important man in the Valley. Maybe you could sway others to my cause. Folk might listen if they heard it from you—rather than some anonymous letter."

He thought for a moment. "I suppose I could try. But it's a tough sell."

"You'd be helping a great many people."

"Of course. Though, I am a busy man already. What could possibly make it worth my while?"

Laurel sensed the innuendo, wondered if she could dodge it. "Altruism?"

"Ha. I do enough for the Valley already."

"Farmers aren't sharing in the wealth your family brings."

Pyxis didn't appear convinced.

"Why," she added, "it's only through your charity that I'm wearing this dress."

"It'd probably be easier to give every girl a dress than sway the vote," he said.

Laurel had to play his silly game. She batted her eyelashes. "Well, Mister Pettifog, surely there's something you want, some price that could convince you."

Pyxis raised an eyebrow. "Yes. Surely."

The dance tapered to an end, Laurel curtseyed, and Pyxis bowed.

"Think on it," she said.

She wasn't sure she should be saying it, wasn't sure she should be implying what she was implying, offering what she was offering. She wasn't sure, if it came down to it, she'd be willing to give it. But Pyxis appeared hooked and had a hard time letting the next male dancer cut in.

Twenty-Five

Jacob kept his distance from Vela like a shy animal, lured by primal desire, stayed by primal fear. He had danced with half a dozen women and scanned a hundred passing faces, keeping his eyes sharp, his neck loose, with a constant awareness of where Vela was at all times. Presently he danced with an older lady (he'd forgotten her name; he'd forgotten all their names)—a plump thing in a silken emerald dress. She plied him with questions, complimented his fine dancing, but he did not speak to her. He hadn't spoken to any of them, as much out of indifference toward them as Vela's presence was a distraction *from* them. He was biding his time, waiting for an opening.

He and the plump lady twirled close, twirled away. He could see Vela, he could not, then he could again. Each twirl matched the pulse of the waltz: close-and-a-way-and-then-seen-and-un-seen-and-a—. The silver comb atop Vela's head gleamed like a beacon that flickered in bursts, interrupted by a passing gentleman in a high fur collar, or a red-haired woman in an ivory mask, or a servant carrying a tray of sparkling wine, or another man in black. Gleam, now twirl; gleam, hidden; gleam, now stop.

The waltz came to an end, and Jacob could not bear another lesser dance. While all the partners on floor bowed their farewell bows and curtseyed their farewell curtsies, Jacob spun away from the plump lady without so much as a nod. He slithered through the crowd toward Vela, and when she came up from her own curtsey he was there before her, silently waiting for the music to begin again.

Her silver comb shone as a steady beam now, as did the ruby at her heart, but her dark eyes were greater jewels still. They beheld him and ensnared him as if by the power of some twin mystic amulets. This was the first time she'd looked upon him in thirteen years; he never wanted her to look away again. Those eyes, like two black suns, a pair of voids drawing him in. Her face was hidden by her raven's mask but those eyes…

The strings introduced the next dance. Jacob bowed deeply then offered his hand to Vela. She looked at it, looked at him. Hesitation, Jacob thought, or recognition? Could she see him through all the black he wore, see him the way he saw her? For a moment he thought she might refuse his dance, and he had to fight the impulse to speak, to blurt out 'Vela, it's me! It's Jacob!'

The moment passed, Vela curtseyed, and put her slender hand in his. It fit perfectly in his palm, and even through his glove and hers that touch was like no sensation Jacob had ever known. Numb did not describe it, for his hand had become less than numb. If Vela's stare were a window to some dark, perilous void, then her touch was passage into it—a dip into a Stygian pool. Jacob was powerless within its grasp, yet power seeped into him:

the power of dream, the power of possibility, the possibility that time itself might be transcended the way they'd transcended thirteen years to this very moment.

Jacob slid his right hand around Vela's trim waist and pulled her close. He smelled her perfume—sweet, a hint of cinnamon. Their eyes remained locked, and they stepped into rhythm together. Neither of them spoke. They merely moved, with a grace beyond grace, two black birds in an interweaving flight pattern. Vela didn't smile, didn't flinch, offered nothing but perfect, silent counterpoint to him, her silent counterpart. Jacob savored every silent step.

This reunion he had staged was meant to settle Jacob's uncertainty once and for all. Yet their shared silence only deepened the mystery. Did she recognize him? Did she *love* him? Jacob could read nothing in the void of her eyes or in the numbness of her touch except what rapture he brought with him. He so wished for her to give him some sign of her feelings; yet he dare not disturb this moment—which, for all he knew, could be their last together.

The waltz ended in a cruel cadence, and Vela's grip slackened in his. But he kept his hand on the small of her back a moment longer, holding her close, closer than any partygoer had thus far dared. The beak of her mask kept his face at a distance, else he would have brought that closer too. They tarried there a moment, locked in one another's gaze, then she tilted her head and brought her lips close to his ear. He felt her breath across his lobe—even through the cowl he wore. He listened intently to that breath, waiting for a whispered word come like a song from the sea.

But no word or whisper came. Without realizing, he'd let his hand drift away from her back, and in that instant she spun from the crook of his arm. She curtseyed to him, and he bowed clumsily in return. Then she disappeared into the crowd, as sultrily and vaporously as she'd appeared.

As the next waltz began, Jacob remained on the dancefloor, stricken dumb by the very dance he'd come to dance.

Twenty-Six

Laurel told herself she would dance with Willem Whitehead once, and he wasn't difficult to spot in the crowd. He wore tight black slacks tucked into high, sandy brown boots. His tight shirt opened in a V halfway down his sternum and revealed his broad, blonde-haired chest. Atop it, he wore a black coat that hung down to his knees. The coat's high collar was made of pale grey wolf's fur. He was the only guest at the ball who wasn't wearing a mask—a rule, in his case, no one would try to enforce.

Laurel's eyes met his across the room, and he approached. He moved like a juggernaut through the dancers, and they gave him the same wide berth they gave Pyxis Pettifog but for very different reasons. In the time it took him to reach her, another masked gentleman approached and requested a dance. Before she could accept or deny, Willem stepped up and stared him down. The gentleman shrunk away without an answer from Laurel.

Willem turned to her. He did not bow, and she did not curtsey.

"Mister Whitehead," she said. "A pleasure seeing you again."

The next song started, and he offered her his hand. Laurel had to muster a little courage to take it, but when they stepped into the rhythm together, she found Willem more gentle and light-footed than she would have guessed.

"You sold your fah-arm yet?" he asked in his Uphill accent.

Innuendo, Laurel reminded herself. When Willem had visited her farm, he'd declared he would make his offer the next time he saw her. Depending on how she answered now, the man might get down on one knee right there on the dance floor. But she supposed there wasn't much she could do about that.

"I have not," she said.

Willem kept dancing and replied: "I read your letter."

That caused Laurel to miss a step. *Who in Long Autumn Valley* hadn't *read it?*

"I never wrote you a letter," she said.

"I read it all the same."

"How do you know I wrote it?"

"The spoken word travels faster than the written one."

"And just as far, it seems."

Lady Idlevice. She was the only one who knew Laurel had written it—aside from Pavo Linenpest, but what reason would he have to spread the letter about, least of all to Willem Whitehead? The lady had stopped sending Laurel suitors but she was still matchmaking from afar.

"What did you think of it?" she asked.

"You don't belong here," Willem replied.

Her eyes locked on his, demanding an explanation.

"You're a poor fah-arm girl," he said.

"So?"

"But you're smarter than most girls. And most men."

Her tone softened. "So?"

"So you plan to use your wits to get in with these folk?"

Laurel looked about at the other dancers. "You're here. Aren't you one of these folk?"

Willem didn't take his eyes from her. "These folk are Blackhead twits."

"I'm a Blackhead too, remember."

"So you're a Blackhead twit trying to be a greater Blackhead twit."

"Mister Whitehead, really?" she complained.

"This way of life will drain your wits," he said. "You waste them playing at something that comes naturally to these people."

"And what is that?"

Willem didn't answer, but he didn't have to. He wasn't fooled by this sophisticated disguise Laurel wore. Yet neither did he pigeonhole her as dull-witted or incapable simply because she was a woman. In a brash sort of way, Willem was complimenting her, and Laurel had to admit to herself that she felt a little flattered.

"I'm not trying to *get in* with these people," she said. "I'm trying to get more than eighteen-fifty an acre. Someone here with money—a lot of money—could profit from it in the process."

She explained her plan to him, and she thought she saw that thin grin of his show for an instant.

"And you're here to sweeten the deal," he said.

Laurel sighed. "I'm here to *seal* the deal, any way I can."

Willem pirouetted her. He was *much* more graceful than he looked. "You don't sound very happy about it," he said.

"I'm not aiming for happiness," she said. "A little independence would be nice."

Willem humphed. "How will you manage that?"

Laurel looked out to the crowd of dancers. "I don't know. I used to want to change things—Linenpest's laws, the Valley. But what can I do? Write letters? I doubt they'll change much. But a woman can have a husband and share what he has. So why not have a husband who has a lot?"

She didn't believe what she was saying; at least, she didn't think she believed it. But the logic of it was sound. Practical, realistic. She *did* want to be *those* things.

"And that's independence?" Willem asked.

"In a way. Some of these men are so rich, I wouldn't need to change what I can't change anyway. I'd be above Linenpest's laws, free the Valley's judgments. Like Lady Idlevice."

Willem shook his head. "That old witch isn't free. She has to wheel that bag of bones around."

"Her servants, I'm sure, can help with that."

"But she's still stuck with him, stuck here."

"Not a bad place to be stuck, if you ask me."

"But if you're stuck, then you're not free."

Laurel supposed no woman was free in the Valley, not truly. But she'd like to be as free as she *could* be.

The dance slowed to an end and the two separated. Again, Willem didn't bow, and Laurel didn't curtsey.

But he said, "I'll give you twenty-seven fifty an acre."

Good to his word, Willem had made his offer. It was the first Laurel had received—aside from Linenpest's, so, the first she'd *attracted on her own*. She was thrilled; this was what she'd been working so hard towards. But she knew, at least in the case of Willem Whitehead, there would be a catch.

"Twenty-seven fifty," she said, "and my hand in marriage, you mean."

"My family owns a hundred times the land as the Idlevices. There are places you can look to the horizon in any direction and not see so much as chimney smoke. *That's* free."

He'd trapped her there. She'd come here for a buyer and used herself as bait. She'd argued marriage could be a practical endeavor, and here one was presented. Willem Whitehead was crass, brutish, but tonight he'd proven to be a little more, a little better. Could she really marry him—marry a Whitehead? Could she really marry anyone just to sell the farm?

"I'll consider it," she said.

"Running out of time," Willem replied.

"I have five days."

Willem's eyes assessed her, perhaps debating whether she was leading him on. Laurel couldn't honestly answer that herself. She'd come this far. Dare she go much further? All the same, she raised her chin and met Willem's stare evenly.

Willem nodded and said, "I'll expect an answer by Wednesday."

He was about to leave but Laurel stopped him. "Thursday," she said.

Without reply, Willem turned and strode out of the ballroom, his business concluded.

Twenty-Seven

Yrion watched folk dance about the Boarsiks' barn. His mother and Aunt Carina, locked at the elbows, pranced in circles, their skirts held up in their free hands. Uncle Cetus stomped his massive boots and shook the floorboards. Young children hopped about like fleas. A few older couples who stood off to the side clapped their hands, providing a rhythm for the fiddle player— one of Aunt Carina's Nudnik cousins.

Candles glowed inside gourd lanterns hanging from the rafters and filled the barn with orange light. Yrion's streamers weaved among them. Wreaths of sticks hung on the support beams. Bundles of dried cornstalks stood in the corners and against the walls. Hay bales served as seats and were stacked two-high as substitutes for tables.

Yrion stood off on his own. The children were too young, the parents and grandparents too old. Laurel was at her ball, and Caelum had no reason to come without her. And no one seemed to miss Corvus' presence the way Yrion did. The serving plates were a little fuller, the dance floor a little emptier. They all seemed, well, *happy*. The only thing Yrion was happy about was that he wore a mask. With it, he didn't have to fake a smile.

Yrion remembered the one year when he'd grown too tired to dance anymore and Father scooped him up and sat him atop his shoulders. Yrion bounced and bounced up there and everyone cheered him on. That was one of his earliest memories; in fact, he couldn't remember an earlier one.

Father, he thought, *you always carried me*.

He slipped out of the barn into the night. A sharp, cold wind blew, but his mask shielded him from it. He went around the side of the barn and followed the fence line of Banyon's pen. The horse stood at the far corner of it, away from the racket in the barn. Yrion and Uncle Cetus had gotten the blanket over him without incident. The black, sheep's wool cover concealed his dun coat; only his pale neck and head could be seen.

Yrion continued to the far end of the fence where the horse stood. He sat on the lowest rail.

"Lonely night, eh Banyon?" he said.

Yrion reached into his pocket and pulled out a yam he'd saved. He let Banyon take it from his hand. The horse gobbled it up then lowered his head through the rail to nuzzle at Yrion's arm.

Yrion giggled and nearly spilled over. "Sorry, boy, that's all."

Light shone in a thin line under the closed barn doors on the far side of the pen. Clapping and cheers and the thin squeal of the fiddle carried out into the night. Uncle Cetus' boots stomped, thud after thud. The wind whistled its own tune through the drying corn crop. No moon shone in the sky, as if the Valley itself was celebrating Everdark.

Yrion wondered how Laurel was faring at the ball. She didn't seem excited about going. But a lot of rich folk would be there, and she wanted one of them to buy the farm. If they didn't, Mayor Linenpest would. Either way, the Blights would be moving on— to where, no one seemed to know.

Everything's changing, Yrion thought.

He didn't know what to do about it. He didn't want to do anything about it. But he knew he was supposed to do something. To grow up, to be the man of the house, whatever that meant.

To be like my father.

Yrion didn't know how.

Uncle Cetus was stomping away, and Banyon snorted uneasily.

Yrion said, "If his boot comes down on someone's foot it'll squish like a mulberry."

Banyon stomped his hoof a few times.

"Don't worry, boy."

Banyon wheeled his head and trotted away. Uncle Cetus' boots thudded on; somehow, his stomping seemed to grow louder.

"He can't go on much longer," Yrion said. "He'll wear himself out."

But his assurances didn't settle the horse. Banyon fussed and neighed.

"Banyon," Yrion called, "settle down now. Settle down, boy."

But Banyon would not. The horse charged to the other side of the pen.

Then a familiar scent wafted across Yrion's nose, and he rose from the rail. A fog had gathered along the fence line and was rolling quickly down the trail. He knew what it was, all too well, and hurried down to meet it, as if standing in its path would somehow block its passage or drive it away.

He held his hands out. "Get, get!"

When the fog reached the corner fencepost it seemed to halt and rose in a tall wall before Yrion. He took two hurried steps back, and the Nightsteed emerged, its front hoofs reared-up. It dropped to all fours, and the ground quaked.

Banyon shrieked.

Yrion's mother, his aunt and uncle, they were fifty yards away. Surely they heard Banyon's fussing, felt the ground shake. If they came out, they would see the Nightsteed for themselves and believe what they otherwise wouldn't, what Yrion wouldn't dare tell them.

But they didn't come out.

Yrion reclaimed his two steps toward the Nightsteed.

"Go on," he hissed. "Get on out of here!"

The Nightsteed snorted, cast the gleam of its onyx eye at Yrion, but didn't budge.

In vain, Yrion tried to calm Banyon again, but the dun was spooked to the point of madness. It bucked about the pen, searching for a way out. In a last, desperate move, it charged straight at the fence where Yrion had been sitting.

"Banyon, no!" Yrion hollered.

The middle rail hung as high as Banyon's chest. When he crashed into it, he split the rail like kindling. Yrion cringed. Without breaking stride, Banyon charged blindly on, up through Uncle Cetus' drying rows of corn. He could break a leg running through fields in the dark.

Yrion turned to the Nightsteed. "See what you've done!"

The Nightsteed stomped its great hoof and snorted again, unfazed. It cared nothing for some smaller, skittish horse of this world. It had come for a rider—it had come for Yrion, and Yrion it must have.

And Yrion. This was all his fault. The Nightsteed wouldn't be here if not for him; if he'd entered the Hall of the Nightfather like he was supposed to, none of this would have happened. The black beast would keep coming till…

Yrion took hold of its shaggy coat, climbed up. The Nightsteed bolted straightaway. Within seconds, they were at the top of Uncle Cetus' cornfield where the mound the Blights and Boarsiks had built to keep the curse at bay ran along the property line. The Nightsteed leapt over the mound and into Yrion's cursed field. Black pumpkins splattered under the beast's hoofs, intensifying the stink of the curse.

Up ahead, Yrion saw Banyon galloping at full speed. But the Nightsteed gained on him.

"Banyon, move!" Yrion hollered. That only drove his black mount faster, and neither beast altered their course. The Nightsteed drew closer and closer—close enough to bite Banyon's tail!—but it did not waver, not for brush or tree or hillside, certainly not for a lesser horse. It would trample Banyon like another pumpkin on its way to the Hall of the Nightfather.

They were right on top of Banyon.

Neither horse broke stride.

They were past Banyon.

Neither horse broke stride.

No bump, no shriek, no snap of bone.

Yrion looked back, and there was Banyon still, charging madly on—now as if it were chasing the Nightsteed. The distance between the two grew, and Banyon seemed to fade like a ghost. But, looking down, Yrion saw that it was he and the beast that bore him who were fading from this world.

The flashing tunnel, the black-leafed canopy, the corridor between two mirrors. Yrion had grown familiar with them all. He closed his eyes and let them pass. He knew this ride and knew his destination. The darkhouse in the distance. *The Hall of the Nightfather.*

The stink of the curse grew, sweet and sick and sharp. It burned his nose and throat like wood smoke, crept over his tongue and into the spaces between his teeth. He salivated like his charging horse, and he spat. He put his head down and waited.

When Yrion opened his eyes, the Nightsteed was gone, the thundering of its hooves was gone, and he stood once again at the Nightfather's door. All was as he'd left it—black leaves, black vines, black limbs, stilled by the Nightfather's curse. He felt the fog at his back, thick over placid water.

He wiped the slaver from his face and stepped up to the door. He closed his eyes again and waited for what he knew would come like a windless storm.

The voice of his father.

"*Yrion.*"

It crawled up his shoulder like a spider and whispered in his ear.

"*Yrion.*"

Yrion shuddered with as much longing as fear.

"Father," he whispered.

"*Yrion.*"

Corvus' voice was all around him now, pleading but directionless. It came from above, from below, from the fog behind, through the doors ahead. Yrion raised his fist.

You've come this far, he told himself. *This is where you belong.*

He knocked once. The old, dead wood was spongy beneath his knuckles, and the knock barely made a sound, just a low, mossy thump. Dust sprinkled down upon his head. Yrion thought he heard a sigh, as the right-hand door opened a crack.

"*Yrion,*" his father's voice came once more, almost pleadingly.

Yrion opened the crack just wide enough to slip inside.

Twenty-Eight

Laurel danced with Pyxis Pettifog again, and this time his drunkenness diminished his gracefulness. He led them recklessly across the dance floor, bumped them into other couples. His once-straight spine now sagged as his many drinks weighed upon him. Laurel felt like she was the only thing holding him up. His eyes were half-open behind his mask, and the words dribbled from his lips as if his mouth had no more room for them.

"I am ready to naaaaaaame my price," he said.

"Mister Pettifog," Laurel replied, "should you be bargaining in your state?"

"My lady, I assure you, I am crystalline."

"I'd hate for you to fall down and shatter."

Pyxis threw his head back. "Ha! My, you *are* clever, aren't you?"

Laurel focused on keeping the man on his feet.

"But honestly, *honestly*," he said, "I've decided on my price. I have. Honestly."

"Very well. So long as it's honest."

"Though, you see, it's not really something I can say. Rather, well…"

Pyxis tried to compose himself into some semblance of seriousness and sobriety and did his best to look into Laurel's eyes. Laurel looked back and saw his pupils crossing and uncrossing. When he leaned in, she turned her head to the side and moved her face past his. His lips landed sloppily on her ear. She cringed.

"Mister Pettifog," she said into his ear. "Am I to understand your price is a kiss?"

He pulled his head away. "Yes. Well, no. In a way. That is, I'd consider a kiss a down payment."

"Oh-ho. And how many kisses will pay the debt in full?"

"Many. Many, many. But kisses are like pennies to dollars, if you follow."

Laurel understood *this* innuendo all too clearly and it was a price she would *not* pay.

"Mister Pettifog," she said, "I don't know that your proposition is wholly appropriate."

He tried to smile his charming smile but it came out crooked. "No need to be coy, Miss Blight."

"Oh, I do have a need. This is a formal occasion."

"Let's sneak away then. I know of a few places—I'm very familiar with this house."

Laurel shook her head. "I won't invite such a scandal."

"No scandal. No one will see. That's what the masks are for."

"Even so."

"Come now."

Pyxis moved his hand from Laurel's waist to the small of her back and pulled her close. Laurel tried to pivot away, but he stepped with her, bringing his lips close once more, blowing the stink of wine into her face. His first kiss landed on her mask, his second on her forehead. Before he could land a third, Laurel took her right hand off his shoulder and swiveled.

Pyxis couldn't stop his drunken momentum—it didn't seem as if he even tried. He toppled, lips still puckered, and of fell flat onto his face. He lay still a few moments, looking dead on the floor, while the surrounding dancers stopped in their steps. Then, groggily, he stirred, like a bear from its winter's nap, and looked about as if he'd forgotten where he was and how he'd gotten there.

Laurel, meanwhile, was almost equally stunned and unsure of what to do. Pyxis might be hurt or angry or both. And, frankly, she didn't want to help him up.

Then, in a dark flash, another gentleman stepped between them, took hold of Laurel's hand, and spun her back into the song's rhythm. He led her into the crowd of dancers, and within five steps they were out of Pyxis' line of sight. Laurel caught a glimpse of Pyxis rising and staggering along the line of pillars, hurrying as fast as his wobbly knees could carry him. His movements told her he would be sick at any moment.

Laurel turned to the gentleman stranger. He was dressed all in black: black jacket, black slacks, black gloves; black mask—saggy-face and tired eyes, but wholly black; he wore a tight black cowl that covered his entire head and neck. He had pale blue eyes, and when he blinked Laurel saw that their lids had been painted black as well.

"Good timing," she said. "Thank you."

The stranger in black didn't respond—which was fine with Laurel. It gave her time to recover from the incident. That Lady Idlevice had even introduced her to a man such as Pyxis! Not that Vela could control him; not that Pyxis could control himself with all he had drunk. In any case, Laurel wouldn't sell to him, not even if he offered a fair price with no marital strings attached.

Well, she thought, *maybe you would, no strings attached.*

But she hadn't come this far to give up now. She still had a farm to sell, and the ball wasn't over yet. Besides, there were other gentlemen present. Willem Whitehead had proved charming, if a little forthright (which wasn't a bad thing), just as Lady Idlevice had said. And here was the gentleman in black, her rescuer in a way, whom Laurel had met all on her own.

"I'm Laurel Blight," she said.

But again the stranger said nothing. He seemed preoccupied—perhaps keeping an eye out for the drunken Pyxis to return.

"You're a quiet one," Laurel said, "the first I've danced with tonight. They claim females are the talkative sex, but some of the chattiest people I've met have been men—especially when they're talking about themselves."

The stranger spun them about in broad, deliberate, three step loops—*one* two three, *one* two three, *one* two three. He felt a little stiff in Laurel's arms. Perhaps, she considered, he was too busy concentrating on the steps to talk.

The music hummed, and though relatively few instruments were present, the guests were entranced by its melody and rhythm. Above, the dancers' reflections swirled kaleidoscopically across the skylight. Laurel realized, to her surprise, she might actually be enjoying herself, enjoying the silence the stranger provided.

Still, the task at hand…

"I don't suppose you're looking to buy land?" she asked. "We have a fine parcel of Copperwood—thirty acres or so—just up the road. Borders this very estate."

One two three, *one* two three.

"Some farmland too," she continued, "though I must be honest: it's not worth a thing. The curse…a few months back. But the Copperwood is strong."

They finished out the song. The gentleman hadn't uttered a word, but after they exchanged bow for curtsey, he offered Laurel his hand again.

"I shouldn't," Laurel said—though she wanted to. "Perhaps later."

He bowed again in acknowledgement and slipped away.

Twenty-Nine

Yrion stood inside the Hall of the Nightfather. Windows lined the walls, wooden support pillars equally spaced between, with a wide aisle up the middle. The pillars were as warped and grey as the doors. In a way, it reminded him of town hall, only there were no benches, and the windows were filthy.

Here the curse reeked strongest of all. Though the air was still and stale and musty like a barn full of rat droppings, the sickly sweetness permeated it, permeated everything, as if things here weren't cursed things but the curse itself taking on different forms. And if that smell bothered Yrion less than other people in Long Autumn Valley, his tolerance ended here. He put his sleeve to his nose and scanned about.

Along the walls and against the pillars and on the floor, people stood and squatted and sat motionless. Cobwebs stretched from the ceilings onto them, as if they were dummies in a tailor shop that had been closed for ages. Dust coated their clothing. None moved, yet none were sleeping. Like Yrion's mask—which he still wore—their eyes sagged and faces drooped with restless exhaustion, but they were all awake, as if forbidden by enchantment to sleep.

And at the far end of the hall sat the Nightfather.

He sprawled atop a backless chair shaped like a U, knees thrown over one arm, his head and neck over the other. He stared listlessly at the ceiling, and his long, brittle white hair grazed the floor. His arms were lanky and splayed out, his skin paler than parchment, his clothes dustier than any in his hall. He looked like a pint of curdled milk poured into a broken cup. The only sound to be heard was his knuckles rapping upon the floorboards, like piano ivories striking broken strings, too bored to manage any sort of rhythm. His wrist was so skinny it was a wonder he could lift his fingers at all.

Yrion was too afraid to move, to disturb the stillness of the hall. The place seemed familiar to him—the dust, the smell. He could hear his father's voice pleading:

"*Yrion.*"

The Nightfather's knuckles stopped rapping, and his face twitched as if a moth had landed upon his nose. Yrion remained still. If he didn't move, perhaps the Nightfather would mistake him for another restless guest waiting for Everdark. Maybe that was what the other dummies were doing: keeping still to avoid the Nightfather's foul temper.

"*Yrion.*"

It sounded as though it were coming from within these walls, flitting about like that pesky moth, trying to find its way through a windowpane.

"*Yrion.*"

Yrion looked about and realized something: the people here, they were not the restless spirits of children like the stories told; aside from himself, they were all grown men. Just as with the Nightsteed, the tales had been slightly off. So what else had they gotten wrong? The thought made Yrion think back to his rides, to the flashing visions in the dark tunnel, the visions of his dust-covered father.

Tears began to well in his eyes.

"*Yrion.*"

Those visions—*that dust*. It was *this* dust, the dust all about him. And his father's voice that seemed to flit all about him here, inside this hall, really *was* coming from inside this hall.

One of these dusty dummies was Corvus Blight, trapped by the Nightfather's enchantment.

"*Yrion.*"

The Nightfather sighed in his chair.

It can't be, Yrion insisted. It made no sense. Corvus Blight was the hardest working man in Long Autumn Valley. *It's impossible*. But no matter how Yrion tried to reject it, he knew it to be true—sensed it, the way he sensed the Nightsteed's urge to ride, the way he sensed the coming snow. The tales were wrong; Corvus was here.

Why, Yrion couldn't fathom—and more unfathomably: why was *Yrion* here? He was nothing like his father. If this was where his father belonged, then Yrion surely belonged someplace else.

Why did the Nightsteed keep dropping him here? It just didn't make sense.

"*Yrion*," his father said.

The Nightfather had finally heard enough. Without turning his head, he shouted to the ceiling: "If you're coming in, do so and close the door!"

Yrion squeaked and jumped back out the door.

Thirty

Laurel danced twice more with the stranger in black, and he was her last partner of the night. Not once had he spoken—not to brag about his wealth or nobility, not to make inappropriate advances. Laurel found this a welcome relief from the game she was playing and, oddly, a comfort for feelings of defeat.

When their last dance ended, the room erupted in applause, cued by a new sort of tune begun by the strings. The cellos drove an ominous, marching rhythm, not something one could dance to. The violins swelled and subsided like haunted winter winds while leather drums accompanied them with deadened thumps.

The guests turned to face the empty stage at the far end of the room, and the floor became crowded as they competed for a view. The music swelled, and anticipation swelled with it. One cluster of women surged forward and bumped Laurel aside. A gloved hand took her by the arm and pulled her close; the stranger in black.

The music mounted to its crescendo, a tense, atonal trill that cut short without resolution, and the double doors behind the stage opened. Two figures materialized from the darkness of the hallway beyond: Lady Idlevice in her raven-beaked mask pushing Lord Percy Idlevice in his wheeled chair. The chair had been decorated with shredded cotton cobwebs like that on the bannister of the spiral stair. He wore silk robes as black as his lady's gown. A massive ruby hung at his chest, attached by a thick gold rope.

Unlike his guests, Lord Idlevice wore no mask. Yet his countenance was weariest of all. The bags beneath his eyes sagged heavier than ever, and his gaze wandered vapidly across the skylight overhead.

Percy Idlevice upon this throne, presiding over the Everdark festivities, hundreds of weary-faced guests in his hall. Percy Idlevice, Nightfather. As lord of the house, it was his role to play. In his physical state, what other role *could* he play? It was a cruel sort of irony, though Laurel couldn't decide if it would be crueler to hide the old man away and carry on his family's tradition without him.

"Ladies and gentlemen," Vela said, "your host."

The crowd cheered and, slowly, Lord Idlevice's right hand lifted. Vela stepped aside and presented her husband with a gesture of her hands, and the crowd cheered all the more.

"I thank you, one and all," she continued, "for attending what has been, without a doubt, the best Ball of the Nightfather yet. I wish you all a safe journey home. There are rooms for those of you who must find your rest before then—some of our guests, I believe, have found it already."

The crowd chuckled at that, and the strings resumed their ominous march.

"Until next year."

Then she turned and exited through the double doors, leaving Percy on the stage.

Laurel knew what came next: the ceremonial Dousing of the Lights—*Everdark*—which brought the festivities to a close. She looked to the high chandeliers and wondered how the lady would manage to darken them with so many guests crowding the stage. Then she saw, above the candles in those crystal nests, silver caps like bells without clappers, one above each candle, attached by a silver chain. The chains met a single cord the center, and the cord ran through a pulley and down to the pillar where it was tied off to a brass cleat. Even now, servants were manning each pillar and undoing cord from cleat as the music began to swell once more. The guests clapped and cheered and whistled.

Laurel couldn't help how she felt. She'd danced with a dozen gentlemen tonight, most rich enough to profit from Laurel's plan, but hadn't received any more offers. A few seemed interested, but more so in her than her plan—which she knew she should expect but had trouble accepting.

Her sigh became lost in the cheers, and she shrugged.

Might as well give it one more try, she thought and leaned sideways to the gentleman in black.

"I had a lovely time," she said.

The stranger didn't respond.

"I'm wondering if we'll ever meet again," she added.

He kept his gaze forward. The din grew.

Laurel had to raise her voice just to hear herself. "I'd like to meet the man behind the mask."

All the servants were in place, and the cheering peaked.

Laurel had to yell. "Can I at least know your name?"

All at once, the servants loosened the cords, and the empty silver bells dropped onto the candles. The room went dark, the music stopped, and the crowd fell silent. The symbolic peace of Everdark settled like a sable sheet over the room.

Laurel felt the stranger lean close, his breath in her ear.

She knew the voice.

"Caelum Cronewetter," it said.

Thirty-One

Jacob stepped onto the stage. With the lights doused, no one could see him. Blindly, he walked to and through the double doors where Vela had gone, following the cinnamon scent of her perfume.

The warning in his mind had returned and demanded an explanation. He'd come for a dance, hadn't he?—for one touch. And he'd gotten it. A victory, not a loss. A farewell memory he ought to walk away with.

But he could not walk away. He could not leave this party without confronting her. The disguise, the secrecy, they had brought him here, but that hadn't been enough. Did she know him? Would she have him? Could they start again?

Before long, he saw orange light in a line on the floor, beaming out from a closed door on the right. He put his ear close to it, heard someone beyond. Her perfume was still strong in the air. He knocked softly.

"Yes?" Vela's voice said.

He pushed the door inward. It was a small room. Vela sat on a cushioned stool before a mirror. Her mask lay among a scattered mess of jewelry atop the table before her. Jacob's eyes wandered up the subtle, sensual s-curve of her spine. Her slender hands were undoing the comb from her hair. She turned to him, beheld him, and paused for a moment. She removed the comb and lowered it into her lap. Her raven locks fell upon her bare shoulders.

Jacob stood there, scarcely breathing, lost once again in the dark voids of her eyes.

"Come in, Jacob," she said, "and close the door."

Thirty-Two

Yrion fell to his back and felt a squish. A few stars fought their way through the mist. The sickly-sweet stink of the curse threatened to gag him. All was quiet save for a lingering echo, the tail end of his own name spoken in his father's unmistakable voice.

"*Yrion.*"

He rose to his elbows and found he was lying in his own farm field. The mushy lump beneath him was a black, cursed pumpkin. In the starlight he could make out a trampled trail across the crops. Banyon's, the Nightsteed's, or both, Yrion couldn't tell.

What was happening to him? What *was* all this? Why did the Nightsteed bring him to the Hall of the Nightfather? *Why* was his own father there?

Yrion was tired. Tired of these rides. Tired of coming and going. Tired of being tired.

He buried his face in his dirty hands and wept.

Thirty-Three

Laurel and Caelum stormed down the carriageway from the Idlevice estate, masks in-hand. Laurel's pace matched her anger, but Caelum was moving just as fast. What right did he have to be angry? she wondered.

"Do you mind telling me what you're doing here?" she asked.

"I was invited," he said.

"Why?"

"What? I can't be a suitor too?"

"Oh, *that's* what you're calling it?"

"I bowed, didn't I? I danced."

"And didn't say a word."

"You talked enough for us both—and had a *lovely* time."

Laurel cringed at him quoting her. "I don't have time for games, Caelum."

"I thought that was why you're here: to play some game."

"Not with you."

"Well I didn't come as me," he said.

"Caelum—"

"You didn't even recognize me."

He was right; she hadn't. Not after three dances, not even his pale blue eyes. But she didn't owe him an apology for that; he was the one being dishonest.

"What's your point?" she asked.

He stopped her in the gravel. "That you don't know what the hell you're doing."

"I'm doing just fine, no thanks to you."

"Hey, I'm the one who got you away from Pyxis Pettifog— the drunk fool."

"I was handling it," she said.

"*Handling* it? Why are you even putting yourself in this situation? Why—"

"Look, I'm not going to have this argument again."

Caelum crossed his arms. "So what happens next? I pretend to be interested in your farm?"

Laurel started walking. "You're the suitor, you figure it out."

"Or am I so charmed I propose on the spot?" he called after her.

"Willem Whitehead did," she called back.

"You're serious?"

Laurel heard him start to follow. "Twenty-seven-fifty an acre," she said.

"Just like that?"

"Just like that. I guess *that's* what suitors do."

Caelum caught up and touched her wrist. She stopped, turned.

"Twenty-two," he said.

"Twenty-two what?"

"Twenty-two an acre. *No* marriage."

Laurel pulled her hand away. "Stop."

"I have some money set aside, and I'm partner now so I'm good for the rest."

"Stop."

"It's a good investment," he said. "I'll have it logged out and sell what's left to Linenpest."

Laurel put her fists on her hips. "Who's going to log it out?"

Caelum shrugged.

"Linenpest already has his own outfit picked for after the vote," she said, "so they won't do it for you. That leaves you the Whiteheads or their cousins. But Willem's your competition now, so they won't either."

Caelum ran his fingers through his hair. "I'll find someone outside the Valley."

"And eat up your profits on travel expenses."

Caelum threw his hands up. "Then I'll buy an axe, Laurel!"

"Uh-huh. And *I'm* the one who doesn't know what she's doing?"

"So that's it?" he said. "You just...*marry Willem Whitehead*?"

Laurel looked away. "I didn't accept his offer."

"But you didn't refuse it. You've only got a week left."

"Five days."

Caelum paced in tight, sloppy circle. Laurel wasn't sure if she wanted him to stay or go. She had a lot to think about without him distracting her.

"Twenty-two an acre," he said. "No marriage. That's all I have. But it's the best offer you're going to get, whether you want to admit it or not."

Now it was his turn to walk away.

"I'm not going to bankrupt you," Laurel replied. "What kind of person would I be?"

He didn't look back. "I don't know anymore."

Laurel let him go.

Thirty-Four

Jacob pushed the door closed behind him. Vela remained in her chair in front of the mirror, as if waiting for him to say something. He said nothing; he had so many things to say that they choked one another out. He stared dumbly at her, in awe of her beauty, in disbelief that this moment had come to pass.

"Take off your mask," Vela said.

His mouth was dry. "How did you know it was me?"

"Did you think you could hide in plain sight?"

"Yes—*no*. I mean, from everyone but you."

"I think you succeeded."

"Why didn't you say something?"

She didn't answer, but it didn't matter now. She'd recognized him—*really recognized him*. Slowly, he pulled back his cowl and raised the mask so it sat atop his head. Vela looked at him for a long, silent moment, her face expressionless, unreadable. It felt to Jacob as though she were staring into him, through him. He wondered if she wanted what she saw.

The moment passed and she smiled. "You look thin, Jacob."

Jacob looked down at his gloved hands and black garb. "Business keeps me busy."

"And out of the kitchen, it seems."

"Out of the Hall of the Nightfather."

"But will it keep you out of an early grave?"

Jacob submitted with a nod, and they stared at one another some more. He could look at her forever.

Eventually, she pointed to his right. "Why don't you sit down?"

It was a small room, and where she pointed a brass-railed bed stretched wall to wall. He went to it, and she swiveled on her stool to face him, palms in her lap. She kept smiling, but that smile hid everything about her. Jacob needed to break through it, needed to know what she felt.

"The side door," he said. "You still leave it unlocked."

"Besides the staff, I think you're the only one who knows."

Jacob scanned that statement for meaning and couldn't any for certain. Did she leave it unlocked for nostalgia's sake? For him?

"Though," she added, "I would have formally invited you, if I'd known you were back."

Jacob shrugged. "I wanted to surprise you."

"Consider me surprised."

She didn't look surprised. She looked unmoved. Every sterile formality they exchanged left what needed said unsaid. Jacob had to get her to open up. He had to *push*.

"You could have mailed an invitation," he said. "Thirteen of them."

"Mailed them where? A rumor one county over?"

"Pavo Linenpest didn't have trouble finding me."

"I wasn't aware you wished to be found."

"You rode off. With *him*. Told me to *go*."

"Probably saved your life."

Jacob let out a long, quiet breath. He needed to push, but he didn't want to argue. Not now, of all times. "I was trying to prevent a scandal."

"Well, scandal came anyway. You disappeared, and people's imaginations ran wild, unchecked."

"You could have checked them."

"Could I? For all I knew, Percy had hunted you down."

Jacob leaned forward. "So you were worried about me?"

Vela paused. It titillated him. "Of *course* I was worried."

Jacob let that absorb. He needed to hear it. He had *come here* to hear it and so much more.

A knock came at the door and someone's head poked in. It was the olive-skinned foreigner who wheeled Lord Idlevice around. He noticed Jacob out of the corner of his eye, then stuck his head in further. The fellow glowered at Jacob.

"Yes?" Vela said to him.

"I've shown Mister Pettifog to a room," the servant said.

"Have one made up for Mister Le'fever here."

The servant's eyes darted between her and Jacob.

"And put Lord Idlevice to bed," she added.

"Yes, my lady."

The servant shot Jacob one last glare before pulling the door closed.

"I don't think that one likes me," Jacob said.

"Suhar?" Vela replied. "He's very devoted. I couldn't get by here without him."

Jacob tried to be tactful. "You have no...children to help?"

"We tried for a time, but nothing came of it." She said it casually, as if she never really wanted them—or had at least made her peace with not having them. That she had no children pleased Jacob the same way Percy Idlevice's failing health did: it might be sad, unfair, a curse even, but Jacob wouldn't dare wish it any other way. Destiny, it seemed, had laid a path that would reunite them.

"I'm sorry to hear it," he said. "The end of the Idlevice line. What do the doctors say?"

Vela waved 'doctors' away. "They're calling it a *nonspecific degenerative disease*—which sounds a lot like old age to me."

Jacob rested his forearms on his knees. "He looks well cared-for, anyway." He felt such tension on the edge of his mind, on the tip of his tongue. All his thoughts and feelings were ready to boil over, demanding to speak, demanding to be heard.

"Have *you* any children?" she asked.

"I don't."

"A wife, surely."

Jacob shook his head. "Business keeps me busy."

"I see. And has business brought you back?"

Formalities couldn't hold Jacob back any longer. "It's strange how our lives have paralleled one another's."

It took her a moment to respond. "Have they?"

"We're like two rails of the same track, bound for the same places, passing through circumstance after circumstance."

"I'm not sure I follow, Jacob."

"So much has changed, but not us." Jacob came off the bed and knelt before her, taking her folded hands in his. "Thirteen years I stayed away, and all the things that could have happened—a wife, children, death—*didn't* happen. To either of us. Thirteen years has carried us back to this night, unchallenged and unchanged. I'm realizing, now, that time doesn't change some people; it hardens them."

Vela thought about it. "Time hasn't changed me," she said, sampling the notion.

"You never stopped loving me," he declared.

"You never stopped loving me."

He pushed himself up, brought his face to hers. She didn't lean in, she didn't back away. She didn't resist when he kissed her. She'd been waiting for Jacob, and this proved it. She loved him; she hadn't changed. He lingered there and she lingered there and time itself seemed to linger as if granting them a ceremonious reprieve from its relentless passage as reward for their hearts' perseverance.

When Jacob pulled away, he said, "Come with me."

"Where are we going?"

"Anywhere—the Copperwood. We'll sneak away to our secret place."

"Oh, Jacob," she said. "Always the romantic."

He stood, keeping her hands in his, but she did not rise.

"No need to sneak away," she said and pulled him down to her.

They kissed again.

Thirty-Five

Laurel received a single letter Monday. Her name was written across the front, but that was all. Knowing it wasn't scribe work, she took it to the dying fire where her mother sat knitting in her rocker. The letter read:

Dear Miss Blight,

It seems I owe you an apology—perhaps several, but as I am unable to recall most of my deplorable actions at the ball, please don't take my lack of specificity as insincerity. I offended many that night, but I fear none more than you, upon whom, most of all, I wished to make a lasting impression. Alas, it seems I accomplished that in the worst manner.

If there is any way I can make reparations, write me, call on me, stop me in town. I don't expect I'll hear from you, and I don't deserve any of your time, past or present. These words have taken too much already. I won't write again.

Ashamedly,

Pyxis

Laurel read it twice more. It seemed heartfelt, but it was too late for that. She put the letter back in the envelope and set it in the fire. The hungry flames licked it up.

"What was it?" her mother asked.

"Nothing."

Pyxis Pettifog was one of the finest, richest, upstanding gentlemen in Long Autumn Valley. But an uncorked bottle let his true character pour out: aristocratic condescendence, entitled arrogance, unchecked lust. Laurel accepted his apology, though she'd rather he had made an appropriate offer. *I'd consider that reparations.*

Willem Whitehead offered more and drank less. He'd impressed Laurel, proved to be insightful if direct. And that rugged charm of his was growing on her. But could she *marry* him? The idea in and of itself sounded preposterous. But, factoring her family, her financial interests, and her father's only damned wish, it wasn't *impossible*.

Caelum's proposal was just as preposterous. She didn't know *what* she was going to do about him.

"You have yet to tell me how the ball went," her mother said.

Laurel watched the last of the envelope burn. "Didn't think you were interested."

"Of course I am. We need to sell before Friday."

"I'm aware."

Laurel hadn't been thinking about anything else since and had been going in one big uncertain circle. The facts were plain, the offers made, the pros and cons weighed. Yet all this quantitative information (what she was really good at) wasn't helping her decide. It didn't fall neatly into place. There were these, well, *conflicts*, intangible forces pushing and pulling her this way and that. She doubted her mother could help; she needed *Caelum*. But Caelum was a factor in this problem, not a solution.

"Willem Whitehead offered twenty-seven fifty an acre," she said.

Her mother waited, as if expecting Laurel to say more, then replied. "That's a fine offer."

"Twenty-seven fifty and my hand in marriage."

Laurel looked to her mother; Lyra didn't look surprised. "And how much would he pay without your hand?"

Laurel looked back into the fire. "He wouldn't."

She didn't mention Caelum's offer. She knew what her mother would say. (*Such a fine young man*). He was a damned fool, willing to bankrupt himself to save them from this mess. (*We should all be so lucky to have such a fool*). *Salvation*, Laurel thought bitterly, *the grandest form of charity*. He was making this much more difficult than it needed to be.

"Well," her mother said, "Linenpest's money is as good as anyone's."

"Eighteen-fifty an acre? That's half what this land's worth."

Her mother paused, perhaps to let out a silent sigh. "We'll get by."

On what? Yrion had gone back to Cronewetters' today, but they couldn't pay him enough. And Laurel hadn't even told her she'd lost the scribe work. "Have you heard back from Oldfather's Inn?"

Laurel knew she hadn't and wouldn't. Mister Oldfather no doubt had opted for a younger launderer to hike up and down four flights of stairs a hundred times a day.

"We'll get by," Lyra repeated, a little more confidently.

"*Will we?*"

Her mother set her knitting on her lap. "Well, what choice do we have?"

Laurel shrugged.

Her mother's eyes slowly widened with realization. "You're thinking of *marrying* our way out of this? What about your principles? What about your pride?"

"Pride and principle are luxuries we can't afford."

"Nonsense. Your pride won't accept the Boarsik's help."

"So I want to make my own way then, Mother. To have what I have having paid for it."

"For that you'll sell yourself for an extra nine dollars an acre?"

Laurel crossed her arms. "It's what Father wanted."

"And after all that arguing, you're giving in *now*?"

Her mother was sounding a lot like Caelum. This was *Laurel's* choice, her sacrifice to make.

"Willem Whitehead can give us land, Mother. As much as we want. We could start over."

Her mother rose from her chair, and her knitting fell from her lap. "I can't believe I'm hearing this. You're talking about marriage and *not* to Caelum Cronewetter?"

"Caelum hasn't proposed to me, Mother."

"He hasn't proposed to you because you've made such a fuss about it!"

"It doesn't matter because he can't afford to save this farm. It's a curse either way: ruin him by selling to him or ruin myself by marrying Willem Whitehead."

"You're ruining more than yourself."

"What is *that* supposed to mean?"

"You're breaking *Caelum's* heart! *Why? Why* are you willing to *do* such a thing?"

Because I want some control. The curse, her father's death, this damned railroad. All of them were out of her control. She was just supposed to flow with them. Well, she was tired of flowing; she wanted to steer, and if it meant steering against the current, so be it. But she didn't expect her mother to understand; Lyra never had ambitions of her own.

"So be it," her mother said. "If you want Whitehead lands, go get them, and take the twenty-seven fifty an acre with you. Every penny. But I'm not coming. Yrion and I are going to stay with the Boarsiks."

Laurel threw her hands up. "I go out of my way to help this family and this is the thanks I get?"

"You want to make your own way, so make it. But don't begrudge us our refusal of *your charity*."

Her mother went to the door, began slipping on her shoes. She had Laurel trapped. Laurel was trying the help, but if they didn't want it what could she do? And without them, what did she have? Her choice? How important was that to her? Important enough to go through with this, alone?

"Willem is coming before Thursday," she said. "I'll introduce you."

Her mother pulled the front door closed behind her.

Thirty-Six

Yrion had heard his mother and sister arguing in the cottage from all the way out in the family cemetery. He sat on the far side of his father's gravestone, his back to it. He was supposed to be down at Cronewetters' Clockworks, but he couldn't face Caelum.

He didn't have the strength. He didn't even have the strength to find himself a decent hiding place.

He wrapped his arms around his knees.

Father, help me. Tell me what to do.

So much had gone wrong. They were going to lose the farm; Laurel was going to marry some horrible Whitehead; even poor Banyon was still missing. And each one of those problems could be tied to Yrion. If he'd learned more about politics, if he'd stayed away from Banyon's pen, if he could keep a job, if he'd been *a man*, maybe he could have helped instead of hurt.

But how could he become a man if children's stories came to life and held him back?

Father, please, talk to me.

"*Yrion?*"

Yrion flinched, then peeked around the side of the gravestone to see his mother standing at the edge of the cemetery.

"What are you doing in there?" she asked. "You're supposed to be working."

He wiped the tears from his eyes.

"Come out," she said, "and tell me what's wrong."

Yrion stayed put.

"I broke Caelum's figurine," he said—which wasn't the right place to start but he just kept blubbering—"and I failed the needle test. And the Cronewetter children there laughed at me—they're half my age! And Caelum is mad at me. And I'm just too clumsy to be a watchmaker, Ma. My hands don't work right."

Lyra came around to the side of the gravestone. "Calm down. You don't have to be a watchmaker."

"But I have to do something, Ma. Laurel's going to marry one of them Whiteheads. I don't understand—I thought she would marry Caelum."

"It's her choice, Yrion. It's got nothing to do with you."

"But what am *I* going to do?"

"We'll figure something out. Now, get up from there; it's no place to be sitting."

Yrion didn't budge. He was so tired—tired of hiding, tired of everything.

"Remember when I asked if you ever feel Father's presence?" he asked.

"I remember."

"Well, I do, even if no one else does. And not just feeling him. I'm *hearing* him."

His mother was silent. He looked at her but couldn't read her expression.

"*Really* hearing him," he said. "He's calling my name, Ma."

"You hear him now? At his grave?"

Yrion didn't, but he wished he did. He wished his father would speak to him—to both of them now—and explain what was going on, what his son was going through. But Yrion would have to do the speaking; he couldn't go on like this.

"Not here," he said. "In the Hall of the Nightfather."

His mother didn't blink, didn't flinch.

"I've seen him, Ma. And I've seen the Nightfather too. The Nightsteed takes me to them. That's why I've been so tired. It scared Banyon off, and I'm scared too. I don't want to be a lazy boy, but I've heard *Father's voice*. He's calling to me, Ma, and I don't know why."

He felt so ashamed saying it—he knew it sounded mad. But his mother would understand; if anyone could, she would. She always did. What he was going through wouldn't put food in their mouths or fetch a higher price for their farm, but it had to mean something. Father was calling to him and him alone; that had to make him useful. Didn't it?

His mother still didn't move. She stood as still as the dummies in the Nightfather's hall.

"Mother?" he said. "What am I going to do?"

Lyra crossed her arms the way Laurel did. "Yrion. This needs to stop."

"Ma?"

"*Now.* You're too old for these stories. I work hard to keep this house in order. And your sister works hard too—look what she's putting herself through for us."

"But, Ma—"

"No more daydreaming. Your sister says I coddle you, and your father said the same. But that ends now. You need to find work—if not with the Cronewetters, then somewhere else. I'm sorry you can't farm with your father, but he's gone and his land is cursed and the time for grieving is over."

"*Ma—*"

"I said *enough*. Your father didn't work himself to death for you to dream up this nonsense."

Yrion began to sob. She'd never been so stern with him, and she looked truly disappointed. He rose to his feet and brushed himself off, but he stayed there and gave her one last, tear-filled look.

She pointed to Witching Hour Road. "*Go.*"

Yrion obeyed as fast as his legs could carry him. He headed south on the road, not knowing where he would go, what he would do. He was on his own now; if Mother didn't believe him, no one would.

Father, where are you?

A mile down the road, he came upon three men standing about. He recognized Mayor Linenpest's fat belly and bright attire. Yrion wiped the tears from his eyes and did his best to compose himself. He wanted to step off the road, or turn back, but already the mayor had spotted him and was waving him on.

The two other men were standing at a tripod with some sort of tubular lens mounted atop it. It was pointed up the road. They peered through it one at a time, turned a little dial, and peered through it some more. They murmured numbers to one another and didn't pay Yrion any mind.

"Young Master Blight," the mayor said, "what brings you down this way?"

Yrion put his hands in his pocket.

"We're taking some final measurements," the mayor said. "For the railroad."

Yrion looked at the tripod, up the road, then back to the mayor.

"Have you given any thought to letting the local trust buy your farm?" the mayor asked.

Yrion shrugged.

The mayor rubbed his pink hands over his fat belly. "We're offering a premium rate through Friday."

"I think Willem Whitehead's going to buy it," Yrion said.

The mayor's eyes narrowed a bit. "Willem Whitehead," he said, as if the name tasted bad.

"Yes sir."

The mayor looked away. "Well, if you change your mind, come see me. I'll take good care of you."

The mayor rejoined the other men at the tripod, apparently all interest in Yrion lost. But Yrion didn't mind; he was glad to get away.

Thirty-Seven

Jacob stayed as a guest in the Idlevice house for two nights and days. The staff waited upon him. He walked the halls as he pleased, unmolested, save by the occasional glare from Lord Idlevice's driver. He had his meals with Vela. Together they strolled through the many gardens and fields of the estate. He told her of all the wild places he had travelled, of the foreign lords and dignitaries he had befriended, of the fortune he had earned.

They spent the nights together, inseparable. Each moment for Jacob was the realization of a dream—an impossible dream made possible—one from which he did not wish to wake but which rewarded him each morning by finding Vela in the bed next to him. Thirteen years' longing, sated. How had he ever doubted?

On the third evening in the house, he wandered into the southwest study. In the curve of the tower sat Percy Idlevice, facing outward. Jacob stepped behind him and looked out from the lord's vantage. The sun fell warm through the panes. Fields and pastures and gardens spread out like a patchwork quilt. A fine view—one Percy could no longer enjoy. Though present in the house, he was no longer a presence. Jacob marveled that this was how their rivalry had ended: without so much as a whimper. Percy Idlevice was little more than a life attached to a name scribbled on a deed, one that allowed Vela to remain under this roof. Now that Jacob was here, she would no longer need that name.

Jacob rested his hands atop the handles of Percy's chair, pushed it gingerly forward and backward a few times. The handles were wrapped in fine leather, soft and earthen brown. The right one, however, felt lopsided in his hand—an odd, uncomfortable defect for such a modern contraption. He ran his fingers along the underside, felt a grooved protrusion. He squeezed it.

Without warning, Lord Idlevice's right hand lifted from the armrest.

Jacob released the handle, and the lord's hand fell. Jacob squeezed, the hand rose; Jacob released, the hand fell. Jacob smiled.

That's one way to cast a vote.

"Jacob?" Vela said behind him.

He turned and beheld her in the doorway—an even greater view than Percy's. She wore a violet gown; she dressed herself in the very finest, always. A true lady. She moved toward the tea table in the far corner of the room and gestured for Jacob to join her. Jacob tarried, savoring her seductive strides, always. When she reached her chair at the table, he went to the door, closed it, then joined her.

They looked at one another in silence for some time, which they often did. Being in her presence still awed him, still felt surreal. Every painful worry about missed opportunities had died—regret had died—killed by the reality of the present. Now, all the things Jacob wished he could share with her were no longer a matter of hoping and dreaming but a matter of planning and doing.

"I've been thinking," Jacob said. "I have some business to address in the east. Why don't you come with me?"

He watched her watch him.

"It's quite a sight," he added. "The coast. And if you like what you see, we'll keep going."

He could see temptation flare in her eyes but also reluctance. "Keep going where?"

"Anywhere. Anywhere in the world. I can take you places where they have masquerades every night. You'd be a queen."

That was how he saw her; that was what she deserved. She folded her hands atop her lap, as if to cover temptation and reluctance. His Vela: too much a lady to show her true self. But she need not hide from him.

He smiled, warmly. "Our lives aren't over yet."

She returned the smile. "Our lives aren't over."

Jacob basked in that smile. Here they were, conversing as if thirteen years hadn't passed. That he had ever doubted coming to the estate baffled him.

From seemingly nowhere Vela said, "Why don't you stay?"

Jacob gave her a puzzled look but shrugged. "All right. But I can't put it off forever."

"I mean here."

Then Jacob understood her. He hadn't considered actually *living* in Long Autumn Valley, well, ever, really. Percy had always been a threat. And there was a curse on this valley, besides. Though, Percy was no longer a threat, and the curse didn't seem to worry others. They endured it, anyway.

"There are still good plots around…" he supposed aloud.

"Jacob. Stay *here*."

Jacob *hadn't* understood her after all. "On the *estate*?"

This was Percy's home. Jacob needed nothing from *him*. Jacob had worked hard for his own fortune, could buy this estate five, ten times over. He could buy it and let it go to ruin like Rotbottom farm—put the curse of Jacob Le'fever on it. Sell it to Pavo Linenpest and let him run his railroad all over the grounds, turn the place into a carnival.

"But I could build us a home," he said.

"*This* is my home."

Jacob pointed to Lord Idlevice over in his chair. "He could cast me out at any time."

She let those ridiculous words hang in the air.

Jacob moved his glasses to the top of his head. This was not the future he had envisioned. Could he really stay here, in the home of his former rival? Had he spent thirteen years earning a fortune he no longer needed? Well, he *was* staying here already. *A fortune plus a fortune isn't a bad thing*. Why not set aside his pride, for her?

He looked at her—tried to look *into* her, the way she seemed able to look into him. He leaned close. His hand trembled. He set it atop hers to steady it. "Will you marry me?"

Jacob saw it again, temptation paired with reluctance, battling behind her eyes. But a plan came to him, there on the spot, crystalline and perfect, as if handed to him by destiny itself.

"Jacob—" she started.

"Sell me the estate."

Jacob watched temptation and reluctance get washed away by shock.

"Your staff and Percy will stay on," he said. "When he finally finds rest, you and I can be married."

Vela looked anywhere but at him, for now he had her cornered. It was an undeniably good plan, one that benefited them both. If ever she had set their love aside for some other advantage—wealth, social standing, her own security—now she could not. Jacob could provide it all.

He put his other hand atop hers.

Finally she looked at him, deeper and more focused than ever before, as if searching for some basest of truths to unify all things. Yes, look, Jacob thought, you will find it here, in me. *I am that truth*. This was where destiny had led them; this was where their paths would merge.

"I married once," she said.

"Not to me—"

"I see no need to go through it again."

Her words didn't seem meant for him. Surely they were the start of a conversation with someone else, some new topic unrelated to Jacob. Her servant must have walked in. Or she was calling to her husband by the window. Or she was talking to herself, shaking out all the last vestiges of resistance. She was speaking gibberish—crude sounds, an uninterpretable language.

Alas, no. Her eyes were fixed upon him—*within him*— those cruel words were for his ears. How could she reject him? How could she not love him? It was *impossible*.

"Vela," he begged, "don't do this. Come back to me."

"Jacob," she said. "I am here."

His eyes pleaded silently with hers. Hers looked down her nose at him—that thin, perfect nose. If she felt hope or doubt or desire, he could not see them. She hid them from him, hid it all.

"Not all of you," he said.

She said nothing but drew her hand away.

Jacob sprang up from his chair and nearly fell over. His limbs tingled, no longer felt like his own, as if he'd fallen asleep on all of them at once. Despair swarmed like flies in his head, fighting to feast on pieces of him dying inside, and he didn't know if it was clouding his judgment or clearing the way for it.

"You didn't build this home," he said. "You stole it. You take and take and give nothing back. What is your husband but a coin purse, and his servants your slaves? And here you ask me to become both, a man without a wife or home of his own—a man to warm your bed and fatten your purse.

"No, I am more than that. I am the man destiny made for you. Thirteen years it has been preparing a path for us, and now is the test: I will give you everything; you must give me this."

The ultimatum. The one he couldn't bring himself to give her thirteen years ago. Here their paths had met. Would they merge, or would this be a crossroads?

Vela remained in her chair, arms now atop the rests, all emotion hidden.

"Time does not change some people," she said, her tone flat, cold. "It hardens them. You once told me that. But what is true for you is true for me: I wouldn't marry you thirteen years ago, and I won't marry you now. I will not marry again."

Jacob reeled, and Lord Idlevice came into his line of sight. Jacob hated the man. What oafish cruelties had Percy subjected her to that had tainted marriage for her? Had he spent thirteen years breaking her—breaking the unbreakable? Had he exhausted himself in the effort, brought himself to his pitiful, crippled state?

Crippled. But still the man stood in Jacob's way.

Jacob stomped over to him, took his chair by the handles, and wheeled him about. Vela had risen to her feet—and what was that? Did Jacob catch a glimpse of concern cross her face?

"*This* is what you want?" Jacob said. "Some rotting vegetable?

"Jacob—" Vela started.

"He does make a good puppet, though, doesn't he? Let's ask him." Jacob leaned down and spoke into Lord Idlevice's ear in a tone fit for a puppy. "Who's a good puppet?" When Jacob squeezed the right handle violently, Percy's hand jerked up.

"And who thinks Jacob's proposal is a good one?" Jacob asked.

Percy raised his hand.

"All in favor of Vela coming to her senses raise your hand."

Percy raised his hand, and Jacob did too.

"Jacob," Vela said, "stop this."

But Jacob couldn't stop. "Who thinks Jacob is the better man? Whose buffoonery drove Vela from his bed in the first place? Who is going to *die* and leave Vela with *nothing.*"

Percy raised his hand three times like the flapping of a broken wing. Jacob rolled him back and forth in place, thrusting him like a weapon at Vela. His head bobbled limply about atop his shoulders while Jacob plied him with question after rhetorical question.

One thrust of the chair went too far: Jacob pushed him forward like a battering ram, and when the chair stopped short, Percy, wrapped tight in his cocoon of a blanket, tumbled forward like a caterpillar falling from a branch. His body made a sort of *flump* sound but his head connected with the tea table with a thud. Blood immediately began to spit from his scalp and quickly pooled on the rug.

Vela slid off her seat and knelt at her husband's side, took his head in her hands. Jacob stood there dumbfounded. He hadn't meant to spill Percy out of his chair like that—hadn't meant to hurt the man. But, then, no—what did Jacob care? Percy was his rival; if it weren't for Percy's *nonspecific degenerative disease,* these past two days might not have happened. He might have already shot Jacob dead on the streets of Brodhaven.

"He has no sons," Jacob said, "no heirs."

The crimson pool grew.

"This isn't your home now. You have no man to keep you on."

The pool touched Vela's knees, disappeared into her violet dress.

"Leave this place, Vela. Leave with me. I can take care of us."

Vela laid her husband's lifeless head down.

"I *need* you," Jacob pleaded. "Finally, you need me."

Vela, at last, raised her head and laid her eyes upon him. And no matter how he searched them, he could find nothing there, neither love nor hate, neither hope nor despair. Nothing. Just two empty black pools—so empty, so black, they sucked all hope from him, the way her dress sucked the blood from her dead husband.

She spoke a single word to him—one word was all she would give: "*Go.*"

Thirty-Eight

Yrion didn't go to Cronewetters' or anywhere else for a job. He made his way south and east through the Copperwood till he found the mucky gully, the dank crack, the hidden basin. And there he found the Nightsteed, waiting for him.

He spurred it onward at a speed he had yet to experience. His boots in its ribs seemed to release something from the beast that yearned to be free, something that could only be beaten free. Its slaver stung his face like pebbles. Yrion himself felt mad, his hair tangled and matted. Tears streamed back across his temples.

This would be his last ride, come what may. He couldn't look for a job, couldn't become a man, couldn't show his face again in the Valley without answers, without guidance. His own mother had driven him away. But fine, she didn't have to believe him about the Nightsteed or the Nightfather. So long as he confronted it.

Father, speak to me.

Yrion arrived as he had before: the Nightsteed had suddenly vanished between his knees and he found himself standing on the Nightfather's doorstep, wrapped in utter darkness and the smell of the curse. The fog over the water behind him pressed close, urged him onward. But he needed no urging. He pulled upon both handles and spread the doors wide. Their hinges creaked and dropped flakes of rust down the jambs, and dust and splinters sprinkled upon his head.

Yrion strode in with as much confidence as he could muster.

The Nightfather sat on his throne. His knees were spread wide and he rested his elbows upon them. The bags beneath his eyes looked like a separate set of sagging cheeks. Deep, permanent creases cut into his brow. His brittle, white beard nearly touched the floor. But he managed to keep his head up and his pale eyes upon his new guest.

Yrion stared back, drew in a heavy, dusty breath, and sneezed.

"Well," the Nightfather said, "out with it, noisemaker." His voice was a dry hiss, like tearing paper, and the stink of his breath wafted across the room. It smelled like the pure, sickly sweet source of the curse.

Yrion shivered, but he had to remain strong. "What," he started, but his throat felt as dry as the Nightfather's sounded. He swallowed. "What do you want with me?"

The Nightfather gestured to the left. "Find a place to stand and quiet down."

"I don't want to stand around in your hall. I'm a...a busy man."

"*No visitors*," the Nightfather said. "Close the doors on your way out."

Yrion didn't budge. "Your horse. It's disturbing me."

The Nightfather let out a humph. "I stole that horse, so it's not mine. Besides, I turned it loose ages ago."

"Well it keeps bringing me here."

The Nightfather dismissed that with a lazy sweep of his wrist. "You're the one who keeps climbing up on it."

"I have to. It insists."

"Oh the damned thing just likes to run."

Yrion didn't understand. He'd *felt* the Nightsteed's need, he'd shared it, the need to run, the need to ride. Why then did it leave him here? He hadn't asked to come here—had he? He looked around to the solemn guests.

"What is this place?" he asked. "Who are these people?"

"I don't know who these people are," the Nightfather said, "and I don't care."

"Then why imprison them here?"

"*Imprison* them?"

"Till Everdark."

The Nightfather reached up and massaged between his eyes with his thumb and forefinger. "They can stay so long as they *keep quiet*. But none of this coming and going business. Look"— and he pointed to Yrion's feet—"you're tracking in leaves."

Yrion looked down and saw blackness stuck to his boots: black maple, black oak, black sumac.

"Sorry," Yrion said. "They'll sweep up easy enough."

The Nightfather shot him an icy glare. "They wouldn't need sweeping if you didn't track them in."

Yrion looked to the cobwebs hanging from the rafters. They draped over the guests, forming wispy bridges from one shoulder to the next. More black leaves gathered in the corners, behind columns, and between the guests' feet. This hall hadn't been swept once. Yrion sneezed at the sight of it, and a few of the Nightfather's guests stirred.

"You're disturbing my hall, boy," the Nightfather said.

Whatever the Nightsteed wanted, whatever this place was, Yrion *had* come for a reason.

He puffed out his chest. "I'm here for my father," he said.

The Nightfather leaned his elbow against his throne's right armrest. "He might be here somewhere"—and he raised his voice—"too many layabouts to keep track of."

"Corvus Blight is no layabout. He's...he's the hardest working man in Long Autumn Valley."

"Oh ho? And what's that got to do with anything?"

Yrion glanced about. "He doesn't belong here. This is a hall of restless spirits."

"Hard workers are some the most restless spirits I know—why do you think they work so hard?"

Yrion shook his head. He didn't want that to make sense. Corvus Blight couldn't have wound up in a place like this. It was backwards, it was unfair. But Yrion had seen the visions on his Nightsteed rides, and he'd heard his father's voice. But no matter how backwards and unfair, Yrion couldn't deny it. Maybe Corvus *was* a restless spirit.

"I heard him," Yrion said. "Calling my name."

"Most vexing, I'm sure."

Then a third voice whispered: "*Yrion.*"

Yrion looked around. "Father!"

The Nightfather looked around too. "Pipe down, you hear?"

Yrion finally moved, going into the crowd of guests. The hall was more densely packed than it appeared, and he could hardly slip between them. All the weary faces looked the same: dust caked on thicker than aristocratic powder, cobwebs hanging over them like veils. He could hear his father whispering his name, but his voice was lost in the tangle of bodies. It didn't help that the Nightfather mocked him as well, parroting, "Yrion, *Yrion.*" Some of the guests seemed to look back at him, as if they briefly mistook Yrion for one of their own loved ones. Most stared blankly ahead, not asleep but not awake, simply waiting, waiting for Everdark.

Yrion found Corvus in the front corner of the hall. In life, his father had never seemed to tire; now, his brow was as furrowed as the Nightfather's, his face saggy, his crow's feet pronounced. But they were his father's eyes, blue, like Laurel's, and having a constant, subtle squint, as if every muscle in Corvus' face were working to keep those eyes open. The same eyes Yrion remembered. He realized, now, that he'd never seen his father any other way than exhausted. Corvus never slowed down, but it wasn't effortless, and long before the man was dead, he was dead tired.

Yrion wrapped his arms around him all the same. "*Father*."

Corvus didn't hug him back; his bony shoulders sagged beneath the pale undergarments he'd been buried in, the last garments Yrion had seen him wearing. He felt as though he might crumple in Yrion's embrace.

"*Yrion*," Corvus whispered, a puff of dust blowing from his lips.

"*Yrion, Yrion*," the Nightfather hissed.

Yrion's tears soaked into his father's shirt. "Father, why are you here?"

"There, there," his father said. "It's not so bad. No tilling, no chopping."

"But, Father, it's so dusty and sad and folk are just…standing around."

"Aye, but it's nice to stand around sometimes."

Yrion didn't understand. "Father, how did you get here?"

Corvus didn't respond; by the look on his face, Yrion wasn't sure his father heard him. He seemed to be drifting into a trance.

"Father?"

"But what are you doing here?" Corvus asked.

"You were calling to me, Father."

"*Yrion*. Aye, I remember now. You should not be here."

Yrion hugged him again. "But you're here. Can't I stay?"

"No, little daydreamer."

"But things have gone so *wrong* since you left. We have to sell the farm, and Laurel's going to marry Willem Whitehead—"

Corvus lifted his head, puffed out his chest. "*Willem Whitehead*?!"

"Will you shut that racket up!" the Nightfather bellowed.

Corvus lingered a moment longer in his attentive state but soon deflated. His shoulders slouched and his head looked too heavy for his neck. "Sell it. Get what you can."

"But, Father, you're…" Yrion didn't know how to say it.

"No sense hanging onto it for my sake. Just one more rotting thing on cursed land."

"I'm just so lost, Da."

"You'll find yourself," Corvus said. "I know you will."

"How? You never taught me."

"Didn't I?"

Corvus drifted away again—whether to reminisce or else in the grip of whatever spell lingered over the guests in this place, Yrion couldn't tell.

"Father?" Yrion said.

Corvus shook his head out of the trance. "I didn't need to. You're a natural."

Yrion didn't understand. "A natural what? I don't know how to *do* anything."

"Come now. Who builds the fires? Who predicts the snowfalls?"

Yrion stuffed his hands into his pockets. "I do."

"And who rides the Nightsteed?"

Yrion kicked at the floorboards. "That's no good to anybody."

"*Yea*, that's a rare gift, son."

"But what do I *do* with it?"

"Use it to find its use."

Yrion whimpered.

"*Trust* it," his father said. "It's not just for daydreaming anymore."

They both flinched as the Nightfather pounded his fist on his throne's armrest. "Do *not* make me come off this chair!"

"You should go," Corvus whispered.

"Come with me," Yrion said.

"Oh, no. No more travelling for me."

"But, Da, you shouldn't be here either."

Corvus smiled. "I have a tough time slowing down." He patted Yrion's head, shaking dust loose from his sleeve.

Yrion sneezed again. Then a heavy thud came from the far end of the hall. Turning, Yrion saw the Nightfather standing on wobbly knees, his overturned throne at his heels. The thud of the throne disturbed some of the other spirits who murmured as if half-awakening from a dream, and the Nightfather's sudden standing sent up a swirl of dust. The swirl was so great that other guests began to sneeze as well. The stillness of the Nightfather's hall erupted in a ruckus of sneezes and coughs and grumblings.

"Now you've done it!" the Nightfather bellowed.

Yrion hugged his father one last time.

"Go," Corvus said.

Yrion moved to the doorway, turned, and squared off with the Nightfather.

"Sit down, Old Lazybones!" Yrion shouted.

The Nightfather's eyes widened and he pointed a long, trembling finger at him. "Mind your tongue, Yrion Blight," he said. "I'll put a curse on your land."

Yrion pointed back with a steady finger of his own. "You already did that."

The Nightfather's brow furrowed. "Oh. Did I?"—and, like Yrion's father, he paused in either the grip of reminiscence or his own sleepy spell. Then he shrugged and extended all his fingers. They released some invisible force, a hard wind that flung his unwanted guest through the doorway.

Yrion landed on his back, the breath rushed from his lungs, and the doors slammed shut.

Thirty-Nine

Jacob stumbled through the Copperwood. His breath came out like locomotive steam. He moved from tree to tree, torn between the need for caution and the need for urgency. The moon was a useless wedge in the sky. The trees all looked the same, and when the wind shifted them, light and shadow danced and disoriented him.

Thirteen years and nothing about this forest looked familiar.

He'd gotten a head start on the servants and needed to keep moving, but he had no direction. Panic had scoured his senses—lifting one foot in front of another was a random sequence—and exhaustion had him ready to fall to his knees and give up. Maybe, he thought, he could still turn back, apologize. It had been an accident after all. Or perhaps he could turn himself in to Mayor Linenpest; Jacob was certain he could buy *that* man off. But images of muskets and torches and dogs—and Suhar, Lord Idlevice's driver, the biggest and meanest dog of them all who'd been hungry for Jacob's flesh since the beginning—drove Jacob onward.

Go, she'd said.

How had it come to this? Where had he gone wrong? The proposal?—no, by the time he'd made it, she'd had him trapped. The nights since the ball?—no, he'd already been trapped then, too. Not the kiss, not the dance, not even the decision to come to the ball. He traced it back to a single moment, one still etched in the wavy glass of his mind: when he first saw her through the Cronewetters' window. From that moment on, he'd been lost, set upon a path he could not turn from. Now, it wasn't exhaustion that had him ready to fall to his knees and give up; it was despair. He ought to turn and face his pursuers. Perhaps Suhar had pulled the Idlevice flintlock down from the wall, taken it up in his lord's stead; perhaps Jacob should let that foreign dog finish what Percy hadn't.

Go, she'd said, toneless, heartless.

He should have sold the farm and left the Valley forever— sold it to Linenpest right there on the platform and gotten back on the very same train. Every step after had been folly, a warped dream—a fevered bout of delirium—that he'd tried to force into a reality.She'd never loved him. She was incapable of love. And she didn't deserve it. Jacob had already known these things. Hadn't he? Known it for thirteen years. Every whispered warning from deep inside him had insisted upon it. Yet he'd willfully disregarded them, suppressed the sense that had always led him to success.

Some dreams shouldn't be dreamt, it reminded him. Some dreamers shouldn't dream.

Jacob stopped, planted his hand against the nearest tree. There wasn't enough air in the Valley to fill his lungs. He turned his ear to the forest behind him. Fallen leaves rustled in the breeze. The canopy swayed. Jacob's thudding heart drowned out the rest. Perhaps he could slow down now. Unless…

He held his breath, and he heard them.

Hounds barking at the moon. Far off, but not far enough.

He stumbled on, faster now. He crested a gentle hump of a hill, burst through a crowded line of evergreens, and beheld the first useful glint of light he had glimpsed since sundown. Below him stretched a wide basin. On the far side, more evergreens lined another gentle hump. The basin's floor was covered with a shallow pool of water. Above it, moonlight fell through the gap between the trees. To the left, a massive birch stood in the center of the pool. At its base, a horse drank the still waters.

It was the biggest horse Jacob had ever seen, close to seven feet at the withers. Its coat appeared dark, but the light was still too dim to tell its true color. But what did the color matter? Jacob needed a horse—one at this very moment—and here one stood, as if destined.

Fortune, it seemed, had not abandoned him, not entirely.

Jacob scurried down the slope. His boots hardly caused a ripple in the pool. The horse looked up from its drinking and snorted. Its ears twitched. Jacob took two steps toward it, and it backed two steps away. Jacob saw that it had no saddle, which would make riding it all the more difficult. He wasn't a good rider—he knew that—but this was no time to be particular.

He took another step, and the horse reared up.

"Easy now," Jacob whispered.

The steed settled, turned its head.

"That's it."

The horse let Jacob draw a few steps closer, but it turned away from him. The moon glinted wildly off its eye. Jacob could sense its impatience; it wanted to bolt, but so did he.

"Easy. Take me with you."

He got as close as its hindquarters, and there he debated how to actually mount the thing. Gently, he laid his hand atop it; skittishness ran through it like lightning. But they needed to hurry—the dogs would soon be upon them.

"Easy, now."

A howl shattered the calm. Jacob flinched, and the horse flinched too. In a panic, it raised its hind leg and kicked.

Its hoof connected with Jacob's temple.

Forty

Yrion sat up. Grey sky lightened between the branches overhead. Dawn had come to the Copperwood. The sickly sweet smell of the curse was strong, stronger than he'd ever remembered in these woods. Flecks of dust clung to his jacket, dust from the Hall of the Nightfather.

Father.

He hung his head, wanting to cry, but noticed a darkness below him, around him. He rolled aside, stood. There, on the forest floor where he'd been lying, was a slick layer of leaves in the outline of his body, leaves like leaves off any tree, only black. Black maple, black oak, black ash. Black and oily and infused with the reek of the curse.

He reached into his jacket pocket and removed the single black maple leaf he'd brought back from a previous journey to the Nightfather's Hall. Now there were many more, too many to take with him even if he wanted to.

Then, from over the hill to his right, he heard voices. Folk out hunting, probably, but something tickled in Yrion's head. A thought. A sense. An *intuition*.

He stuffed the leaf back into his pocket and dropped to his knees. Hurriedly, he raked up other leaves—red ones, orange ones, yellow and brown ones—and pushed them atop the black ones. Faster, faster, for the voices were drawing nearer.

He stood up just as the hunters appeared at the crest of the hill. Half a dozen with as many hounds plus two horses marched along the ridgeline. It looked like they'd caught their game; one horse had a limp kill slung over its back. Yrion glanced down at his pile, kicked one last foot's worth of orange over black, then waved to the party. The last hunter in line waved back, and they kept moving.

Yrion waited for them to pass out of sight then looked again to his pile. The thought still tickled. The intuition. Like a choking fire. Like the smell of a coming snow. Only sickly sweet.

Yrion knew what he had to do.

Forty-One

Laurel found her mother in her rocker before the hearth. Dawn had come, and the fire had long since died out. Lyra wasn't sleeping, just staring into the empty hearth.

"Mother, it's freezing in here," she said.

Laurel tried blowing on the coals but revived none of their orange life. She restacked some wood upon it, tried starting it fresh. It didn't want to light.

"Yrion," she hollered. "Yrion, come get this fire lit."

"He's not here," her mother said.

Not here? Yrion never rose this early. "The Cronewetters aren't open yet."

"He didn't come home last night."

"Didn't come—"

Laurel looked at her mother, found Lyra's face ashen. Lyra rocked a few times, kept her eyes on the fireless hearth. Seeing her worry so made Laurel worry a little too. It wasn't like Yrion to wake up early but it was even less like him to stay out late—the kid was scared of the dark.

Still, Laurel shook her head. "I guarantee he's off playing some game with himself."

Lyra dropped her eyes to her lap. "I told him he had to find work."

"It's a job, Mother, not a death sentence. But he already has one with Caelum."

"He said it wasn't working out."

"Wasn't working—he's only been there *one day*." Laurel almost went on a rant about his laziness but it was too early to get into it again. The fire began to sputter and smoke, which was good enough for her. "So long as he comes back with work."

Lyra rose from her chair and headed back to the bedrooms. This was the longest conversation Laurel had had with her since they'd argued about Willem Whitehead's proposal.

Willem would expect an answer any day now. Laurel hadn't ruled out the possibility—the *opportunity*—but neither had she made her peace with it. She could, in a way, become a princess— of a wild, brutish family, but a princess nonetheless. A princess with thousands of acres. Resources. Capital. Maybe even influence, the kind all rich families had. Wasn't that what she always wanted?—the chance to make a difference, especially for women. So she'd have to marry for it. She had never wanted that, but at least she had a choice in the matter. Unlike Father's death. Unlike the curse.

But what about the Blight *family*? Yrion and Mother were going to live with the Boarsiks. Would they come visit Laurel in the Uphills? Would Laurel come down to visit them? Would the curse, Corvus' death, and this railroad vote tear them apart? Had it torn them apart already?

Like it had torn her and Caelum apart. She hadn't heard from him since the ball, and the way they had left things, she didn't know if she'd ever hear from him again. Whom would she consult now? To whom would she confess? *He* certainly wasn't going to visit her in the Uphills. Could she really never see him again? The thought put a lump in her throat.

She swallowed it.

These questions caused her nothing but grief, so she turned her mind to something tangible, quantitative. She fetched the pen Lady Idlevice had gifted her and dug out a scratch piece of paper (wishing she hadn't burned so much of it the day she lost her job). She used them to calculate how long a family of three might last on twenty-seven fifty an acre, twenty-two an acre, eighteen-fifty an acre. How much coal could that buy? Firewood? Food? How many seasons rent could it pay? These were questions Laurel could come close to answering. And they might keep thoughts of Caelum from cropping up.

At eleven o'clock, Yrion burst through the front door. For the first time in Laurel's life she thought he looked determined, looked like their father. He came straight to the table and dropped a thin envelope atop her figures.

"Eighty-three acres at eighteen-fifty an acre," he said, "is one thousand five hundred and thirty-five dollars. And fifty cents."

Laurel looked back and forth between her brother and the envelope. Their mother came to the table and flipped back the envelope's fold to reveal a single sheet of paper. Laurel recognized the red watermark crest across its top. It was a banknote.

She looked to him. "Where did you get this?"

"The mayor said we could stay on till spring," he said. "He won't break ground till then."

Laurel was slow to understand her brother's words, as if her mind were rejecting them, protecting her—protecting *him*—from their implications. "Yrion, what have you done?"

"I'm going down to tell Uncle Cetus we're coming to stay."

He couldn't have. Not Yrion. Not the boy who shirked all responsibility. Not the boy who needed his fingers to count to ten. Not Yrion, the daydreamer.

"Yrion, what have you done?" she repeated.

Her brother looked at the floor for a moment. She thought he was going to start shifting from one foot to the other. But he didn't. He looked back to her.

"I sold the farm," he said.

The room began to spin. She gripped the edges of the table to brace herself. The envelope became a fuzzy white rectangle, and her brother became some blurry, nightmarish ghoul. She felt ready to vomit.

All her hard work. All that she'd put herself through—for this family, for *him*.

He said, "I know you wanted to get what it's worth—"

Laurel stood up fast, and her chair tipped over. "I can't believe this. I can't *believe* it!"

"But soon it won't be worth anything."

Laurel grabbed her fine pen and whipped it across the room. It hit the hearth and shattered into its composite pieces. A starburst of ink stained the stone, and more dripped from the mantle.

Their mother didn't flinch. "Yrion," she said, "what do you mean it won't be worth anything?"

Yrion's held his trembling hands at his sides and glued his eyes to the envelope.

"Yrion?" their mother repeated.

Slowly, he reached into his pocket and produced a broad leaf. He almost laid it atop the table, but thought better of it; instead, he held it up by its stem. It was a perfect maple leaf: broad, symmetrical, undamaged by wind or bug. Only, it was black, black like every crop, root and vine in their field. Laurel and her mother backed away from its familiar smell.

"I found this in the Copperwood," Yrion said.

Laurel looked at her mother, at Yrion, at the leaf. "So?"

"The Copperwood is cursed," he said.

Laurel and Lyra exchanged another glance.

"The Copperwood is strong," Lyra said.

"The Copperwood is cursed," Yrion repeated. "And it's going to spread fast."

Laurel saw concern on their mother's face, but she wasn't sure if it was because Lyra thought Yrion was as crazy as Laurel did or if Lyra actually believed him.

"Oh, how would you know?" Laurel said. "No one knows that kind of thing."

"I don't know how I know. Call it an intuition. And when people find out—"

"I can't listen to this—"

"—*and when people find out*, no one's going to want the land. Not for logs, anyway. And not for eighteen-fifty. We're talking thousands of acres, Laurel. Maybe millions."

"Not millions,"—he had no idea how big an acre was.

"Thousands then. Point is, we'd be *really* broke. Rotbottom broke."

Laurel threw her hands up. "So the boy wakes up one day and decides he wants to be a man. Makes the biggest decision this family has had to make in six generations—on what? An *intuition*? When did you even learn that word?"

Yrion's hands were at his sides again, the leaf back in his pocket. "Now you won't have to marry Willem Whitehead."

She'd strangle him. She'd stuff the banknote down his throat. Her voice came out like a bear's: *"It's my choice!"*

"Yrion," their mother said, "go down and see your Uncle Cetus."

Yrion scampered out of the house. Laurel had to fight the urge to chase after him. Everything she'd worked for, all the horrible things she'd convinced herself she was ready to do, gone.

She wheeled to her mother. "So I guess you got what you wanted."

"Laurel—"

"Your son's all grown up and you didn't have to lift a finger."

"Laurel, you're upset."

"You think this was easy for me? Courting and gowns and fancy balls? That's not me, but I *made it* me!"

"And made yourself miserable in the process."

"I've been miserable since Father—" Laurel let her shoulders slump. Still standing, she bent over, rested her forearms on the table, and hung her head. She had nothing: no job, no home, no choices. Nothing, not even herself. She'd convinced herself she was willing to give it all up—all her principles, all her pride—because it was the practical thing, the *smart* thing. Corvus died, and her idealism had to die too—she had to *kill* it, didn't she? She had to grow up, as much as Yrion did, if in a different way.

Her mother took both Laurel's hands in her own and gave them a firm squeeze. "You're wound so tight. Like your father. The two of you never slow down, never give in. It killed him, you know."

A tear dropped from the bridge of Laurel's nose onto the table.

"Yrion, he's easy," her mother said. "Flighty, but he always manages to land on his feet. I try my best with you, but your father handled it better."

"Father and I did nothing but fight."

"It seemed that way. But it made you who you are. It tested your convictions. Don't let his death shake them. Forget the sale, forget the whole damned railroad. Get back to the things that are really important to you, back to the things you're good at."

The things she was good at; she didn't even know what they were anymore. She'd been toiling at things she *wasn't* good at for—how long had it been? How long had it been since she'd done something well, done something right? How would she get back to that?

Laurel squeezed her mother's hand back. Maybe her mother didn't understand what drove Laurel to these extremes, but she did see Laurel's limitations. And she never made Laurel feel as though those limitations were shortcomings or failures. Laurel did that to herself. That was the Corvus in her, that constant, nagging push, the need to keep moving. She hadn't grieved his death, but neither had she let him go; it was as if, in some twisted way, she'd been trying to serve as his substitute.

Just then the front door opened and Yrion stuck his head in. "Laurel, you have a visitor."

"Send them away," she said, rising from the table and wiping a tear from her cheek.

Yrion lingered a moment. "It's Willem Whitehead."

Of all the times. Laurel was in no state to be receiving guests. Or marrying herself off. *Or maybe this is as good a time as any.* If she needed to stick to things she was good at, disappointing people was high on that list.

"I'll be right out," she said.

Yrion pulled his head back through the door and left it open a crack. Laurel tucked some wild hairs behind her ears and dabbed her face dry on her sleeves. Her mother gave her an encouraging nod, and Laurel went out the door.

Willem Whitehead stood in the front yard, arms crossed over his chest. He wore the long coat Laurel had met him in, with the high, wolf's fur collar. His long hair blew in the breeze. Up on the road, an ashy, piebald horse waited.

"Mister Whitehead," Laurel said, doing her best hide her distress. "I suppose you're here for my answer?"

Willem nodded.

"Well, I'm sorry," she said. "I can't sell you this farm at twenty-seven fifty an acre. We already sold it for eighteen-fifty an acre. To Pavo Linenpest."

Willem eyed her evenly. "That's a bad deal."

"Apparently I have no say in the matter. I'm sorry you came all this way."

"I'm not."

That gave Laurel pause. "Naturally," she said, "this changes the terms of your offer."

"It doesn't."

"Mister Whitehead. I have no farm to sell you."

"Eighty-three acres at twenty-seven fifty an acre. I'll pay an even twenty-five hundred."

"Twenty-five hundred for what? My hand?"

Willem nodded without flinching, and Laurel saw again that charm Lady Idlevice had told her about. It wasn't so much his confidence that she admired, but his directness, the way conducted himself no matter the business at hand.

But Laurel had to laugh. "That's your price, huh?"

"What's yours?"

Laurel looked back at her cottage, around at the Copperwood. "Good question."

"It's a good deal."

A good deal. That's what all this was about, wasn't it? Some women married for love where romance is the currency, and they hoped to get a good deal. Some women married noblemen where social status was the currency, and they hoped to get a good deal. Some married for money where *currency* was the currency, and they hoped to get a good deal. Why would Laurel marry? What was her currency? Control? Martyrdom? She didn't even know anymore. It all seemed so silly.

"It is a good deal," she said. "Maybe the best I'll get. But my answer is no."

Willem Whitehead remained unmoved. "Five thousand."

Laurel wondered how far he would go. He seemed to be a man who was used to getting what he wanted—if not taking it.

"Twenty thousand," she said, "and my answer is still no. I'm not for sale."

Willem eyes narrowed as if he were trying to read some subtext in her words. But there was none. Laurel had nothing to hide from him, no ulterior motives; she wasn't playing any more games. When he finally understood this, he nodded one last time, uncrossed his arms, and strode up the front path.

"Good luck at the vote," Laurel called after him.

He mounted his steed and galloped off without response or farewell.

Laurel watched him go, glad he was gone. One more worry off her plate. What was left, she wondered. Her farm was sold, she'd lost her job somewhere along the way, this suitor business was through...almost, anyway.

She started walking, south on Witching Hour Road. The air was crisp, but the breeze brought up the stink from her cursed field—from Pavo Linenpest's field, now. She looked up at the canopy of trees: yellow, orange, red, brilliant even under cloudy skies. Could it really succumb to the curse? *The Copperwood is strong.*

Yet, she had always considered herself strong, too. What had happened to her in the past month? To what pressures had she succumbed that made marriage to Willem Whitehead—marriage period—a good idea? She didn't know, and she was too tired think about it. Thoughts themselves had piled up and become a weight she could veritably feel from the tops of her shoulders to the soles of her feet. She was tired, tired of feeling tired.

The streets of Brodhaven were busier than Laurel ever remembered, teeming with window shoppers, peddlers' carts, wagons being unloaded by their drivers who whisked their wares into the stores. Goods flowed up from the railway stop, and when the vote passed they would flow down from the Uphills. The town seemed ready to burst. Behind the line of shops on the main avenue, new buildings were being erected: more stores and narrow residences in a row.

Laurel stopped out front of Cronewetters' Clockworks. A dozen clocks ticked away the last minutes of the hour. She wasn't there long before the bells of the front door rang and Caelum was standing before her, his pale eyes bright and cold, his gaze level and deep. If Laurel had read nothing on Willem Whitehead's face because of its blankness, she could read nothing on Caelum's because of its complexity. There was so much written there. To passersby, he might look angry or resolute or like a man patiently listening to a customer's complaints. Laurel, who knew his face so well, saw all that and more, every subtlety in his sinew, one emotion contradicting the next.

"We sold the farm," she said.

"Oh?"

She couldn't hide the defeat in her voice. "To Pavo Linenpest."

"Oh."

Laurel soon found herself shifting from one foot to the other, like her mother and brother.

"Is that all you're going to say?" she asked. "*Oh?*"

"You're the one who came down here. You don't have something to say?"

"I said we sold the farm."

"Aye, to Pavo Linenpest."

Laurel looked away. This used to be easy—*they* used to be easy. They used to understand one another. She supposed it was all her fault though. Just one of her many bungles this past month. She'd been acting like a fool.

That last thought came out strong, and she audibly said, "Fool."

"Fool?" Caelum said. "I told you to stay away from Vela Idlevice."

Laurel stood there, unable to dispute him. But she didn't blame the lady for any of this. Laurel had gone to her for help, and the lady tried to help as best as she could. If Laurel would have known herself a little better, she might have handled herself a little better. She might have bowed out earlier. But somehow Caelum had known. He knew her better than herself sometimes. All she could *do* was stand there; it was probably the first time she have a rebuttal ready.

That, apparently, tripped Caelum up. "I still don't—how is Willem Whitehead an *option*? The man's a, a—a"

"What do you want from me?" Laurel asked. She wasn't here to talk about Willem Whitehead—or Pyxis Pettifog or Lady Idlevice.

Caelum ran his fingers once through his hair. "How about I tell you what I don't want?"

Laurel waited for him to speak.

He said, "I don't want you to marry me."

Laurel looked away from him. "But what if I did?"

Caelum threw his hands up. "So now you want to?"

She shrugged. "Humor me."

He ran his fingers through his hair. He really wasn't used to this, her letting him speak so plainly about them. But, in a way, she'd broken that bond they shared—and it wasn't a fragile thing either. She had to let him let it out, to hold nothing back.

He pointed back and forth between her and himself. "No one else understands this but us—at least, that's what I thought. Do you? Do *you* understand what this is?"

Laurel did understand. It wasn't easy for her to talk about or even think about or even admit to herself. But she understood it, like an intuition, one she'd been choosing to ignore.

"I don't want to own you," Caelum said, "or command you or prove to others that what we have is real. But I need to know you understand. How I feel, how you feel. I need to know you understand it. I need—"

"My heart," Laurel said.

Caelum looked her in the eye. He looked ready to cry. "That much I need."

He wasn't offering to take care of her; he was offering to help her take care of herself. He was offering her exactly what she wanted. Laurel had come very close to choosing much worse, choosing some stranger, choosing for choice's sake. But what she and Caelum had went beyond offers and choices; they had companionship, maybe even love. And she wondered: why not love? Their *own kind* of love. Their own arrangement, taking all the good and leaving the hollow traditions behind. *Exactly* what she wanted.

"All right," she said.

Caelum put his hands on his hips. "All right as in agreement?"

"All right as in agreement."

He did his best to hide his smile. "All right."

Instantly, a tremendous weight seemed to lift from Laurel. The air thinned and crisped and flowed deep and free into her lungs—she hadn't realized until now how heavy it had become. She felt unburdened, from obligation and things unsaid, ready to think freely.

She said the first thing that came to mind: "I need a job."

Caelum gave her a sly glance. "You know, steady hands run in your family."

Laurel's blood tingled, but she had to ask: "What about Yrion?"

"You tell me. He hasn't shown up for two weeks."

"I told you he would wander off." She looked at him earnestly. "You think I'll be good at it?"

Caelum took both her hands in his. "I know it."

Forty-Two

Yrion and Uncle Cetus stopped on Witching Hour Road halfway down the hill to Brodhaven. Sunday the Twenty-Sixth, the day of the vote, had finally come, and the road was busy with southbound horse- and foot-traffic. Yrion recognized many of the travelers as Whiteheads by their wolf's fur coats. He'd never seen so many come down from the Uphills.

"Look at them," Uncle Cetus said—but he wasn't talking about Whiteheads. Out on the meadow-covered hills surrounding Brodhaven, townsfolk stood facing Yrion and his Uncle's direction. "Like they're out to watch some fireworks. Probably have blankets and picnic baskets too."

Yrion turned to see what the onlookers saw: flecks of black peppered the Copperwood's orange and red canopy. In places, patches of it dominated where whole trees had already turned. Yrion's intuition had proven correct; the Copperwood was cursed. Within a day of him selling his farm, black leaves started appearing throughout the forest, and each day since townsfolk had been coming out to the hilltops to watch it progress. Its sick-sweetness hung so heavy that everyone could smell it; some of the fancier ladies could be seen holding perfumed kerchiefs to their noses.

"Come on," Uncle Cetus said, "best get this over with. Going over to the Nudnik's later today to look at a horse, if you want to come."

Banyon hadn't been seen since the Everdark festivities. Yrion had even gone out looking for the horse a few times when he wasn't helping Uncle Cetus on the farm.

"Where do you think he is?" Yrion asked.

"Banyon? Probably food for buzzards, lying in a ditch with a broken leg. Or maybe he found himself that mare he's always been a-searching for. Who knows?"

"Poor Banyon," was all Yrion could say.

They crossed into Brodhaven and went straight to town hall. The bell out front was ringing, calling all to the meeting. Inside, Uncle Cetus signed his name in the big book. Yrion, who no longer owned land, did not sign, and one of the door wardens touched him on shoulder.

"We're expecting a full house today," the warden said.

"He's with me," Uncle Cetus said. "Going to show him how this gets done."

Uncle Cetus dwarfed the warden, and the warden thought better of disagreeing with him.

They found a seat on one of the last benches. Yrion saw Caelum standing near the front of the hall, looking very serious, talking with some other gentlemen. Yrion looked about and noticed that there were, indeed, more Whiteheads here than at last month's meeting, and there seemed to be far fewer townsmen present. Maybe the townsmen were all up on the hillsides watching the Copperwood turn.

When the bell outside the hall stopped ringing, folk were still filing in, filling the outer aisles along the windows and the upper loft. The boards overhead creaked with the weight of them. Yrion heard the doors close. The pulpit at the front of the room stood empty, as did the long, low table stretching across its front. Folk soon began to grumble over the growing heat and stuffiness in the air.

Fifteen minutes passed before the clerks and Mayor Linenpest arrived. They appeared on the left of the pulpit and table, whispering amongst themselves.

"Move it along, Linenpest!" someone shouted.

"We haven't got all day!" barked another.

The clerks slid into the spots behind the table, and the mayor huffed and puffed his way up to the pulpit. His face looked redder than ever, and his jowls glistened with sweat. Even his white sash looked wrinkled, as if he'd worn it to bed on a restless night.

"Calling to order," Linenpest said, sounding as bad as he looked, "this, the seventeen hundred and thirty-eighth Brodhaven assembly, Twenty-Sixth October. Our doors have been sh-shut. Let no one open them. Till we're through."

The mayor had to pat his forehead dry on his sleeve before continuing.

"Let us begin with announcements. As I'm sure you are aware, the curse has taken the Copperwood. This has very serious—*grievous*—implications for our good town, for Long Autumn Valley. We have been working tirelessly to organize a thorough investigation. And with confirmed incidents in the west, charities are, uh, somewhat stretched, as it were. We ask that you, our generous members, pass what donations you can through my office and we'll see that it reaches those who need it."

Half the room grumbled at that. The other half laughed outright.

"Now," the mayor continued, "now I'd like to open the floor for any public announcements—"

"Get on with it!" one member shouted.

Another hollered, "Aye, we came to vote, not to hear who's getting hitched."

Aye, aye, the assembly agreed.

"Oh, ah, yes," Linenpest stammered. He'd grown so red he looked like a blood-filled tick ready to pop. "In light of recent events—the curse in the Copperwood, I mean—it would be, uh, indelicate, as it were, to proceed with our planned agenda. I move we postpone the Witching Hour Railroad vote to November Thirtieth—"

The hall erupted. "*Nay! Nay!*" the Whitehead clan shouted.

Mayor Linenpest began ringing his rusty cowbell, but it only incited further *nays*. Then, the big Willem Whitehead stepped into the main aisle and raised both his hands. His clan fell silent. With that kind of control, Yrion thought, he ought to be presiding today.

"Let us put *that* to a vote," Willem said. "Show of hands, who wants to vote today?"

An overwhelming number of hands went up, most of them Whiteheads, accompanied by unrequested *yeas*. Uncle Cetus raised his hand too.

"And who doesn't want to vote?" Willem asked.

An underwhelming number of hands went up. Yrion wondered if some hadn't raised their hands either time, afraid of the rowdy Whiteheads.

"Mayor," Willem said, "the yeas have it. Proceed."

The Whiteheads nodded to one another and murmured agreements. Mayor Linenpest leaned over the front of his bench and whispered to his clerks; they seemed to be arguing.

"Linenpest's in trouble now," Uncle Cetus said.

"Did he break the rules?" Yrion asked.

"Opposite. He's done everything by the book—the book he himself helped write—and now he's got to follow through. See, his yes-men and money-men who wanted to build this railroad aren't sure they want it built anymore. Want to see how bad the curse really is. That's why a lot of them didn't show up today; they're afraid to hitch their horse to the wrong post. Now, if the mayor loses, it'll have cost him a lot of time and money and maybe the next election. But if he wins, then he has to buy up all that worthless acreage."

"Oh. Do you think he'll win or lose?"

"Well, I wouldn't blame folk for voting yea if it means they'll get something for their cursed land. But the Whiteheads look after their own. I don't think they came all this way to let Linenpest get what's theirs."

The head clerk stood and began reading the lengthy Witching Hour Railroad proposition in its entirety while the others passed out pamphlets covering its main points—the same pamphlets Brodhaven had already distributed via mail. The Mayor really had everything worked out in advance. Everything except the curse.

The Whiteheads began to grumble again, demanding that the reading be skipped and the vote be taken, but in this Mayor Linenpest would not bend. He insisted that it be read in its entirety, according to procedure, perhaps to stall the inevitable, perhaps to drive a few impatient Whiteheads out and increase his chances. By the time the clerk finished, his voice was crackling like leaves on a breeze.

The voting started immediately after and it moved swiftly. Yrion tried to keep track of yeas and nays but lost count. The mayor kept his head down, unable to face the assembly, and each nay weighed upon his shoulders more and more.

"Nay," said Uncle Cetus when his name was called.

The nays won it one hundred fifty-five to one hundred thirty-four. Considering Linenpest required three-fifths to win, this was a landslide defeat. Also, a record number of landowners had attended, more Whiteheads than anyone expected. The Whiteheads looked about at one another, arms crossed and pleased.

The mayor's voice barely made it past his mustache. "Any new business?"

But already someone had opened the hall's double doors and men were filing out.

"I have," came a voice from the front. It was Caelum. He stood up on his seat and yelled to the back. "I have new business."

The departing members slowed a bit, but their faces said 'this better be good.'

"My proposal is simple," Caelum said, "but it will change everything: how we write our laws, how we conduct our business. It's a change happening everywhere else. It's time Long Autumn Valley changed too."

Folk seemed honestly interested in that. Some of those moving to the door stopped.

"Whom do we trust to watch over our lands when we're here to vote? Not Brodhaven. To watch over our homes while we work the fields? Not Brodhaven. Yet we came very close today to—"

"Ack, spit it out, man!" someone shouted, and the assembly grumbled in agreemen.

Caelum raised his hands to silence them. "I'm proposing we let women inherit land. We let them own businesses. We invite them here to participate in our decisions; we let them vote."

The men lingered for a silent moment, as if they'd all taken a bad step and had to steady themselves. Yrion loved the idea— he'd wanted that all along. The way the others lingered, exchanging glances, if only for that silent moment, they seemed to be considering it. But the moment passed: their brows furrowed, they grinned at one another dismissively, and their grumbling resumed.

Caelum remained standing and speaking, if only to their backs.

"It's going to happen anyway," he said. "You can't halt progress."

It didn't stop anyone from leaving, but their leaving didn't stop him from talking. Only when Mayor Linenpest began ringing his cowbell to officially dismiss the assembly did Caelum step down.

"Don't think folk are quite ready for that," Uncle Cetus said. "Anyway, better get a move on. Day's wasting."

"Uncle Cetus," Yrion said, "I'm going to wait for Caelum."

His uncle patted him on the shoulder. "Don't be too long, or I'm going to the Nudnik's without you."

Yrion stood up on the bench and let everyone else file out. Caelum was still up front talking with a few men who'd gathered around him. By the time the assembly had thinned enough for Yrion to reach the front, Caelum was saying his farewells to the circle.

"Yrion," Caelum said cheerily, "can you believe it? We won."

"Aye. But no one liked your idea."

"Oh, that's all right. A few did. Though it's really Laurel's idea."

Yrion shrugged. "I liked it."

"The next time they hear it, it won't sound so strange."

The day Yrion sold the farm, Laurel had gone to Brodhaven, found herself a room to rent and a job with Caelum at the clockworks. They hadn't seen much of her since. Yrion supposed she was still sore with him about selling the farm.

"How is she?" Yrion asked.

"Why don't you stop by and see her?"

"Oh, I don't know."

"Come on."

The hall had mostly emptied, and Yrion and Caelum walked out together. The news of Mayor Linenpest's failed railroad vote buzzed in the streets. Yrion could see the long line of Whiteheads in the distance, marching their victory march north up Witching Hour Road, back to the Uphills.

Yrion and Caelum found Laurel already out in front of the clockworks, taking in the news.

"Look who I found," Caelum called to her.

Yrion didn't know why, but he was embarrassed to make eye contact with his sister. "We won."

"I heard," Laurel said.

"Wait here," Caelum said to Yrion. "Got something for you."

Caelum went into his shop, leaving Yrion and Laurel alone. Yrion stuffed his hands in his pockets and shifted from one foot to the other.

"Well," Laurel said, "you were right about the Copperwood. Don't know how you do it."

Yrion shrugged, sheepish. It almost sounded like Laurel was complimenting him.

"Anyway," she said. "How's Mother?"

"She hopes you'll come see us soon."

"I will. Been busy here."

They stood there a few moments, and Yrion didn't know what else to say. He kicked at the ground some, and Laurel looked around at the passersby. Then Caelum came out of the shop and handed Yrion a bundle of cloth with something hard inside.

"For you," Caelum said.

Yrion pulled back the folds to reveal a pewter figurine: ten inches high, locked in a frozen charge, mane blowing in a still wind; the Nightsteed. The little boy Yrion had broken free clung to the horse's neck again. Yrion could see bright metallic seams where Caelum had re-adhered and reinforced him.

"I know how much you liked that one," Caelum said.

Yrion blushed. "I'm sorry."

"Don't be. Fragile as it was, I could never have sold it. And with the seams, I can't sell it now."

"I'm sorry—I mean thanks." Yrion folded it back up.

Caelum raised his hand high enough to pat Yrion on the head but stopped. Then he lowered the hand and held it out to Yrion. Yrion shook it.

They said their farewells, and Yrion made his way out of town, testing the weight and feel of the statuette in his hand. He folded back the cloth and looked at it. He remembered only a few weeks back how the thing had entranced him—how all the statuettes had. He had wanted to set money aside to buy one. Yet now, holding one of his own, he felt less enchanted. It was amazing work, and he was very grateful that Caelum had given it to him, but something had changed.

Yrion hadn't seen the Nightsteed since the Nightfather cast him from his hall, and he didn't expect he would ever see it again. He felt a sense of completeness about it, about his father's death, about a lot of things. It was a new feeling for him, or maybe just a new way of looking at a feeling he'd felt before. He wasn't sure yet, but he felt ready to figure it out, figure it out without looking for it. It would come to him.

He passed under the Copperwood's darkening canopy. The clouds had covered up the sun, and pale light filtered orange and yellow and red through the leaves. Yrion knew this was one of the last times he would see the forest this way. This would be a short autumn for the Copperwood, the last autumn. The smell of the curse was strong and deep. Complete. Soon, every leaf and branch would turn black. Yrion sensed it—another of his intuitions. He liked that word, *intuition*. It sounded smart.

Yrion couldn't say what would happen to the forest after that. Would the trees rot and crumble? Would they remain standing and make the place a haunted forest? Was the curse just a precursor to something like Everdark, a darkening of the whole valley, of the whole world? Intuition told him nothing about that.

A thud sounded off to his right. A chill ran through him, and he stopped short. Then came a crunching sound, leaves beneath something very heavy. *Thud. Thud. Thud. Thud.*

He was afraid to look. Hadn't he just felt complete? Would the Nightsteed haunt him forever?

Closer now. And closer. *Thud. Thud. Thud. Thud.*

He *wouldn't* ride it again. He'd climb a tree. He'd shoo it off. But he *would not ride it*. He turned, ready to square off with the beast.

Through the trees came Banyon, stepping lazily along.

Yrion exhaled. "*There* you are."

The dun still wore the black sheep's wool blanket Uncle Cetus and Yrion had covered him with the night of the barn dance. Flecks of leaves and burrs and briars clung to it. But Banyon didn't seem stressed. He just moseyed towards Yrion as if he were back in his pen sniffing for a handout.

"Uncle Cetus was going to replace you today. Is that why you turned up?"

Banyon came out onto the road and stood next to Yrion, even let Yrion pull a few burrs from his blanket.

"Look at you all scuffed up. You need a good brushing."

Banyon snorted.

"You don't think so, huh? Better come along anyway."

Yrion started walking. Banyon followed alongside.

Forty-Three

Laurel was sitting at Caelum's workbench at the back of the Cronewetters' workshop when she heard him approach. She slid her scrap of metal close and covered it with her hands.

"Just got the news," he said. Then he saw her conspicuous hands. "Let me see."

"The news first," she said.

"They just settled Lord Idlevice's will."

Long Autumn Valley hadn't stopped talking about the Idlevices since Lord Percy *and* Jacob Le'fever died within six hours of one another. After Jacob assaulted the lord, the Idlevice servants claimed to have found him in the Copperwood already dead from an apparent blow to the head. Common suspicion held that the servants had dealt Jacob their own brand of justice, but without witnesses to contradict their story no arrests were made.

But even more talked about than this double tragedy was the will. Most assumed Lord Idlevice's estate and all his wealth would go to some distant relative no one had ever met. Pavo Linenpest, after his railroad upset, no doubt wanted it to go to the public trust. It certainly wouldn't pass to Laurel or her family so she didn't care much either way.

"Lord Idlevice left everything," Caelum said, "to his driver."

Laurel hadn't expected that.

"Suhar," she said, absently.

"Can you believe it?"

It made sense on several levels, depending on how deeply (and cynically) one chose to examine it. On the surface, Lord Percy had developed a special bond with the servant who had tended to him through his long wintering. Or perhaps his undying love for Vela compelled him to set aside family pride for her, even if it meant leaving everything to a servant—and a foreigner at that. But Laurel couldn't imagine Lady Idlevice, manager of the estate's affairs, had nothing to do with the fortunate circumstances that allowed her to remain under its roof. Vela controlled her own destiny.

"Yes," Laurel said, "I can believe it."

Caelum shrugged. "You know her better than I do." Then he turned his attention once more to her hands. "Now, let me see."

Laurel hesitated, and he had to poke her in the side to wrest the scrap metal from her grip. He held it close to the lamp on the table. The light glimmered off loops and lines etched into the metal's surface, the letters L, A, U, R, and E, Laurel's name carved over and over in different sizes and fonts. Laurel fiddled with a burin while Caelum examined her work.

"This is good," he said.

"Sure. All you need is a customer who wants my name engraved on something."

"We'll have you doing watches in no time."

"Can you sell a watch made by a woman?"

"*Engraved* by a woman to start. We'll ease them into it."

Laurel crossed her arms and grumbled something inaudible even to herself.

"These things take time," Caelum said.

"I don't know. I don't know if I'm right for this."

"Are you kidding? You're—"

The four brass bells rang from the showroom.

"Customer," Caelum said and hurried away.

Laurel looked about her workspace. Half a dozen burins with different tips stood upright in a little wooden rack. Other scrap plates lay in a pile, covered front and back with random letters and words. She'd been back here for weeks trying to improve her skills. Caelum insisted she was a natural, but his cousins who sat in the workshop with her, some of them a third her age, were just as good if not better. And if Laurel was going to make any money at this, she needed to start producing things meant for sale.

She sighed. *These things take time.*

Caelum poked his head back into the workshop. "Laurel, customer to see you."

She rose from her stool. "Me?"

She moved uncertainly to the front of the workshop. Caelum held the door for her, and she entered the show room alone.

Vela Idlevice stood in front of a glass display case.

"Lady…Vela," Laurel said.

Vela Idlevice glanced about the shop. "Laurel. I see you've landed on your feet."

Laurel didn't know what to say to that, so said, "I was sorry to hear about your—about Lord Idlevice. He was…a very gracious man."

The lady looked at a few clocks, but didn't seem particularly interested in them—or chatting about her late husband.

"Can I help you with something?" Laurel asked.

"I believe so." Vela reached into a fold of her dress's sleeve, produced a trifold stack of papers. "I read a letter recently."

She set the papers atop the glass counter. The front page had a decorative banner across the top quarter wrapped about large block letters that read "The Longest Autumn." Hand-written words streamed beneath the banner in a perfect, steady script. Laurel knew every letter.

"How did you come by it?" Laurel asked.

"Oh, it's making its way around certain circles."

That phrase was almost ominous to Laurel. The last letter she'd written had caused her a bit of trouble, but it had also helped get the Witching Hour Railroad vote stricken down—if only in a small way. The one laying before her was bound to cause more trouble; she hoped it would help make bigger changes. And this time her employer supported her—already Caelum had proposed big changes at the town meetings.

"Did you write this letter?" Vela asked.

Laurel looked at it. "Newsletter, really. Hoping to make a monthly serial of it."

"Then I would like to subscribe—if subscriptions are offered."

Laurel nodded slowly. "They can be."

"In here, it talks of women organizing. Discussing."

"That has yet to happen."

"I hope you'll include me when the time comes. And I know others who are interested."

Laurel nodded and a moment passed.

"I should be going," the lady said. "Pleasure seeing you, Miss Blight. As always."

Vela left the shop. Laurel returned to her workspace and found Caelum waiting for her on her stool. She could sense a lingering suspicion from him, with a dash of disapproval.

"Well?" he said.

"She wants me to send her a newsletter."

"Quite the readership you're gathering."

"And?"

He relaxed a little. "No ands. You should be proud."

She shooed him off the stool and observed her latest practice scrap in the lamplight. The loops of her cursive script were too fat; it was tough to do sharp curves so small. She puffed out her lower lip in concentration and concern. Caelum must have noticed because he went to another bench and returned with a pincushion that looked like a pumpkin. He set it down and removed a tiny needle—Laurel had never seen one so small. Then he plucked a hair from his head and held them both out to her. She gave him a puzzled look but took them.

"Now," he said, "at arm's length, thread the needle."

Laurel stared at the thread and needle. They felt almost the same thickness in her fingertips, and when she stretched her arms out they looked identical.

"You've done this?" she asked, eyes on them.

"Oh, sure," Caelum replied.

She looked at him, saw half a grin, but his cousins had come off their stools and were gathering around. Laurel lowered her hands, took a breath, and stretched them back out. They caught the lamplight the same way, looking like two strands of gold. She rested the edges of her palms together, rolled the needle back and forth in her fingertips to position the eye. Then she gave Caelum one last look before advancing the hair with one subtle but fluid movement.

The hair didn't bend, but she might have missed the needle completely.

Caelum's eyes widened.

"Bravo," he whispered, and the cousins oohed and ahhed.

Laurel brought her hands close. The hair had gone through the needle's eye.

"What did I tell you?" Caelum said. "Steady hands."

Laurel smiled.

99976197R00129

Made in the USA
Columbia, SC
14 July 2018